**MARTHA GELLHORN**, well-known for her novels, short stories, and outstanding journalism, began her distinguished career as a war correspondent for Collier's in Spain. She also covered Finland, China (her travels there are described in TRAVELS WITH MYSELF AND ANOTHER), England, France, Germany, and Java. In 1966, she became war correspondent for the London Guardian in Vietnam and in 1967, Israel. THE FACE OF WAR is a collection of her years of war reporting.

Ms. Gellhorn has written several highly acclaimed works of fiction, including THE TROUBLE I'VE SEEN, A STRICKEN FIELD, THE HEART OF ANOTHER, LIANA, THE WINE OF ASTONISHMENT, THE LOWEST TREES HAVE TOPS, and most recently, THE WEATHER IN AFRICA.

# THE WEATHER IN AFRICA

## MARTHA GELLHORN

 A BARD BOOK/PUBLISHED BY AVON BOOKS

AVON BOOKS
A division of
The Hearst Corportion
959 Eighth Avenue
New York, New York 10019

The Dodd, Mead & Company edition contains the following
Library of Congress Cataloging in Publication Data:

Gellhorn, Martha, 1908—
  The weather in Africa.

  Novellas.
  CONTENTS: On the mountain.—In the highlands.—By the
sea.
  I. Title.
PZ$_3$.G28We 1980 [PS3513.E46] 813′.5′2

First Bard Printing, September, 1981

FOR L.

# :I: ON THE MOUNTAIN

There was much talk when Jane and Mary Ann Jenkins came home to Mount Kilimanjaro. Mary Ann had been gone for only two years in an American city no one ever heard of, called Cleveland; but Jane was away for twelve long years, cutting a swath in Europe, so the locals understood. Gone into the wide world, far from this mountain, to make their fortunes, and returned to the ancestral hotel with no fortune and unmarried, both of them.

All the Europeans knew the Jenkins family and all had something to say about the surprise reappearance of the Jenkins daughters. In Moshi, they talked at the hotel bar, the post office, the best general store, the petrol station, the bank; up and down the mountain, they talked in the farmers' homes when the ladies had a bridge afternoon, at Sunday lunch parties, in matrimonial beds. Henry McIntyre, who'd farmed coffee on Kilimanjaro longer than living memory, delivered the majority verdict: 'Those poor gormless girls have made a proper balls of it.'

His wife said, 'Girls?' lifting her eyebrows.

Jane was thirty-two and Mary Ann thirty.

Everybody sensed defeat, the end of great expectations. Bob and Dorothy Jenkins, the parents, were overjoyed. They had no idea that people were talking about their children.

But everyone agreed that Bob and Dorothy were getting on and it was only right for the girls to come back and give them a hand. The older generation remembered when Bob and Dorothy showed up, thirty-five years ago, and bought land on a dirt road, back of beyond on the east side of the mountain, to start a hotel. The neighbouring farmers thought they were mad. Who would come to it and why? The hotel was nothing but an overgrown log cabin in those days, with five bedrooms the size of broom cupboards. Bob and Dorothy named the place Travellers' Rest, and were undaunted.

There were forty bedrooms now. The log cabin had expanded into a long central building, two stories high, still faced with split logs, that was its charm, that and the great wistaria circling the verandah pillars by the main door, and the golden spray and the mat of ficus leaves and bougainvillaea against the dark wood. Inside there was a fine bar and stone fireplaces and a lounge with comfortable chairs and writing tables and a dining room tricked out in daffodil yellow cloths and napkins. The bedrooms above were chintz-draped, with plenty of first-class tiled bathrooms.

Eight bungalows, four on each side, stretched in a semicircle from the main hotel: sitting room, bedroom, bath and a little verandah for private drinking before lunch, too cold in the evening. The bungalows were the last word with Swedish type furniture, Dorothy had said, and curtains and upholstery of bright jagged modern designs. The swimming pool was an ornamental blue lake set in the lawn; no one but tourists would be fool enough to plunge into that ice water. Behind the bungalows nearest the entrance drive, they built a tennis court for the young. Landrovers were on hire. All of this was buried in a garden like a huge flower bed. Old Bob was a true gardener, he'd suffered when he had to cut down trees for the new construction. Anything grew with so much rain and mist and unlimited water in the mountain streams.

No one was disagreeable about the Jenkins' success. They had earned it. Everybody knew what a sweat it was to make a business thrive in Tanganyika, now Tanzania. The watu, the Africans. You had to be on your toes twenty-four hours a day: they forgot everything; they broke everything; they were naturally unreliable and mindless; you couldn't begin to imagine what idiocy they would invent next. Specially in a hotel where foreigners didn't understand and expected slap-up service. Dorothy was after them day and night, checking, instructing. And Bob was a darling. Everyone loved Bob.

All the resident Europeans found a chance to take a good

look at the prodigal daughters. Everyone was curious about the changes wrought by time and absence. Jane had been a dewy English rose, with golden hair and big blue eyes, spoiled rotten by her parents. The dew had definitely dried off, which gave satisfaction; Jane had been too fond of herself, too pleased with her appearance, though no one could say she was by any means a hag now. Mary Ann looked pretty much the same. She didn't look like her parents, any more than Jane did. Jane the beauty. Mary Ann, officially the homely one. Mary Ann was all shades of brown and average features. Jane had the tall lean elegant body of a fashion model; Mary Ann was short, with a bosom and hips and a waist. No man thereabouts had ever laid a hand on either of them. It had always been an unspoken sour assumption that the Jenkins girls were waiting for a better bet: Kilimanjaro and environs were not good enough for them.

America had improved Mary Ann. She didn't dress as sloppily. Before her Cleveland adventure, Mary Ann cut her hair with a nail scissors and wore any old trousers, or dresses like flowered chair covers in the evening. Now she did things to her hair, sometimes piling it on top of her head, sometimes wearing it in that odd younger generation way, as if you'd got out of bed and forgot to brush it, hanging down all over the place; sometimes in a pony-tail with a scarf knotted and floating behind. And miniskirts and well-fitting slacks and pullovers that enhanced her breasts. American clothes. Clothes were reported to be very cheap in America.

Aside from losing dewiness, Jane seemed to have picked up an extra dose of the haughties in Europe. From the way she behaved, they were all watu to her now.

'I like how they talk,' said a newcomer, the young bank manager in Moshi, who weekended at Travellers' Rest, and enjoyed the company and the tennis. Moshi was a dead little town, the week was long and lonely. 'Where did they get that accent?'

'Chagga,' Henry McIntyre explained. 'Chagga English.

They spoke Chagga first, running around with the kids in the servants' lines and the village up there. Considering how they grew up, it's funny to hear Jane now. She sounds like a typical old colonialist Memsaab. God knows the watu drive you batty but there's no malice in them, poor sods. No reason for Jane to go on as if they were monsters. Half the watu in the Jenkins hotel have been there all Jane's life; she used to play with a lot of them. Though I will say she bossed the hide off them, even as a child.'

Mr and Mrs Jenkins beamed, Bob from behind his gold-rimmed spectacles, Dorothy from her sharp darting black eyes. They beamed and relaxed, glad to see the girls taking over. It was the girls' hotel, they had made it only to give to their girls. Dorothy, who seemed never to have sat down since the moment the hotel opened, now often took her ease by the big fireplace in the lounge or in a woven plastic chair on the verandah. And Bob, who had grown stooped and half bald on this mountainside, looked younger from happiness in having his daughters home.

Bob and Dorothy agreed that the girls shared out the work wisely. Mary Ann supervised the staff, the supplies and the office. Jane attended to the guests. Jane had real poise and style after her years in Europe; the guests were charmed by her; and she'd become a linguist too. Very important now that they got so many nationalities on these tours. Jane handled them beautifully, speaking French and Italian. The guests were thrilled to hear that their daughter was a celebrity, the famous singer Janina, resting after triumphs in the capitals of Europe. Jane knew the amount of French and Italian needed in a hotel; she'd used those words, living in hotels. The guests sometimes wondered who the little dark girl was, rushing about in the background.

At the age of seven and a half, Mary Ann's eyes were opened painfully and permanently. They had returned for their first Christmas holiday from boarding school, Jane from Tanamuru Girls School, the most expensive establishment for young ladies in Kenya, and Mary Ann from a modest little place near Arusha, practically next door.

Jane said, 'How's your school?'

'Very nice.'

'I'm *so* glad.'

It was like being hit in the face. Mary Ann could not have put it into words; she was not skilful with words at thirty, let alone at seven and a half. But she knew by Jane's smile and voice and the look in her eyes: the golden-haired princess was graciously condescending to the peasant. That was how Jane saw them and meant them to be. From that day, Mary Ann ceased to follow and adore her older sister.

She wanted to strike back; she wanted to hurt Jane. She hid a small harmless snake in Jane's underwear drawer and Jane, screaming with terror, was petted and stroked and kissed and cuddled by Mummy and allowed to sleep in the parents' room until the fear passed. She broke Jane's favourite doll, claiming an accident, and Daddy bought Jane a new and better doll. Mary Ann realized then that she was not clever enough to fight Jane. Her parents didn't love her, they had found her in a basket, she was not their child, she would run away and live in the forest like Mowgli. Mary Ann was unhappy for the whole month.

But since Mary Ann was born to be cheerful she gave up worrying about Jane and ignored her, which was easy to do as Jane spent less and less time at home. Bob and Dorothy paid more attention to little Mary Ann, thinking she would be sad without her sister. Mary Ann rejoiced to be alone with her parents and back on the mountain, where she always wanted to be.

'Jane's so popular,' Dorothy would say with pride and some sorrow. Jane wrote about the wonderful time she was having at Ol Ilyopita with Cynthia Lavering, at her family's enormous farm in Kenya; Sir George and Lady Lavering, Jane noted. She had been to the Nairobi races in the Hallams' box with Stefanella Hallam; Mr Hallam owned the best racehorses in Africa, Jane explained.

'Jane's making fine friends,' Bob Jenkins would say, awed that his daughter bloomed in the fashionable society of Kenya where he would have felt out of place and miserable.

Bragging, Mary Ann thought, big fat show-off: a hideous offence. But who cared, the more Jane stayed away from Kilimanjaro the better.

They would never guess how Jane sucked up to Cynthia and Stefi, the richest, grandest, prettiest girls in school, and how brutally they mocked and rejected her. Nor how she had wooed their mothers, at a school festivity, clinging wistfully to the great ladies until the mothers gave the desired invitations and ordered their daughters to be civil. There were no further visits in those realms of splendour, as Cynthia and Stefi turned sullen and unmanageable; but Jane continued to write to her parents about the Laverings and the Hallams, while accepting third and fourth best offers of hospitality. She hated Cynthia and Stefi who made her beg for what should be hers by right. And she was determined that one day she would be where she belonged, at the very top, looking down.

Bob and Dorothy were to blame, of course, aside from the mysteries of genes and chromosomes. They had read no books on child psychology or any other psychology and believed in their simple old-fashioned way that love was the best guide in rearing the young.

'You're my little princess,' Bob would say, holding Jane's hand, parading her through the lounge for all to admire.

'You look like a little princess,' Dorothy would say, smoothing a new dress, giving an extra brush stroke to shining yellow hair.

To Mary Ann, Bob would say, 'Be my good little girl and bring home a fine report this term.'

And Dorothy would say, 'Tidy your room, darling, don't dawdle, there's my good little girl.'

So they bent their twigs, as parents do, with the best intentions. Jane had to conclude she was a princess in exile since princesses do not stem from pub-keepers with 'The customer is always right' as their royal motto. Mary Ann had to conclude that being a good girl was the highest aim in life, or despise her parents as fools. The Jenkins' friends and neighbours agreed unanimously that Bob and Dorothy were making a perfect mess of Jane though Mary Ann was a dear little thing.

Jane was a beauty, no getting around that fact. Mary Ann accepted that fact as she accepted Jane's cast-off, cut-down clothing. It was pointless to resent being plain and plain girls automatically got second best in everything. While Jane took singing lessons in London, she learned shorthand and typing in Mombasa because her parents needed a competent secretary. If Jane wanted to dazzle London, let the silly bitch go to it; her life was here on the mountain, helping to run the hotel. Everyone couldn't be beautiful; she was happy as she was. Jane, for all her looks and privileges and the blind adulation of her parents, never seemed happy.

When she returned from the secretarial college and worked with them every day as an equal, Mary Ann finally understood her parents and forgave them. They were loving and humble and very much ugly ducklings and, for no explicable reason, after six years of marriage when hope was gone, they had produced this swan, Jane. Mary Ann realized that Jane was the achievement of their lives, not the hotel. It had never occurred to them that building a hotel 7,000 feet up Kilimanjaro, out of sight of the famous sugar loaf top, on a bad road, was an act of folly. Ignorant and confident, they had built and worked, built more and worked more; the hotel, filling no previously felt want, was a success from the beginning.

But Jane was a dispensation from heaven, a miracle. Merely by looking at a photograph of Jane they felt singled out for divine favour. Mary Ann, small and cosy and dark, was what they might have expected: an ordinary person like themselves, to be loved, not worshipped.

Neither of the girls talked to each other or their parents

or anyone else about their years away from Kilimanjaro. Jane buried memory under layers of pride. Pride had kept her going and pride reminded her that she was Janina, temporarily resting at her family's stylish hotel in East Africa until her agent proposed a worthwhile engagement. But waking at night from a bad blurred dream, she could not forget the last memory. The Savoy, in Harrogate: the too large chilly provincial dining room and the terrible band and the clients, often gathered in determinedly hearty conventions, middle-aged, middle-class, safely accompanied by their wives. She had finished her number, microphone returned to Sammy, the band leader, herself slipping behind the curtain to her dressing room, when she was stopped by a voice from the past.

'Hello, love. Don't you recognize old friends?'

He was fatter and more common but also richer; he looked oiled with prosperity. Jeff Parks, her secretly married husband of less than a year; a man, scarcely a man then, who had walked out on her when she was twenty-one. She remembered every instant of that final scene and every word. He'd said, 'You're as cold and limp in bed as a slab of plaice. And you better live in Africa where you've got all those blacks to do the work, no man wants to come home to a pigsty and feed off tinned beans. And besides that, Goldilocks, you'll never be Lena Horne, never, got it? You'll never never never make the Savoy.' Then he left, and his face was alight with relief and gaiety as he closed the door behind him.

Now he said, 'Congratulations, Goldilocks. You made it after all. The Savoy.'

Jane fled from him; she did not cry then, as she had not cried when she was twenty-one. She stood in this bleak cubicle where no artist could ever have received baskets of flowers, throngs of admirers, flattering telegrams, and stared at her face. Her eyes looked crazy with fear. She left a note for the manager, mentioning a cable from home, packed her bags and caught the night train for London. She kept the taxi while she cashed a cheque at the London bank where, year after year, Bob and Dorothy deposited her allowance; it was the least they could do to help their gifted child, all alone in the costly cities of Europe. Then she drove to the airport and waited until she could get a seat on a plane for Dar-es-Salaam.

The road had been long and stony and cold: singing in coffee bars on the King's Road, and later in shabby night-clubs in Soho, snubbing men, after Jeff Parks, not wanting them anyway, wanting only her name, Janina, on bill-boards, in newspapers, on records, engagements in great hotels, the stage, films: fame. Then the Left Bank in Paris, a series of basement boîtes, hateful people to work with and the male customers assuming that a girl nightclub singer was also a whore. And always the dead time, between jobs, resting in smelly hotels, listening to her gramophone, practising before the mirror, patting her face with creams and astringents, brushing her hair, exercising her body, fighting off loneliness and doubt and four walls. Until Rome.

In Rome, there was Luigi, three years younger though she never told him, and beautiful with tight black curls and a glorious profile and satiny olive skin and eyes to drown in and a soft voice murmuring praise and tenderness. He worked as a salesman in a men's shop on the Via Frances-cina; he was poor but superbly dressed, they made a stunning couple as they walked arm in arm along the Via Veneto. Her allowance and salary were enough for them both.

With his touch, Luigi woke the frozen sleeping princess at last. She had not imagined that life held such wild happiness; her singing showed it. Five months of unclouded delight. She felt young and carefree, protected, truly loved, a woman fulfilled. The solitude and ugliness of the past vanished; she had Luigi, the golden present in this magical city, the glowing future. One night Luigi came to the Club Aphrodite glum and Luigi was never glum, always gay, warm, proud of her, passionate. He said he'd lost his job but did not say the boss called him a lazy bum who better find a rich old American to keep him like all the other lazy bums. He was sick of Rome, Luigi said, noisy shoving people; everything cost too much. He was going back to his paese, anyway he'd been getting angry letters from his mother, telling him his duty was to return, his wife was about to drop another bambino. The third, Luigi said, making a face, shrugging his shoulders.

Jane believed that Luigi had not offered her marriage because he was poor; she understood all the aspects of pride. He had explained that he was learning the business from the bottom; his uncle planned to set him up in a shop of his own. When Luigi had his shop, Jane knew he would speak. Her relentless endurance and ambition seemed absurd now, except as a means to this end. Her career had been a trick of destiny to lead her to Rome and Luigi. What was the lonely dream of fame compared to the joy of being Luigi's wife? It was only a matter of time, a little waiting, but enchanted waiting, until Luigi's male pride was soothed by the possession of his own shop. They had invented the name together: Palm Beach. Jane wondered whether she could work with him, be near him by day as well as night, or would a woman's presence lower the tone of the most elegant men's boutique in Rome? She would learn to cook and to sew; she meant to serve Luigi tenderly, ardently, in every way, with her whole heart.

Jane's arm moved by itself. She hit Luigi hard, swinging her handbag like a club. He clutched his cheek, glared at her with fury, and ran from her dressing room. Jane locked the door and wept, for the first time, until she felt cold, faint, blinded and choked by tears, too weak to move. A broken heart was a real thing, a knife pain in the chest. And in the mind, black despair. There was no one in the world to turn to; she was alone with this anguish, she was freezing to death from loneliness.

But no one must ever know, no one, ever. She could not live if people mocked her, laughing behind her back, the proud English Janina fooled by the first Italian who laid her. She would wait here until everyone had gone so that no one should see her ravaged face. A terrible word hovered, pushing itself forward to be heard. *Failure.* There were no tears left, only this sensation of creeping cold, in the airless dressing room on a summer night. Wait, Jane told herself, wait, wait. The couch with the bumpy springs smelled of mildew, the worn green damask was greasy from many other heads.

Later, singing those ritual words – 'Doan evah leave me ... why ya treat me so mean ... youah mah man, I need ya honey, I need ya lovah ...' – there was meaning and emotion in her voice. But now she hated Rome too, hated every beautiful young man with tight black curls, and the streets were full of them. She welcomed a stout middle-aged English gent who said he was in Rome on holiday, the manager of the Savoy, in Harrogate, and a lovely English girl like her didn't belong here with all these slimy Wops, she ought to come home, his clientele wasn't an ogling bunch of lechers, they were good solid English people.

Mary Ann had less to remember and no special reason to forget. There had been eight years of work in the hotel, lifting some of the burden from her parents' shoulders. When she felt she could steal time for herself, she was off up the mountain, passing the Chagga village where she chatted with old friends, into the damp jungly world of the rain forest. She had learned little at school but Miss Peabody, beloved maths teacher, happened to be an amateur botanist and Mary Ann had acquired curiosity and excitement from her. Before that, Mary Ann treated the natural world as Africans usually do: fauna were a nuisance or a menace or something to eat; flora were uninteresting unless edible or saleable. Bob called this botanizing Mary Ann's hobby and was glad the child had an amusement. Mary Ann became extraordinarily knowledgeable, an untutored scientist.

Mary Ann was too busy to think about men and, considering herself plain as a plate, she did not imagine that men would ever think about her. Sometimes, playing with African babies, she was shaken by the lack of her own; but then the hotel wrapped her in its coiling demands, and time passed. Until Mr and Mrs Niedermeyer arrived as guests and took a tremendous shine to her and finally proposed that Mary Ann return with them to Cleveland.

'It's perfectly lovely here,' Mrs Niedermeyer said to Dorothy, 'I can't imagine a lovelier place to live. But don't you think the child should see more of the world and meet more people? I won't make her work too hard, I promise; she'll have plenty of time for parties and fun and young men.' Mrs Niedermeyer had in mind her favourite nephew, thirty-one and single, and though the comparison was disloyal she found Mary Ann sweeter and gentler than the girls she knew around Cleveland; and romantic too, with that little brown face and funny accent and demure manner. If only Jack fell in love with her, everyone would be settled and happy.

Working as Mrs Niedermeyer's secretary was a rest cure after the hotel. Mary Ann had plenty of time and money. She had refused to accept any allowance from her parents, but Mrs Niedermeyer paid her well. With the aid of her new enthusiastic Cleveland girl-friends, she bought clothes and tried out hairdressers. Jack taught her to play bridge and dance. She was surrounded by talkative cordial girls and by Jack, teacher, guide, protector. He was a cautious young stockbroker and took a year to decide he was in love with Mary Ann and was dumbfounded when she thanked him and said No, with a look in her eyes like one who has accidentally hurt an animal, like knocking over a dog in the road. Jack then knew he was passionately in love with Mary Ann. Mrs Niedermeyer had kept her Fred waiting too; she realized Mary Ann was not playing with Jack, the child was truly uncertain.

Jack offered Mary Ann everything and more to come. How could she explain that she didn't want everything; she didn't know that she wanted anything. It seemed to her that she already had too much; why did she need eight lipsticks for instance? Principally, she could not say to Jack or any of these generous American friends that Cleveland

and surroundings produced something like a stone in her stomach, a solid heaviness of depression. She never woke with a singing heart because she knew what lay around her, a vast lake full of filth, an ugly sprawling city, a slum for both rich and poor, a flat weak countryside with spindly trees. She hungered for the air and silence and space of Africa and the great untamed mountain. At first snow had fascinated her; then she watched it turn to yellow slush and she thought it was hell. She had a fur coat, a present from Mrs Niedermeyer, and was cold all winter and in the summer felt she would suffocate. Air-conditioning stopped up her nose. Jack persisted with patience and unflagging will. Competition, Mrs Niedermeyer thought, the breath of life to all of them, even if the competition is only a girl saying no.

Mary Ann reasoned with herself. Who did she think she was, a beauty like Jane, with a queue of suitors to pick and choose from? Jack was the first man to want her and would certainly be the last. He was kindness itself and good-looking though she could never exactly remember his face when she was alone. But marriage was long, look at Daddy and Mummy, forever long, sleeping in the same room. When Jack kissed her she felt embarrassed; he talked a lot and laughed a lot and that was nice but she could not keep her mind on what he said. Perhaps if you weren't attractive to men, it worked the other way too, so you weren't very attracted to them.

Finally, because everyone seemed to accuse her, silently and sadly and somehow justly, of meanness, Mary Ann agreed to be engaged, but a long engagement; she had saved money to see the Far West, already glimpsed in the Moshi cinema, and she also wanted to visit her parents. Jack kissed her with unusual force and gave her a handsome diamond ring which she did not wear unless she was with him, for fear of losing it. Her innocence was her armour. Jack would have been more assertive sexually with a more experienced American girl. He was a bit frustrated but also pleased, as if he'd netted a rare bird of an almost extinct species. Mary Ann set off on bus and train to see America.

She kept thinking it was awfully small. Perhaps it wasn't but the cars and buses and trains and planes and roads made it feel crowded or used up; and there were signs of people everywhere, interminable muck, though when she reached the west and the mountains, it felt better, if not as splendid as in the films. She thought the California desert was like parts of Africa she didn't know, for she hardly knew Africa either, like the country around Lake Rudolf. She went walking, she was always searching for a chance to walk where there were no cars. The desert grew a rich crop of empty beer cans and bottles, and sometimes great mounds of used tyres, and dirty papers and plastic containers blew in the hot wind. She dared not tell Jack that she couldn't face it, so said she was now going home to visit her parents and wrote to him, sick with guilt, on the aeroplane, explaining that she could never make him happy and would he please forgive and forget. He would find his ring in the top right-hand drawer of the desk in Mrs Niedermeyer's guest room.

Her parents misunderstood Mary Ann's misery when she first returned, guessing at blighted love. They were glad when she revived which she did within four months upon receiving a letter, at once perky and hostile, from Mrs Niedermeyer announcing Jack's marriage to a girl born in Cleveland, someone he'd always known, a fine old family. Now, at thirty, Mary Ann knew that she would never marry. But the mountain was there, a gold mine for a botanist except that she never had a minute to herself.

If she'd known Jane was coming home, she might have stayed in Cleveland and married Jack. Daddy and Mummy were crackers; what did they mean dumping the whole hotel on her shoulders as if doing her a favour. Daddy and Mummy sat around boring the guests and making asses of themselves, boasting about Jane, you'd think Jane was Marlene Dietrich. Jane did nothing. She idled in her room with green cement on her face to ward off wrinkles and listened to her gramophone, wah-wah-wah bellowing about love like a sick cow. Or she floated among the guests being lordly or drove to Nairobi to chat up travel agents. What did Daddy and Mummy *mean*? Room boys, waiters, gardeners, kitchen staff, drivers, desk and office clerks, fifty-nine Africans and one Asian, and she alone was supposed to keep them all up to tourist standards. She was so tired and worried she felt sick. She was just about ready to give Jane a piece of her mind. High time someone took Jane down; she'd been conceited enough before she went to Europe and now she was worse. And Amir had gone on leave so there were the accounts as well; too much, too damn much, more than flesh and blood could stand.

Mary Ann had never before given Jane a piece of her mind. Jane stamped into the office where Mary Ann was bowed over a ledger, saying, 'There's an African drinking at the bar.'

Mary Ann went on, moving her lips, adding the long line of figures.

'Since when,' Jane said furiously, 'do Africans drink at our bar?'

'Since Independence,' Mary Ann said, still adding.

'It's the limit. Why do we put up with it?'

Mary Ann laid a ruler to mark her place and made a note. Then she turned to Jane. 'He's the M.P. for this district. A very nice man and an honest one. He even insists on paying for his beer. We're lucky he likes to stop in here when he's visiting his people.'

'Lucky?' Jane said with scorn. 'We certainly don't want African good will and a ghastly lot of African guests.'

'You fool,' Mary Ann said. 'We want African good will like mad. Haven't you heard about Independence? What do you keep under your peroxided hair? We're visitors here. It's not our colony, it's their country. If we insult Africans, we're out. Deported. They can do it and they do.'

'I never heard such rot. I'd rather sell the hotel than crawl to Africans.'

'Would you? Have you got a buyer? My God, how stupid can you be?'

Jane was too stunned by this turning worm to answer properly. Instead she said, 'I'm sure Daddy's put money aside.'

'Think again. They've ploughed the profits back so they could make a big fancy hotel for us, to keep us in our old age. Were you rude to him?'

'He smiled at me,' Jane said, furious again. 'I didn't say anything but I imagine he got the message.'

'Oh for God's sake. Now I'll have to go and try to make up for you. You tiresome dangerous half-wit.'

Jane brooded and fumed and sulked and, for once, her parents backed Mary Ann.

'We've had very few African guests,' Bob said. 'Mostly Ministers. Decent well-behaved chaps. Africans don't really like it here and it's quite expensive for them. But of course we do our best to make them happy if they come; we must, Jane. It's different from when you were a child. They don't want the hotel and they know we're useful for the tourist trade. But believe me, if we offended them, they wouldn't worry about anything practical, they'd kick us out.'

From spite, to show up Mary Ann and her parents, Jane unleashed all her charms and wiles on the next African guest. He was the new African, a young bureaucrat in a grey flannel suit. He came from the coast; there were ancient mixtures of Arab in his blood; he had a sharp nose and carved lips and a beautifully muscled slender tall body. With white skin, he would have resembled a Greek god as portrayed in the statues in the Rome museums which Jane had never visited. His name was Paul Nbaigu, a Christian like the Jenkins. He had a bureaucrat's job in the Ministry of Co-operatives and a European's taste for bathrooms and respectfully served food. Instead of staying with the African manager of a Co-op, he chose to do his inspector's round from Travellers' Rest. At the bar, where he was quietly drinking whisky and soda, splurging his pay on European pleasures, Jane joined him, introduced herself and smiled her best, sad, alluring, professional singer's smile. She might have been moaning more of the ritual blues' words: why doan yah luv me like yah useta do.

Jane suggested sharing his table at dinner, more spiteful bravado: let her family see what crawling to Africans looked like. Paul Nbaigu could not refuse but failed to appear honoured. Jane began to notice him.

'Where did you learn English?' Jane asked. 'You speak it perfectly.'

'Here and there. And at Makerere University.'

She could hardly inquire where he'd learned his table manners which were faultless. He began to notice Jane too, in particular the way she treated the waiter, not seeing the man, giving orders contemptuously. A small flame started to burn in the mind of Mr Nbaigu, who did not love white people though he did not specially love black people either.

'Where did you learn Swahili?' he asked.

'I was born here.'

'Upcountry Swahili,' Mr Nbaigu said mildly. 'On the coast, we rather make fun of it.'

He was not easy to talk to but Jane had never talked with an educated African before, nor talked with any of them since childhood when she ruled as queen of the infant population in the nearby Chagga village. And talk was not really the point. All during dinner – roast lamb, mint sauce, potatoes, cauliflower, treacle tart, good plain English cooking, Dorothy's pride and specialty – Jane felt an alarming sensation, as if waves of electricity flowed from this handsome composed African and rippled over her body. She was babbling like a nervous girl by the time muddy coffee was served. Mr Nbaigu excused himself, saying he had work to do. Jane swaggered across the dining room to her family's table.

'Well?' she said. 'Making Africans happy, Daddy, buttering up our bosses.'

Bob nodded and continued to chew treacle tart. Dorothy's hands trembled but she said nothing.

'He's not one of our better bosses,' Mary Ann remarked.

'And how do you know?' Jane asked.

'I've friends, Chaggas. They don't like the way he stays here and pops in on them, all neat and citified, and asks a few questions and gives a few orders, and hurries off. They think he cares about his job for himself, not for them.'

'You've certainly got your finger on the pulse of the nation. Why don't you become a Tanzanian citizen so you can really shove in and run things? Does he come often?'

'Every few months,' Bob said. 'He's got Meru district too, probably more. Mary Ann's right; he's not popular with the African farmers. A proper bureaucrat, same breed all over the world. Funny how quick the Africans have picked that up. They've taken to government paperwork like ducks to water.'

Dorothy still did not speak; Mary Ann was too angry to look at her sister. Jane's little exhibition had hurt the parents. They were incurably old colonialists, not the wicked ogres of propaganda either, kinder and more responsible employers than Africans were, ready to expend time and thought and money to help any Africans in their neighbourhood who needed help. Mary Ann knew of all the loans, all the transport to hospital, all the home doctoring, all the advising: calls for aid heeded by day and night over the years. Like good officers, they cared for and liked their troops. But there it was: Africans were Other Ranks. By law, Africans were now equal. Laws had not changed, emotions. And the sight of a white woman with a black man roused emotions which Mary Ann did not understand, but knew her parents were feeling now.

Clearly, Jane had been teaching the family a lesson: do not criticize Jane, however gently. They were helpless, and Mary Ann wished Jane would turn into Janina again and depart before boredom and frustration made her sharpen her claws on the old people.

Jane dreamed of the black man several times and woke afraid. Erotic dreams, ugly dreams. She cursed Luigi and knew with fear that Luigi had left her with more than a broken heart and that she was starving and she was also getting older and perhaps she would starve to death, taking a long time over it, a long empty man-less time. She went to Nairobi more often; she sat at the pavement tables of the Thorn Tree café looking at men, to see if she could find someone she wanted. No one. East Africa appeared to be overrun by middle-aged tourists wearing paunches and peculiar clothes, rumpled garments from where they came or instant comical safari kit. Or there were very young men, young as puppies, with masses of hair and occasionally beards to make them sweat more, with shorts little better than fig leaves and strong brown hairy legs. She wanted someone as beautiful as Luigi and far more trustworthy; an Anglo-Saxon of thirty-odd, perfectly groomed, perfectly made, and single.

Paul Nbaigu returned sooner than usual; something was wrong with the coffee plants on a co-operative farm, a bug, a fungus. The farmers were anxious, he had to report. Jane joined him again at the bar but now she was hesitant, not graciously condescending, and he was worried for he knew nothing about his job except how to fill and file all the mimeographed forms. They talked little, locked in their separate trouble, but the waves of electricity flowed even more strongly over Jane, concentrating, it seemed, where Luigi had most expertly caressed her body.

She was staring at Paul Nbaigu, hypnotized, when he turned to her and something unknown happened: she felt herself drawn into his eyes as if they had widened like black caves and she was physically pulled into them. At the same moment, mindlessly, she knew that electricity now moved both ways, that he too felt this hot demanding warmth on his body. She blinked, to break the spell; and they looked at each other, startled, sharing absolute knowledge without words.

Jane did not suggest joining Paul Nbaigu for dinner but sat with her family, lost to everything except the sensation of spinning in a whirlpool, voiceless with terror, and compelled by inescapable force to the dark sucking centre.

'Aren't you hungry, darling?' Bob asked.

'No, Daddy.' Surprised she could speak and surprised by

that voice, someone else's. Her own voice was screaming silently, No! No! No! to another question.

'You don't look well, Jane,' Dorothy said. 'You haven't forgotten to take your Nivaquine? They say there's a lot of malaria in Nairobi now. There never used to be, before, but everything's so changed.'

Mary Ann was silent too, though eating heartily. An Englishman had arrived that afternoon, in a scarred Landrover, and asked a magical question: what was the best way from here into the rain forest? She told him, longing to ask why, and he obliged without questioning. 'I'm a botanist,' he said, and was amazed by the delighted warmth of her smile. Now Mary Ann was debating whether she could seek him out, after dinner, without seeming pushy; wondering, beyond that, if he would let her go along some time to watch and learn.

Mary Ann was settled in the lounge, chatting to a tall skinny Englishman, whose neck was also tall and skinny and badly reddened by sun, obviously a newcomer getting his first dose of the climate, with a skin all wrong for it. Jane pretended to be casual about the guests' register: Paul Nbaigu was in room 24. Second floor of the main building, and there was no reason for her to go up the wide wooden stairs. The family lived in a log cabin of their own, like the bungalows only larger and set back in a private garden west of the hotel buildings. Mr and Mrs Jenkins would circulate a bit, asking the guests pleasant questions about their day, available for complaints or requests, and then take a torch to light their way home. Mary Ann seemed glued where she was, hanging on the Englishman's words. Jane roamed through the bar and lounge and stepped out to the verandah, useful at night for brief star-gazing if cloud permitted or it wasn't raining; in all cases too cold to linger. Paul Nbaigu must be in his room.

She felt now like a sleepwalker at the edge of the whirl-pool, dreaming her helplessness and the force that pulled her. She had stopped thinking of her parents, Mary Ann or any inquisitive guests; she was not thinking at all; she was moving slowly towards the powerful drowning centre. She did not knock at the door of room 24; she turned the knob and entered. He was waiting for her.

He locked the door and turned off the light; a gleam came from the lighted bathroom. He took her face in his hands and kissed her once, but kissing was not what they needed. In silence, in the shadowed room, they got rid of their clothes, pulling them off and dropping them on the floor. Then he held her, close against him, the whole length of their bodies pressed hard together. He groaned softly, softer than a whisper. She felt deaf and blind; all sensation was direct and overwhelming through the skin. He lifted her and laid her on the bed. They made no sound, and muffled the final wrenching cries against each other's bodies.

Much later, Paul Nbaigu looked at the luminous dial of his watch. 'Go now,' he said. Jane obeyed, collecting her clothes from the floor and dressing herself without care. The man lay silent on the bed. When she had her hand on the doorknob, he said, 'Tomorrow'. No other words had been spoken. She moved as secretly as a hunting cat and was not seen or heard on the way to the Jenkins bungalow. The family was asleep; in the morning they would not question her. Adults could not live together if they spent their time questioning. Presumably she had stayed in the lounge, perhaps playing bridge.

Mary Ann found the day difficult. The cook had forgotten suddenly and entirely how to make apple pie. This sort of amnesia was frequent and why not? Africans never ate the European food, had no idea how it should taste and merely remembered - except for lapses - how to cook it and how it was supposed to look when done. Five houseboys sent word they were at death's door having got drunk on village homebrew the night before; the hotel was full. Three Landrovers were out of commission just when everyone seemed bent on making the cold bumpy trip to the Bismarck Hut to watch the sun rise or set over the vast gleaming top of the mountain. Several guests had objected to their bar bills which were inaccurate. The barman, who wrote the chits, had in his eyes a look which Mary Ann knew well; he was withdrawn into the dream world that Europeans cannot penetrate or imagine; all his outside actions were meaningless, he was living elsewhere. Routine, nothing special, nothing to get fussed about. But today Mary Ann was absorbed by what Jim Withers, the botanist, had said last night; she was repeating it to herself; she needed time to sort it out.

He explained himself, he thought simply and clearly, and left Mary Ann baffled.

'I've got a grant for a year,' Dr Withers said. 'Another scientific carpet-bagger. If it keeps up like this, there'll be more scientists than business men here, all carpet-bagging like crazy. Poor Africa. Anyway I comfort myself that I'm harmless, don't cost anyone here a penny and won't destroy anything. It's my sabbatical, I'm a botany don in a university you'll not have heard of, and I've got this grant to work up a survey of the plant ecology of the montane rain forest. Best luck that ever happened to me. I've always wanted to come to Africa but lacked the lolly, of course.'

What could it all mean?

Then they talked about the rain forest; slowly, it seemed that Mary Ann was doing the talking. He listened and said, seriously, 'Look, this is damned unfair. You should have the grant and make the survey and get the recognition. It's your bailiwick and you know it like the back of your hand. Let's do it together, you sign the work too; I'll see you get paid, if need be I'll split the grant. It can't cost much to live here, specially as I'll be camping.'

'Oh no,' Mary Ann said, 'Oh no.'

'Why not?'

'I wouldn't dream of it; besides there's the hotel. My parents have practically turned it over to us, you see.'

'Well, if you can't take time off for fieldwork during the week, I can bring samples and consult you, and you could surely get away on Sundays. I mean it, I want to work with you. It's purely selfish of me, you could save me all sorts of time and keep me from making dumb mistakes.'

Heaven, Mary Ann thought. For the first time in her life, something she wanted to do with all her heart. Not work at all, plain bliss. He was called Doctor, she found out, because he was a Ph.D.; and don meant professor, far better than dear long-lost Miss Peabody.

She was not going to lose this chance. If the hotel fell apart that might make Daddy and Mummy see how lunatic they were, she didn't care, Jane wasn't the only one who had the right to a life of her own. And Dr Withers did indeed need her badly. Mary Ann thought he was wonderfully sporting and eager but not very practical. She hired a safari servant, despite his protests ('I can cook and look after myself, I'm not used to servants'). But camping, Mary Ann explained, was an occupation in itself: gathering firewood and making fires, boiling water, washing up, washing clothes, even if he cooked for himself which was a good idea; and besides someone had to help him in the forest. No, it would be unwise to set up his tent actually in the rain forest, too damp and gloomy, but she knew a sort of glade by a stream where she'd always thought she'd like to stay.

In the late afternoon, between tea and dinner when not much could happen at the hotel, Mary Ann drove up the track and bumped across country to Dr Withers' site, a grassy slope shaded by wild fig and mvule and podo trees, with a stream between high banks, the water creaming around boulders and smooth over brown pebbles. She counted a day ruined if she could not come; her heart lifted when she saw the neat camp. The big tent that was Jim's home and office, Koroga's small tent, the thatched cookhouse lean-to with firewood stacked to keep dry, the careful circle of stones around the charred camp fire, the tarpaulin-screened latrine, the unscreened shower bucket hanging from a branch.

Jim learned a little Swahili before he came; Koroga knew some English after three years at a mission school but Jim had asked Mary Ann to translate in Chagga his one firm

order. 'I didn't come here to spoil the ecology,' Jim said.
'Please explain to Koroga that we'll leave no muck behind
us, we'll keep this place clean, we bury or burn. I never saw
anywhere more beautiful and we won't pollute the stream
either, we share the latrine. Get that across to Koroga like
a darling. I'll raise the roof if I see one tin thrown in the
bushes.'

Jim and Koroga were always there, back from cutting
their way through the forest, collecting samples. The big
plastic bags full of the day's haul lay beside the table where
Jim sorted the samples and wrote his observations in the
field notebooks. Plant presses were drying on two charcoal
braziers. If Koroga was not washing or ironing their
clothes, he might be practising with obvious delight his
new skill of mounting samples with Bexol. Jim said that
Koroga's hands, with the dried bits of leaf and flower and
that oil can of plastic glue, were more adept than his; just
as he said the accuracy of Mary Ann's line drawings in
Indian ink made his look like baby bungling. 'What would
I do without you both?' Jim asked. She adored the feeling
of this place, three workers in the vineyards of science.

She had returned Jim's paint-box and delivered a water-
colour sketch and her information on the habits and habitat
of a plant with a narrow pointed leaf and three-petalled
lavender flower when Jim suddenly put his arm around her
and laughed and said, 'You know what you are? You're
the most wonderful odd little creature who ever lived.' And
kissed the top of her head. That made Mary Ann shy, but
the next day he had forgotten his outburst and was asking
about a spidery moss. Mary Ann found it intoxicating and
incredible that a professor should make notes on what she
said.

Jane had become less of a nuisance. She went off to Dar
where she said there were many travel agents, as yet
unapproached; and then to Arusha, another haven for
travel agents. When at home, Jane seemed detached and
rather sleepy. She made no further exhibitions with Paul
Nbaigu, who stayed at the hotel more often now; and Mary

Ann thought it a good thing that Jane spent so little time with the guests, not having been sure that the guests were as charmed by Jane's queenly intrusions as Daddy believed.

Paul Nbaigu had never had a white woman before. He imagined them cold and proud and thought probably their skin would be clammy, fish-belly white. Jane must be in a class by herself. She was the most passionate and insatiable woman in his wide experience. Sometimes he felt they were eating each other, swallowing each other whole, not just copulating. There was none of the teasing and joking you got with African girls; Jane looked at him, he looked at her, they didn't need more to set them on fire. He hated to admit any of the backwardness of his people but a lot of African girls were still circumcised and you never knew how much they were fooling you and how much they felt. With Jane, you knew. And he had tested her good and proper, he wasn't taking any Memsaab stuff, he made jolly sure she worshipped every inch of his black skin. Beautiful, my God, she was beautiful, and the easy stylish way she wore those clothes that came from Paris and Rome and London. All for him, all to himself, and no other black man before him.

On the other hand, he had to be careful. He did not mean to risk his job for her. A few top African people had European wives, but they were the old boys, in at the start. He doubted whether even a European mistress would be wise nowadays. He intended to end up a Cabinet Minister and saw no reason why not. Though he lusted for her, simply thinking about her made him sweat, he was going to tell Jane she had to stop following him around. She wasn't exactly invisible and he wasn't unknown, being an official; and it began to look dicey the way she was in Dar or Arusha when he was, and he couldn't chance coming to Travellers' Rest so often either. The local Co-ops might begin to wonder why he showed up all the time and make inquiries at the Ministry in Dar and nothing good would come of that.

When he explained to Jane, she beat against his chest

with her fists and cried out with such anguish that he clamped his hand over her mouth. Then she wept in shuddering sobs, the way his womenfolk wept at a death. Nothing would calm her except his body, and he had a frightening vision of an octopus, strong white writhing arms holding him, crushing him. Later he said it again, coldly, 'The way I want or not at all.' Then, curiously, 'Don't you ever think about your family? What if they got wind of this? They wouldn't be very happy.'

'I don't care, I don't care. I don't care about anything except you.'

'You care about me, pretty Jane, from the waist down. If you really cared about me, you'd care about my career too.'

'Oh, career! Don't be ridiculous! What sort of career is there in a stupid little tinpot African country?'

It was the turning point. He did not desire her less but saw her now as the enemy, like all whites, in her heart despising his country and his people and thus himself and his hopes. To Jane, they were servants, people without faces, meant to take orders. She would obey him, Paul decided, and she would eat dirt and like it, and then finally she would beg forgiveness for insulting his nation. Jane followed him to Dar once more. Paul had never told her where he lived. Before, he had come discreetly to her hotel room late at night. This time Paul refused to see her and she had the sense – not because of her family or her reputation but from her knowledge of Paul – not to pursue him to his office or waylay him outside the Ministry door.

Jane returned to Kilimanjaro and waited, suffering the agony of withdrawal symptoms. Dorothy wanted to call the doctor in Moshi but Jane said she was only tired, for God's sake leave me alone, let me rest in bed, send trays from time to time and please please please will everyone get the hell out and stay out. Mary Ann was too involved with botany and Jim Withers to pay much attention. 'Temperament,' Mary Ann said. 'After all, she's the famous singer, Janina.' The parents were distressed by both their girls: one seemed to be hysterically ailing and the other seemed heartlessly indifferent.

Mary Ann was concerned about Jim. February was supposed to be a dry month but instead was one long drip; the man had lived in his tent for six weeks and would soon be growing moss, not studying it. He would turn against the place; he would want to move; Mary Ann could not bear the thought. No, of course not, Jim was a scientist with work to do, and she had never seen a man so concentrated and so disciplined. She had also never seen a man so constantly exuberantly happy. Until the last few weeks. Now something was the matter. Perhaps he only needed a break, a rest, and surely he would enjoy a hot bath. She suggested that he weekend at the hotel.

'Darling Mary Ann,' said Jim. 'It's a beauty hotel but it's expensive as it has a right to be. And my branch of science is not spoiled with money. I've got to stretch that grant a good long way. Besides, this home you chose for me is the best I've ever had. The richest man in England would envy me; imagine having trout out of your own stream for breakfast.'

So Koroga was poaching upstream with poison in the time-honoured Chagga way. Mary Ann gave Koroga a sharp look, Koroga smiled innocently, and Mary Ann decided to forget it. In fact, good for Koroga if trout at breakfast made Jim happy.

'I consider that I am living in the lap of luxury,' said Dr Withers who meant it but also pined for a hot bath and something longer, wider and softer than his canvas cot.

'You had a very expensive room. We've got much cheaper ones. Though I wish you'd come as my parents' guest. We invite friends all the time.'

This was not true and would have resulted in early bankruptcy. Mary Ann knew Jim would not accept that invitation but she could quickly whip the price card off the room door, and there would be no problem with her parents in making special arrangements about his bill.

'We'll see, and thank you,' Dr Withers said. 'We really

ought to set up as a permanent team. You know everything and I can look up the names. Now help me place this uninspiring growth. It's Haloragidaceae, the water milfoil family, of which there are eight genera and . . .'

'How much is your grant?' Mary Ann asked sternly, because she was so afraid of offending him.

'£2,500. Sounds a lot but the Landrover and the camping stuff and air fares all come out of it. I told you my branch of science isn't overwhelmed with money. If I could find a poisonous grass or a flower that killed on touch, and think of a way to plant them wherever our rulers dreamed up an enemy, I'd get a grant of millions. But nobody, I promise you, gives a hoot for botany except some scientists and little old ladies who like to press wild flowers.'

'And me,' Mary Ann said.

'Yes, and you, bless you.'

'Please come to the hotel for the weekend.'

'Mary Ann, I should tell you that I'm married.'

She hoped and prayed that her face showed nothing, not knowing until this minute that there would be anything to show. Now she knew, and it was heavy sad knowledge.

'I don't see how that affects having a bath,' she said.

'No. But it affects me. You see, I'm in love with you. And I don't know what to do. I'm thirty-six and badly married and I have two children and no money to mention and I clamber around the forest all day thinking of you and when you'll come and when I'm not doing that I think about Adele and how frightful it will be to go home to her and then I think about Billy and Mike.'

She took his hand, a big freckled hand with good Kilimanjaro earth under the finger nails. Heavy and sad for him too.

'We have a year,' Mary Ann said. 'No, but more than ten months.'

'It's not enough. I want to spend the rest of my life with you in Africa. Adele is brainless, that's not a crime, maybe not even a handicap. It's her emotions I can't stand. They're all small and competitive and ungenerous. If I walk out, she'd get the boys and I couldn't leave them to be brought up by her; it would be like crippling them. What can I do?'

'Nothing,' Mary Ann said, and felt deep lines forming on her face: old age and loneliness.

'Mary Ann darling, I never stopped to ask if you care at all for me.'

'Yes,' she said. 'I didn't know it until now. I thought it was only botany.'

He laughed and leaned awkwardly across from his camp stool and awkwardly kissed her.

'Oh hell, I must get a sofa up here so at least I can put my arms around you. You darling delicious little brown girl, to think I've made you unhappy too.'

'But will you come for the weekend?'

'Yes. We mustn't waste a minute. And who knows, I might get a brainwave and figure out how to manage life. I can't say I've ever managed anything to date except plant life. Would you mind standing up and then I'll bend down and kiss you without falling off my stool.'

Even that was awkward, due to his extreme height and her lack of it, but gentle and tender and satisfactory to them both.


Paul Nbaigu made no plans but felt himself guided: the words and the acts came of themselves. He was in fact possessed. Cruelty, the power to inflict pain, possessed his mind. Jane's crime – contempt, insult – merged with all the other white man's crimes. She was linked to the outrage of South Africa and Rhodesia and Mozambique; to every offence he had endured before Independence when he was a native in a British colony; to the sneering European professors who sent him away from Makerere after only one year. He hated Jane's white skin for he knew he longed to be white like her, European, rich and travelled and well-dressed and arrogant like her. Insanely, he was revenging all his people by scourging one white woman. He was reckless now, he could not resist the joy of his power. Each humiliation that Jane accepted inspired him with a wild urge to impose worse humiliations. He forgot his precautions about his job. He came to Travellers' Rest every weekend, leaving his work unfinished elsewhere to get the time, turning in hastily invented reports and forged forms to hide dereliction of duty. His salary would not cover this weekly extravagance. It was a special pleasure that Jane had to pay for the room where he made her suffer.

He was not waiting when Jane came to his room now; he was reading.

'Hungry, pretty Jane?' he whispered, since he still had some caution left, enough to know that Mr Jenkins would bar him from the hotel forever if Jane's visits were heard. Jane dreaded that whispering taunting voice, and every word it spoke. She dared not answer back, if she could have imagined any answer, because she knew the certain punishment; Paul would withhold what she craved.

'Take your clothes off,' he whispered, 'and wait until I'm ready.'

And she did, again, as often before, numb with shame, silent, tears sliding down her cheeks. It excited him unbearably to find her aching and arched to his touch, her face wet with this proof of her servitude. He resented his own need, as avid as hers though different. He would only be master when he could play with her and use her and feel nothing.

'What a bore,' he whispered, 'I think I'll take a rest,' knowing he had left her at the peak of that slow undulating yearning climb.

'Paul, Paul, please, please, please.'

'No.' He removed her desperate hands and felt her by his side, shivering like a dog.

'Stop crying,' he whispered. 'You're losing your looks. You go on like this and you'll be so ugly even a white man won't have you. All right. Come here.'

The sob of relief, of gratitude, was delicious but never enough. for he wanted her too; he had not entirely won yet.

He invented games. 'We're going to be two nice simple Africans, pretty Jane. You're a Chagga woman with a big round ass and a bundle of kuni on your head and I'm a big sweaty fellow in from the fields, just passing by and thinking what a nice quick fuck you'd make.'

'*No*.'

'No?' he whispered, mocking.

'Yes.'

'That's better.'

Her mind was empty except for a ceaseless incantation: come to me, come to me, come to me. By the end of each Sunday they were exhausted from cruelty given and received and from the gluttony of their bodies.

The servants knew. Jane had not realized at first what was happening. Imperious as always with them, she ordered Jagi, a houseboy, to empty ashtrays in the lounge, remarking that he was lazy and stupid not to do it without being told. Instead of mumbling some excuse, the man smiled broadly and picked up an ashtray with insolent languor. Jane went to Mary Ann demanding that Jagi be sacked for cheekiness and incompetence. Mary Ann, counting groceries in a storeroom, said wearily, 'It's not your job to supervise staff, Jane, I wish you wouldn't meddle.'

'Is it all right with you if the lounge looks like an African beer parlour?'

It was too much trouble to explain to Jane the routine of the hotel; one houseboy was not detailed to lurk in wait for every stubbed cigarette end, there were regular hours when the waiters tidied up. This was not Jagi's task and Jagi was a perfectly efficient room boy and perfectly polite. Mary Ann knew Jane's manner to the staff and assumed Jagi had simply been fed up and showed it.

'Jagi's been here fourteen years,' Mary Ann said. 'You can't just sack people offhand any more. They have rights based on years of employment. There'd be a huge to-do with the labour office, the whole staff might walk out, and even if we won, there'd be a mountain of bonus pay. For heaven's sake, Jane, calm down and leave the Africans to me.'

After that it was like a nightmare, when one dreamed of running into endless closed doors but now it was endless knowing smiles; every African on the place had that smile, only for her, and only when she was alone, whether she gave them an order or not. The smiles were an extension of Paul's horrible whispers. Jane stayed in her room most of the day and surprised the family by saying that she could not stand the scruffy way Josphat cleaned the bungalow and the body odour he left behind him; she would look after her own room from now on. Since the parents and Mary Ann were seldom in their bungalow, they did not notice the obsessional way Jane took baths, four and five times a day, scrubbing herself with a loofah, muttering frantic promises: I won't, I won't, not ever again . . . Nor, of course, did they notice when she took to drink.

The week, waiting for known misery, became unendurable. Jane could not free her mind of its sickening memories nor could she bear the shame of wanting Paul still. As she was safe from the Africans' smiles with the guests around her, she began to sit at the bar, drinking with them before dinner. When one group left for the dining room, Jane joined another group and so became drunk for the first time in her life. Bob saw this at once and spoke to her gently.

'Jane darling, at this altitude drink goes straight to the head and I think you've had a wee one too many. You don't know about whisky, little girl. It's nice of you to keep the guests company but you'll be safer with tomato juice. I'm afraid you're going to have a bad headache or tummy-ache tomorrow.'

Jane realized that drink had blurred everything, the rooms around her and the people in them, and the agony in her mind and the burning in her body; all had become wavy and far off, not really attached to her; and sleep came as immediate merciful darkness. She had heard the guests talking about drink; Americans especially were partial to vodka.

'Doesn't smell on your breath,' one said.

'Doesn't really taste on your tongue either,' said another. 'But it does the job all right.'

In the middle of the afternoon, in the deserted lounge, Jane risked the barman's inevitable smile and sent him off with a load of soft drinks to the Jenkins bungalow. She then stole a bottle of vodka, slipping it into a large embroidery bag brought along for the purpose. She did not think of driving to Moshi to buy a supply, nor imagine any consequences. That afternoon, alone in her room, Jane drank vodka until the walls began to tilt; the bed swayed and circled when she reached it; she was asleep, dead drunk, when Dorothy came to call her for dinner. Dorothy ordered a tray with a thermos of soup and cold meat and salad to take back to the bungalow later.

'I'm terribly worried about Jane,' Dorothy said. She could talk freely because Mary Ann was dining at another table with her botanist, Dr Withers.

'She looks so dragged down,' Dorothy said. 'It's not fever, I don't think, but something's very wrong. Intestinal parasites maybe? Only I don't see how, with the kitchen so clean; unless she picked up a bug in Dar or Nairobi or somewhere. She won't listen to me. She won't see Dr Ramtullah. I'm really terribly anxious, Bob.'

'Yes, Dorry, I know. I'm worried about Mary Ann too. The child's tired, that's what. It's too much for her; she's practically running the hotel single-handed. Jane's been wonderful with the travel agents but there's nothing more for her to do, and jollying the guests isn't a very interesting job. Probably poor Jane is bored sick, she's used to a much gayer life than we have here. Sometimes I wish we didn't have to charge so much, we'd get younger people; you know they're mostly pretty well along, the ones who come here. Oh my, I'm afraid we retired a bit too soon, Dorry girl.'

'What shall we do, Bob?'

'Well, you're so tactful, love, couldn't you offer to take some of the staff work off Mary Ann; perhaps the kitchen department as a start? I'll tell her I'm tired of sitting around and say I'd like to get back to the office, I think that would ease her quite a lot. And slowly we'll nudge our way in again. But Jane, well, what can we do? You know it's possible after all the time she's been away that the altitude upsets her. Could we suggest she go to the coast for a long holiday? There's that club at Kilifi, I heard it's very attractive and all the smart people from Kenya go there and overseas visitors; it might cheer her up. Then we'll have to see. If she wants to go back to Europe, Dorry, of course we'll help her.'

Dorothy smiled sadly. 'It was lovely while it lasted,' she said.

'Children aren't born to help parents, Dorry dear, we know that, it's the other way around. One day the girls will have their own children to look after.' But as he said it, he saw Dorry's face and knew his own would have the same hurt look of revelation. He couldn't believe it, Dorry couldn't believe it: their babies, born on this mountain, the golden-haired little nymph and the funny little brown muffin, were women in their thirties. It was late, almost too late: no sign of husbands, no sign of grandchildren. Two grown women, their daughters, both looking ill, both stuck here with no future except more of the same, a future like their parents' past.

'I wish to God we'd never built this whacking place,' Bob said with passion. 'I wish we'd saved every penny of the profits and put it in a bank in Switzerland so we could get up and go, now, all of us, to where the girls have a better chance.'

'No, my dear,' Dorothy said and took his hand. 'You mustn't talk like that. We've had a wonderful life here and the girls have a fine business to inherit. You mustn't forget how happy we all were when they were growing up. It's just a bad piece of time now, troubled like, but it will pass, you'll see. I won't have you regretting what we've worked so hard for. It isn't right. Now smile at me and tomorrow we'll begin fixing everything just as you said.'

Mary Ann found out about Jane's drinking in an obvious way: there was a discrepancy in supplies, so much liquor accounted for and so much more gone. In the wine cellar, the vodka was fourteen bottles short. Mugo had been with them as long as Mary Ann could remember; he must have lost his mind to start pinching one kind of drink and in such quantity, and what on earth was he doing with it? He didn't drink himself; Mary Ann could not imagine the mountain Chaggas paying large sums for foreign booze when they got tight as owls on their own homebrew; did he sell it in Moshi? She chose a time when no one was at the bar and, hating to, accused Mugo of theft. He looked shocked and said with dignity, in Swahili, 'I thought you knew, Memsaab Mariani. Memsaab Janny took those bottles, all the time, she takes them to her room and drinks them. Ask Josphat how he finds them in the dustbin behind your house.'

Mary Ann begged his pardon and asked him not to speak of this to anyone.

'Everyone knows,' Mugo said, 'except your father and mother and the European guests.'

Mary Ann felt her cheeks flaming, but managed to say quietly, 'All right, Mugo, and so it must remain.'

Now what? It was too much; it was more than she could take. She walked out into the garden, pretending to inspect the farthest wall where bougainvillaea splashed great sprays of scarlet and orange and yellow. She had problems of her own, secrets of her own, and felt like a trapped rat desperately trying to find a way out. She had sensed a peculiar atmosphere among the hotel Africans, something strange which she could not identify or understand, but clearly this was it.

The eldest daughter of the house was a thief and a drunk. Mary Ann knew the Africans well, knew their laughter, their mockery, even the most loyal would be pleased to see the mighty wazungu fallen, silly sinners like themselves. Word would spread up and down the mountain. How could they hope to keep order in the hotel with the Africans privately laughing at this splendid joke? Especially as it was Jane, who treated them as if she were the Queen of Heaven and they were insects beneath her feet? We've come back to ruin our parents, Mary Ann thought with despair, ruin all their work and spoil their lives. In return for love and kindness, this was what their daughters were giving them: disgrace.

It was a perfect April day, with huge white iceberg clouds floating over a bright blue sky. Pansies, calla lilies, lupins, roses, geraniums, larkspur, violets, in sun and shade flowers gleamed as if lacquered. The air was rackety with birdsong, and Mary Ann wished she were dead.

She would have to take the only action she could think of. The parents were in Moshi, luckily, ordering supplies; Mary Ann had agreed to relinquish some of her duties, not saying it was about time, before she collapsed from running the hotel on her own. And Jane, of course, would be in her room where Mary Ann never went, and Jane was, listening to a successful rival on her gramophone, and drunk though not helplessly so, having learned the dosage of vodka required to dull life but not knock her off her feet. Jane made no attempt to hide the bottle.

Mary Ann said, 'You have to stop, Jane, or you have to go away. Better if you did both. The watu all know you're stealing and drinking by yourself. It's a matter of time before Daddy and Mummy find out, and they must not ever. Daddy wants you to take a holiday at the coast and God knows why you refused. We can't run the hotel if the Africans laugh at us, you know that, you can't have forgotten everything you knew before you went away.'

'Finished?' Jane said.

'Yes.' Mary Ann wanted to hit her; that maddening smile, that special Jane smile, condescending to lesser mortals.

'You doan know the half of it, dearie.'

Mary Ann shuddered with distaste.

'I know enough. Jane, go to Kenya, the coast, I'll see you get plenty of money. You can drink yourself blind, for all I care, just so you don't do it here. Jane, please.'

'Good lil Mary Ann, goody goody lil Mary Ann. Jane's the baddy; Mary Ann's the goody. I'm staying right here. Got my reasons. Got *a* reason.'

'I'll see you get no more drink, I'll find a way, I promise you.'

'Can't stop me driving to Moshi. Buy a crate. Too lazy before but not much trouble.'

'Jane, I beg you, think of Daddy and Mummy, don't you care about anyone in the world but yourself?'

'*Yes!*' Jane shouted. 'Now get out!'

It was a dim last hope and Mary Ann controlled her voice.

'Listen to me, Jane. You're destroying your looks. I had no idea why and Mummy thinks you're ill. Your face is puffy and the skin isn't marvellous the way it was. Your eyes have veins in them. You can't want to spoil all that, you must take care of yourself, you're a great beauty. If you go on like this, you'll be ugly.'

'So I've been told,' Jane said drearily. 'Now get out, will you?'

It was early to drive up the road through the powdery red dust, but Mary Ann decided she had to get away to the peace of Jim's camp. Perhaps she had been right in the beginning when she said she thought she'd loved only botany; she loved this work and admired it, the slow and thorough completion of a task.

She brooded vaguely on Koroga whose family she knew; they were ordinary mountain people and lived in the usual welter of babies, chickens, rags, pots, rubbish. Koroga was a nice boy, perhaps twenty years old, willing to work as a casual labourer on the coffee or pyrethrum farms if he got the chance and also willing to lounge around the village. Koroga was now changed beyond recognition. Had he been infected by Jim's example? Or was it the way Jim treated Koroga, with courtesy and confidence, rather as if Koroga were a student, sharing this project, eager to learn skills and accept responsibility.

Not knowing Africans, Jim found nothing remarkable in Koroga's recent conversion to tidiness and reliability. Mary Ann had meant to warn Jim that the watu got uncontrollably bored from time to time and disappeared for a beer party and dance, or disappeared into their special dream state and forgot all duties. It could be disastrous with no evil intent; Koroga might let the plant presses burn from absent-mindedness. Koroga instead had become a devoted assistant. He only stopped work when Jim asked him to; then they drank beer and talked together companionably about the animals Jim had so far failed to meet in the forest. Koroga would be heartbroken when Jim left the mountain. Pure luck. Well, someone had to be lucky around here.

Oh yes, Jim was happy as a lark. He was thrilled by the work and by its progress. He loved Mary Ann. He hadn't a problem in the world; England, Adele, the boys, the future were blotted out as irrelevant to the exciting present. Mary Ann steered around a deep pothole and told herself that she must not, she absolutely must not take against Jim. No one was guilty; inexperience could not be a sin though it was obviously a hell of a disadvantage.

Jim had been stunned when he realized Mary Ann was a virgin. Well, why not, a virgin of thirty must be a peculiar event; spinster was probably a better word than virgin. He was far from happy then, on the contrary, almost tearful, blaming himself, begging her forgiveness, wretched with the certainty he had hurt her, which he had, though she could not see it mattered so much, it was by no means a fatal wound. She'd had no time to consider how she felt about her initiation into the rites of love, being too busy consoling Jim. It turned out that whereas he was her first man, she was his second woman. He had married at twenty-four, a gawky shy studious young man, a virgin himself, and been faithful not from love but because he had neither opportunity nor confidence to stray. His field had always been botany, not sex.

Innocence protected them both. Mary Ann went openly

to Jim's room when he came to the hotel, and no one remarked on it. They ate at a separate table, obviously wrapped up in each other's talk, and no one gossiped. Sometimes, in the late afternoon, they wandered off into the forest and Jim, overcome by the sylvan idyll aspect, made love to her, and no African spied on them. Hiding nothing, no one seemed to notice there was anything to hide. They were accepted as a pair of botanists, not a pair of lovers.

Meanwhile, inexperience was the enemy. Though Mary Ann was a virgin, Jim assumed she knew the drill on birth control since she did not mention the matter. Adele had managed all that side. Mary Ann was waiting for guidance, to be told what to do next. So no one did anything and the result was known now only to Mary Ann, and known by instinct; she was sick in the mornings, she felt sick and weak all day, her body had never failed her before and now it was a burden. All she really wanted to do was lie on her bed and feel awful and drizzle tears.

It seemed a fearful price to pay for an act which wasn't important to her. In fairness, Jim ought to be sick and sick with anxiety, since he was the one who took such pleasure in love-making. No, she told herself, stop it. Perhaps sex wasn't all that important for women anyway but afterwards was lovely, snug and cherished in his arms, feeling herself special because apparently she was unique and wonderful though she could not imagine why. But now, now: what in God's name should she do now? Not tell Jim at any rate because there was nothing he could do. He might have erased Adele and the boys from his mind but Mary Ann had not.

There were old women on the mountain and Mary Ann knew all about them in theory. They brewed up weird disgusting things and girls drank the brew and aborted, or so the Africans said. She had known of this since childhood, as she knew so much, without relating it to herself; African ways, African troubles, part of her knowledge but nothing to do with her. She had friends among the

Africans, she could be led to one of the old women, probably what worked on an African girl would work on her, or kill her as the case might be, you'd not know without trying. But she wanted to have this child, for herself. Jim would go away and right now she didn't mind, feeling too sick and harassed to care for the cause of her misery. But she wanted a child to love and look after in the long years when she was going to be older and older, struggling with the hotel, alone on this mountain.

The problem was her parents and how not to shame them, for they would be horrified and she understood that. Europeans got married; Africans rollicked around lustfully and had babies all over the lot: two different worlds. She was cleverer each day with little lies. She agreed with Dorothy that she wasn't well and drove to Moshi allegedly to consult Dr Ramtullah and returned saying a liver upset had been diagnosed, and produced a bottle of vitamins with the label washed off as her prescription. She could only be in the second month, and must have a ghastly physique to be sick so soon, but nothing would show for some time. She had planned it all and now Jane threatened her plans.

She intended to plead exhaustion to the parents, knowing they would insist on a rest. She meant to go to the Seychelles, where she knew no one and no one from here ever went, and from there write that she had found a baby she meant to adopt as she longed for a child but would never marry. And have the baby in the Asian hospital in Mombasa, and return with it, fudging dates as best she could, recognizing that she and the baby would be trapped in the lies to spare her parents. Perhaps it wasn't a brilliant scheme but she could think of nothing better. And now there was Jane, who wouldn't go away and wouldn't stop guzzling, and Mary Ann could not leave her parents alone with that blowsy selfish bitch, for Jane would break their hearts.

That was the difference; Mary Ann might disgrace them which was bad enough, but Jane was the one who could break their hearts. It's cruelty to children, Mary Ann said in her mind, pleading with Jane, can't you see? They're as simple and trusting as children inside themselves; wrinkles and grey hair are just on the outside. Jane wouldn't see so it was up to her to protect them. She had become older or wiser or tougher than they were. They lived by the rules they'd been taught by their own simple God-fearing parents. Right and wrong and no complications. They wouldn't understand anything, they'd look stricken and curl up and die of broken hearts.

If only she could spill all this on Jim but what was the use? He couldn't help with Jane and if she told him about herself he'd just be harassed and unhappy too. She was a woman of thirty, supposedly in her right mind, and the man hadn't raped her, and she had to take the consequences of her acts and cope with Jane somehow and she also had to stop this loathsome habit of dripping tears all the time.

Jim was drawing a heart-shaped leaf with a flower like a green and red caterpillar but put aside his work as the Landrover drove up the track. He said at once, 'Darling, you look ill and sad, what's happened?'

'Nothing. Just a bum day at the hotel, I think I ate something funny, nothing really. What's that?'

'You mean to say you've never seen it before?'

'Never.'

Jim seized her in his arms, lifted her in the air, and whirled around before the tent, shouting, 'Oh Linnaeus, here I come! I've discovered a new species!'

'Put me down, idiot,' Mary Ann said. 'New to me. I don't know every foot of the forest.'

'Well yes, but it is wonderful, I can't believe it. It's Piperaceae but I can't find a description of anything like this species in my books. I'll have it checked at the Herbarium in Nairobi and at Kew, if they don't know it, and no doubt it will turn out to be as common as dandelions. But it is exciting, isn't it? Koroga and I set off very early and ploughed on, north-west, much farther than we've gone before and this proves I must move camp and tackle a whole other area.'

That too, Mary Ann thought, now she would not have the relief of the afternoons, the satisfaction of sharing this work to take her mind off the miserable troubles at home.

'Mary Ann, dearest love, you're crying! Oh no, don't. I'm not going miles away, do you think I'd leave you, I couldn't, I need you every way. Just a few miles, we'll figure it out together, it might mean a little longer drive but I'll never get out of range.'

'I'm being silly. We could drive around on Sunday with Koroga and see what's the best next site.'

So they sat side by side on camp stools and Jim gave her his treasure and said, 'You make a drawing of it, darling, you're much better than I am,' and she took up the fine pointed pen while he sorted and noted the rest of the day's samples and her stomach did not feel queasy and her headache went away and she forgot Jane.

All week, Paul Nbaigu had been planning this, he could think of nothing else, he was in a fever to get back to Jane and arrived earlier than usual on Friday evening. That night in his dark room he was kind; the terrible whispers ceased; he made no degrading demands. After months of torment Jane was allowed to take her ecstasy freely and again and again. Pain washed from her mind and body; she felt beautiful once more; she would stop drinking. Sensing the return of her power as the desired object, she was sure she could persuade Paul to let her rent a flat in Dar; night after night like this, all she wanted on earth.

When Paul suggested that she come with him tomorrow, as he had to visit a nearby coffee Co-op briefly, and then they could drive up the mountain and find a moss bed for their purpose, Jane believed her long torture was finished. Something had poisoned Paul, he was a mysterious animal, perhaps he had been gripped by an evil spell cast on him with burning herbs and bits of feather and skin and incantations. She had watched these dread performances as a child, hidden with African children who were deeply frightened while she was only watching. What Africans believed came true. Cobras, Jane thought vaguely, a curse of cobras and now he was released because her magic was stronger.

Paul gave instructions before Jane left his room. 'Walk down the road away from the hotel, I'll pick you up out of sight of here around nine.' Jane was very gay in the car, surprised at how exciting it was to sit near him and move over the daylight world. She could not take her eyes from his profile nor stop thinking of what it would be like under the great trees with sun seeping through to make gold patterns on his smooth black skin.

'Be quick,' Jane said. Paul had parked his car on a track by the coffee bushes, far from the Co-op buildings and the farmers' huts. Paul grinned at her. And he was quick, but not as she'd expected. Jane was smoking and dreaming about Dar, they'd find deserted stretches of beach where they could swim naked and make love in the warm sand, when she heard an African girl giggling. Even as a child, Jane had detested African girls, complete imbeciles the whole lot, giggling and teetering around on their ungainly big bare feet, and she was annoyed at this intrusion on her fantasy, the white beach, the black body, the aquamarine water.

But the giggling was near and insistent, to the left, in the low coffee bushes, and Jane turned her head, meaning to say crossly, wacha kelele, shut up, when she saw Paul. Paul with a little African girl of fourteen or fifteen, giggling her head off, all teeth and wide fascinated eyes and sharp little tits and a neat hard little bottom under her cotton dress, but nothing else under it most obviously. Paul pulling the little African girl by the hand, wheedling, and the little African girl slowly coming closer, giggling less, closer, closer, under the covering bushes but clearly in view from the track, the car; and the girl crouching on all fours, with Paul lifting up her dress and Paul kneeling, his hands holding, reaching, and then and then. Jane watched as she was meant to do until she yanked open the car door and stumbled to the side of the road and retched. She could hear the giggling, renewed now, and a slap like a friendly hand on a hard little bottom, and Paul's voice, amiable and brisk, telling the girl to be off, she was a good little piece, he'd see her again soon.

Jane got back in the car, stone cold, with that bile taste in her mouth. Paul came out on the track, ahead of her, casually doing up his trousers, and looked around, pretending to search for the car and then sauntered towards her. Opening the door on his side he said, 'Funny, I thought I'd left the car up that way.'

'You did not,' Jane said.

He turned expertly and headed out towards the main dirt road but not before he had studied her face, which was white and set and haggard, a ruin of a middle-aged woman. Smiling, Paul said, 'Oh you saw? Jealous, pretty Jane? That's a sweet age for a girl. The kid's been following me around for weeks. I couldn't resist giving her a bit of what she wanted. I like to oblige the ladies.'

'You filthy pig.'

Not taking his eyes from the road, Paul hit her back-handed across the mouth. But he was smiling again, his voice calm and pleasant, when he said, 'Okay, get out here, mustn't be seen driving in together. I'm feeling a bit tired, I'll be taking a nap after lunch if you want me.'

'No.'

'Suit yourself. Now or never, as they say.'

He had passed beyond all caution. After lunch, when the corridors were full of guests going to their rooms, when the servants were all over the place, bringing down luggage, readying rooms for new arrivals: his recklessness added to the excitement, because now he knew he was winning. He only had to prove it finally; if Jane would take this and still come to him, he knew he would feel nothing and be absolute master, despising her far more than she had dared despise his country, his people, himself.

And she did come, reckless too or beyond thought. Jane understood the threat, it was always the same. Now or never. Hating Paul and hating herself, but going to that room because she could not endure the never, knowing herself diseased in mind and body, mad, or under his spell. Paul had paid the witchdoctor, he had watched the medicine mixed on the fire, listened to the incantations to enslave her and drive her insane, it didn't matter, she could not stop herself, she was blind to the startled glances of the servants and only habit made her close the door quickly before any passing guest saw a splendid black body naked on the white sheets.

'Ah, you've come,' Paul whispered, triumphant because her face was no longer beautiful but somehow shrivelled, haunted, with crazy staring eyes. He was well satisfied by the juicy little farm girl and Jane was no one to rouse a man today but there was the last step, to play with her and use her and prove to himself that he felt nothing.

'I forgot how nice that African way is,' Paul whispered. 'All this time fooling around with a Memsaab but I find I like it, maybe best of all. Hurry, take your clothes off, I have to get back to work. You know what to do; you saw.'

Tears burned her eyes, her head hung down like an animal being beaten to death, and yet and still her body ached and yearned and welcomed and clutched and dissolved. Paul stood up, naked and strong before her, revenged on all of them, proud, certain of himself forever. Jane had fallen back on her heels, lifting eyes that had gone dark and blank. There was no pride left in her.

'Now apologize,' Paul commanded.

'What?'

'You heard me, apologize.'

'I apologize.'

'*No*,' he said furiously, 'Apologize for what you said.'

'Said?' Jane repeated. 'What did I say?'

'You said this was a stupid little tinpot African country.'

Slowly, groping for sense and memory, Jane remembered, long ago, that first lesson in misery when Paul told her she must wait his convenience, the first time he had threatened punishment. What he wanted or not at all. Slowly, she recited those words in her mind: stupid little

tinpot African country, and suddenly she seemed to understand.

'That was why?' Jane cried. 'Just for that? That was why
all along?'

Paul nodded. 'And now you will apologize.'

At first Jane hiccoughed and gasped out words, hard to
hear, then he got them patchily, through a choked mixture
of sobs and wrenching laughter. 'Poor little . . . black
boy . . . Jane . . . hurt his . . . feelings.' She was rocking
back and forth on the floor, the laughter swelling to
screams, broken by sobs, her eyes closed with the tears
pushing out from under the lashes. 'Poor little . . . black
boy . . .'

Paul stared at her in terror, paralysed for the moment by
this hideous noise and the sight of her and by that pitying
contempt; poor little black boy . . . hurt his feelings . . .
Then instinct took over, flight, as fast as he could move and
as far from here as he could get. He tore into his clothes and
slammed the door behind him and raced down the passage,
down the stairs, across the empty reception hall to his car,
and was driving at speed towards the hotel gates when Jagi
came into Paul's room. Jagi flung a blanket over Jane's
nakedness and ran for Mary Ann.

'Someone sick,' Jagi said to guests peering out from their
rooms, alarmed by the muffled but incredible sounds, was
it pain, or drunken laughter, what was it? 'Sorry,' Jagi
threw back to them. 'Someone sick. All right soon.' Mary
Ann followed Jagi up the stairs, walking as fast as a run.
She had no idea what had happened but slapped Jane's face
hard and repeatedly, told Jagi to fetch a pail and threw cold
water on Jane again and again. The insane sounds stopped
and Jane sat on the floor, huddled in the wet blanket, silent,
staring at the wall.

Mary Ann gave orders. Jagi was to get a driver to bring
a covered Landrover to the back door, and leave it; Jagi
was to make sure the upper hall was empty and that the
parents were not anywhere around; then Jagi was to help
her take Jane down the back stairs to the car and come

with her to Moshi. Mary Ann managed to get Jane's dress on, but nothing more; she wrapped Jane in a dry blanket and waited until Jagi gave the all clear. Jagi half carried, half dragged Jane to the car, sitting on the rear seat with her as Mary Ann instructed. He stayed with Jane, who was limp and still staring at nothing, while Mary Ann hurried into Dr Ramtullah's office and made the clerk understand he must interrupt the doctor, it was an emergency. Dr Ramtullah followed in his car to the hospital; Jane was put in a private room; Dr Ramtullah injected a strong sedative.

'Now,' said Dr Ramtullah, standing in the corridor outside the closed door.

'I think a nervous breakdown,' Mary Ann said. 'She was hysterical, laughing and crying. I must tell you, Dr Ramtullah, that Jane's been drinking for several months. A lot. Probably because it was a great blow to give up her career and come home; she must have been brooding.' As she spoke, Mary Ann realized this would be the story for the parents, with the drink part excepted, and for guests or friends or anyone who inquired or had to be told. The Africans in the hotel would know, that could not be helped and did not matter, as long as the parents never found out.

'Miss Mary Ann,' Dr Ramtullah said. 'I am keeping Miss Jane here until she is being calm and rested, but then you should be taking her to Nairobi. I am writing to my colleague Dr Kleber, he will be treating her. Here we are not having facilities for such a case. Miss Jane is needing treatment, do not think she is well again in one week, no, from hysteria and alcohol it is longer than that.'

'Oh yes, I agree, Dr Ramtullah. I'll take her to Nairobi as soon as possible, that's much the best. But would it be all right if I told my parents they mustn't come to see Jane? She might be upset or they might.'

'That is very wise, Miss Jane must be having complete rest. You will be telephoning me, I will inform of everything.'

In the Landrover, driving back slowly to the hotel, Mary

Ann said: 'Jagi, what driver brought this Landrover round?'

'Moses.'

'Did you say anything to him?'

'No Memsaab Mariani, only to bring the car.'

'And when you were looking around the back stairs and the hall, did you talk to any of the staff?'

'No.'

'Then you and I are the only ones who know about this, Jagi.'

'Yes, Memsaab Mariani.'

'No one else must ever know, Jagi. If anyone does know, it will be because you have spoken. I do not ask this for Memsaab Janny, but for my father and mother. They have been friends of your family for a long time, Jagi. I remember when your sister Nyamburu pierced her foot on a nail my mother took her to hospital and looked after her and her foot was very big with poison coming from it and she would have died if my mother had not helped. Do you remember, Jagi?'

'Yes, Memsaab Mariani.'

'Then it will be a secret between us. Tell me, whose room was Memsaab Janny in?'

'Paul Nbaigu,' Jagi said promptly. 'That maridadi Swahili from Dar. It was the first time Memsaab Janny went to his room before night.'

Mary Ann hung on to the wheel. Her hands felt weak, she was afraid her unstable body might do something violent like vomit or faint. There must not be a car accident. She stopped the Landrover at the side of the road, the motor idling, and leaned her forehead against the steering wheel. If I'm not careful, she thought, I'll start screaming and crying hysterically myself. So it was not Jane's drinking, not nearly that and all the Africans knew. Jane, who was so beastly to the watu, Jane of all women. It's ended now; I'll get her to Nairobi and then back to Europe; I'll do murder to keep this from Daddy and Mummy.

Jagi had waited silently, behaving as if he were not there.

Mary Ann straightened up and took deep breaths, testing herself. It was safe to drive on and safe to speak. She couldn't lose her grip again until she had cleared away this awful mess and sent Jane far far from Kilimanjaro.

'Jagi, I want you to pack Mr Nbaigu's things and bring them to me, when no one is in the office. He will not be staying at the hotel again.'

'Good,' Jagi said. Well, that was one help; evidently the hotel Africans didn't like Mr Nbaigu any more than the Chagga coffee farmers did.

Bob and Dorothy were beside themselves with anxiety but Mary Ann kept reassuring them, Dr Ramtullah reported that Jane was resting calmly, there was nothing at all to worry about. Believing Mary Ann's story without question, Bob and Dorothy blamed themselves bitterly for having accepted Jane's sacrifice; were it not for them, she would be singing in Europe instead of recovering from a nervous collapse in Moshi. They failed to notice the pinched, drawn face of their younger daughter. Dorothy said, 'If Dr Ramtullah thinks it's better for you to look after Jane, darling, please forget about the hotel; Daddy and I can handle everything. You just take care of Jane.'

Mary Ann stole enough time to help Jim find a new camp site. Jim was glowing with joy because the Herbarium in Nairobi seemed to think he had come up with a new species of Piperaceae, though they were sending the sample to Kew Gardens for a final opinion. Immortality within his grasp: his name attached to a plant. He was also tense with hope because he had finally had a brainwave about how to manage life, yet did not tell Mary Ann lest his scheme turn out a disappointment. He felt crafty and unclean but supposed that if you managed life a certain amount of cunning and dirt rubbed off on you.

He had written two letters, the first to the head of his department, with some colour photos, some drawings, and many notes included. He said that this montane rain forest was an unspoiled marvel and deserved more than a year's study; he would like an extra year, he felt sure he could guarantee then a definitive survey of the plant ecology. Would Dr Harvey put in a word for him with the Murchison Foundation, suggesting an extension of his grant? Obviously this work would redound to the credit of their department and their university (ah, the slyness when you began to manipulate events). There was a financial problem because he realized the university could not pay his salary after the end of the sabbatical year; he would therefore need more assistance to support his family in England, but less money out here. And naturally all this depended on Dr Harvey keeping his place open, in case Dr Harvey agreed on the value of his Kilimanjaro research. Pompous old Harvey, Jim Withers thought, and a fine pompous letter to match.

The second letter went to his wife Adele and jumped the gun. In it, he announced that he would be staying an extra year on the mountain to complete his study and would of course make the best financial arrangements he could for her and the children, but an extension of his grant would not equal his regular salary. This letter caused him some anxiety. If Adele rang Dr Harvey to protest or gum the works, she would learn he was lying in his teeth but he decided Adele was too brainless to be as crafty as he had become.

He expected Adele to have a fit, not because her beloved husband was missed and longed for, but because a woman needs a man around the house for odd jobs and because of the promised money shortage. Adele was neither bad-looking nor old, thirty-two now, and just the sort of woman to mate with a chap who sold insurance or frigidaires or cars, a steady small businessman type, interested as she was in boring useful gadgets and what the neighbours thought and what the neighbours owned.

As for the boys, he could not be certain of Adele's emotions except that the boys were her property, which was the tricky angle, for she was a great believer in property. On the other hand, they got on her nerves; she was the kind of mother who shouted and administered slaps and complained of the endless work of rearing the young. Dr Withers could not believe that his wife loved anyone though admitting that, since he was not a mother, he had no way of knowing how maternal instincts worked when the crunch came.

He was banking on Adele to look out for another bread-winner and man about the house, and then to realize that two lively untidy little boys might discourage a future second husband. At aged eight and five Billy and Mike were too young to be harmed by their mother's lack of intelligence and by the meanness of her standards and ambitions, though they could, he reflected sadly, be having a pretty dull cramped year now. But if only if only Adele left him, Billy and Mike would have Mary Ann for a mother and then choirs of angels would sing and all would be beer and skittles.

He had sent the letters ten days ago. Dr Withers would not permit himself to fret about the answers, having determined that three weeks was the correct waiting period. Meanwhile he had this new section of the forest to explore and Mary Ann was overburdened with her overpainted, overdressed sister who seemed to have developed a nervous breakdown from frustrated vanity.

In the parents' car, driving to Nairobi, Jane was sullen.

'This is all absolute nonsense,' she said.

'Dr Ramtullah doesn't think so,' Mary Ann said, 'And you're under doctor's orders.'

'If you imagine I'm going to hang around the Nairobi hospital for months, you're mad.'

'Until the doctors say it's all right to leave, that's all. What do you plan to do afterwards?'

Mary Ann chanced looking sideways at her sister. Jane was thin and pale and a tightness around the mouth showed the bitter shape of things to come and her hair lay flat and lifeless on her head. At Mary Ann's question, there had been a sudden involuntary sagging of shoulders and face, a sigh or a groan repressed. Then Jane lifted her head and Mary Ann had to admire her. Everything was wrong with Jane, she was an appalling person, but now when she was wrecked, Jane's conceit began to look like pride and took on the quality of bravery.

'I'll go to Europe, of course,' Jane said, head high. 'I was a fool to come home, Daddy and Mummy aren't doddering, they can run the hotel perfectly well without my help. I'm through with Africa. It's the dreariest backward nothing place there is.'

Jagi told Mary Ann when she got home, exhausted from the long drive, that Paul Nbaigu had come to the hotel and been informed by Kibia at the desk that there were no vacant rooms and when he asked for Memsaab Janny Kibia said that Memsaab Janny had gone to Nairobi and was not returning to Kilimanjaro. Thank God for that, Mary Ann thought, no scene, no argument for the parents to hear. She spoke to Kibia saying that he must remember, if Mr Nbaigu came again in a couple of months as he had before, there were never any vacant rooms since Mr Nbaigu was not the sort of guest they wanted.

'He will not be coming back,' Kibia assured her. 'I hear from a man in the Co-op office he lost his job.'

Not only Jane had seen Paul Nbaigu and the giggling little African girl. Two old women, weeding invisibly and silently under nearby coffee bushes, had seen and heard. They told the girl's father, who beat the child until she could neither sit nor stand, and they told the manager of the Co-op. He in turn informed Paul Nbaigu's boss at the Ministry in Dar. The farm people were furious; it was a grave affront and an indecency. This city African, not of their tribe, came to them in his fancy clothes, speaking his fancy Swahili, and debauched one of their girls for his morning entertainment.

Paul's boss called him in and said Paul was the biggest damn fool he ever met in his life, if Paul was so randy why not hire a tart in Moshi, and Paul was sacked on the spot. The boss wanted no scandal which would reflect on his section. Both Paul and his superior knew Paul was finished in government work. Mr Mabari would not stick his neck

out by covering for Paul or slipping him into another
department. Mr Mabari, to keep this dirty little scandal
from his own administrative record, said he would accept
Paul's resignation and if Paul could get a job in private
industry he would write a non-committal recommendation.

Paul knew there was no appeal, and besides he would be
well advised to go quickly and quietly for they might look
more closely into his behaviour if he made a fuss, and thus
learn of the cheating on time and work. The top boss of all
would be outraged enough by the story of the Chagga girl,
and unforgiving about dishonesty towards the government.

Paul walked through Dar, red-eyed with hate and
shaking with panic. Jane, he muttered to himself, walking
on the hot pavements, past the Asian shops, past the reek
of dried fish by the market, on the dirt lane that led to the
small house with its flaking white-washed plaster where
four African families lived. Back to the stinking rooms
shared with his mother and younger sisters. Jane did it;
Jane had picked up his life and smashed it. He was twenty-
five and all he had worked for and dreamed of was lost.
The years at a mission school when he was such a Christ-
loving book-bound kid he wouldn't even listen to a dirty
joke for fear the missionaries would guess and he would
lose what he lived for: the scholarship to Makerere. Slave
jobs in vacations, 'Carry the basket, Memsaab?', 'Paper,
Bwana?', a kid anybody could kick around for a few
shillings. And finally Makerere, the dream come true.

Maybe he had been a little wild, how could he help it, it
was the first time in his life that he had what he wanted,
God he was so happy, free, somebody, wearing a short red
academic gown in hall, living like a European, maybe he
didn't study enough, they could have given him a second
chance. Europeans feared an African with spunk, they
couldn't wait to chuck him out. And how he had grovelled
and scraped to get a desk job in the Ministry, where
boredom was like pain until, only a year ago, he started to
climb, with a car, off on the roads, an official, the liaison
between Dar and the upcountry peasants. The months at

Makerere and this year, out of twenty-five years; less than two years of the kind of life he had longed for and worked for and suffered for. *Jane did it.*

He banged through the room where his mother as usual was washing other people's clothes, shouting at her that he'd been fired, thrown out, ruined, all because of a lying ugly whore.

'Don't shout at me,' his mother said. She was a fat strong-willed woman, long since abandoned by Paul's father, who had raised six children and took no nonsense from any of them. Paul was the clever one, and also the worthless one. Her pride in his looks, education, success, had withered into doubt. If a man was no good inside himself all the fine clothes and fine ways would not hide it forever. 'And don't shout about that woman whoever she is. A man who lets a woman mess up his life can blame himself. You won't find me crying for you. And you better get a job fast, boy, because Mama isn't going to feed you.'

No. He would not plod from office to office, where signs on the doors said: Hakuna Kazi – there is no work. And wait and beg and gratefully, if he was lucky, take a little clerk's job under some unschooled African or sharp Asian, with a serene white man far off in an air-conditioned office, like a king ruling them all. Jane would pay; Jane would provide the work and good work, clean work, pleasant, well-paid work. There was plenty he could do in that grand hotel of hers. And if she didn't feel like it, he knew how to get his way. He'd tell her stupid cheerful old Daddy what kind of daughter Jane was, he'd tell the whole hotel full of rich wazungu coming to his country to have a nice time looking at animals and mountains, he'd make such a bad noise they'd hear it all over Tanzania. But now he had no car; the car belonged to the job, not to him. His hate for Jane festered like an infected wound during the ten-hour jolting ride in a bus, surrounded by Africans smelling of dirt and poverty, laughing and babbling like idiots mile after mile.

He felt fouled when he got off that rickety bus in Moshi,

stinking like all the other passengers, his clothes rumpled and sweaty, and now he had to take another bus up the winding mountain road and walk through the dust. He had come to this hotel before in a car, as well put together as a European, stopping always in a Moshi petrol station first to groom himself in the lavatory, changing his shirt and suit if need be. He arrived as an equal with the guests or better because he was a government man and they were only foreign tourists and if any of them stepped out of line they could be deported; he, Paul, could report them, he had power and they had none. Now he came on foot, tired, soiled, an African out of work, like any of his people, the poor and faceless, and he felt with shame that he belonged at the back door, not in the reception hall. The cold hostility of Kibia at the desk, the flat unsmiling stares of the hotel servants, finished him.

He was defenceless among enemies and afraid. If he made a noise here, Mr Jenkins would call the police. The Europeans always won. They had the money and the real power and they thought ahead and were quiet as snakes and knew what they were doing, and his people were slaves who would serve them, even against their own kind. He walked back down the drive to wait at the lower bus stop. He didn't walk, he shuffled. The strength was gone from the magnificent body which had been his certain source of pride.

Counting every shilling now, Paul spent the night in a cheap African hotel in Moshi. He lay on the lumpy kapok mattress on the iron cot and heard through the slat walls the disgusting sounds of his people, loudly attending to the night's business: peeing, belching, drinking, laughing, talking at the top of their lungs, fornicating, snoring, to the tune of whiney Indian music and solemn news broadcasts on their transistor radios. He felt imprisoned, a man alone, everything lost except his one possession: hatred. Hatred for Jane, for white people everywhere, men and women alike: this passion clamped over his mind forever.

He wanted to kill them, he had no other desire. All that

sleepless night he thought of this: kill them, any of them, all of them. By morning he had thought of a way, without going to jail, and rose with gummed hot eyes and a sour taste in his mouth but no longer ashamed of his filth and stench and his loss of place in the world. He had a new nobler place: he would make his way to the southern frontier and join a camp of Freedom Fighters and sooner or later it would be given to him: the chance to kill white people. He could not reach Jane but there were others, and he knew what he wanted, he would not forget or waver. He would be the sword of vengeance and they would come to fear him before he was through.

Mary Ann brought the two letters, since Jim used the hotel as his mail address, but he would not read them while she was there lest they be dusty answers and he had to conceal defeat. However Dr Withers could not conceal his distraction and Mary Ann, puzzled and rather hurt, left early. Presently Koroga thought his Bwana must be drunk for he was laughing and talking in a loud voice. 'God bless us every one!' Dr Withers said, hugging himself and laughing like a lunatic. 'Oh too good to be true! Too good to be true!' This called for a celebration; first of all he would have a large whisky, normally rationed because of expense, and read both letters again. Tomorrow he would drive to Moshi and on the way invite Mary Ann to a dinner party for two. He wanted special luxuries for the feast: a tin of pâté, a cake, and a bottle of wine. Could he wait until tomorrow night or should he ask her for lunch? No, dinner, so she wouldn't have to hurry back to that cannibal hotel which ate her alive, but would have hours for talking and planning.

Adele had never given him a gift like this; he could almost hear her high complaining voice as he read. He savoured the typical longed-for abuse. Jim, not she, had destroyed this marriage; she knew her duty but Jim felt no obligation to anyone except himself. Did he expect her to sit alone in England another whole hard year, coping with the boys by herself, with not even enough money? She had kept her vows faithfully, but now considered herself free. Unlike Jim, who traipsed off whenever he got a chance – remember Wales, Switzerland, and every weekend he could manage, if he couldn't go farther, he'd leave her for Kew Gardens – there was a reliable steady man in Reading, Mr Billingsley, who owned a large furniture store.

She had met Mr Billingsley some months ago when she went in to price a little table. Mr Billingsley was a widower, childless, somewhat older than herself, with a very good position and lovely taste and manners, and she was no longer going to reject his attentions. She knew Mr Billingsley wanted to marry her and she warned Jim that she intended immediately to consult a solicitor about the divorce laws. As for Billy and Mike, Mr Billingsley had a beautiful home and naturally cared a great deal for furniture and was unused to children, and Jim would absolutely have to take his share of responsibility, she could not be expected to assume the entire burden of bringing up the boys.

Dr Withers kissed this letter reverently, and treated himself to another whisky. Damn the expense. Life was a bowl of cherries. The future shone with a rosy sunrise glow. And Dr Harvey was a dear man not a pompous bore, who said he fully agreed with Dr Withers' assessment of the importance of the Kilimanjaro rain forest, and had written the Murchison people for an appointment and would urge the extension of the grant next week in London. Dr Withers kissed that letter too. What the hell, kissing letters might turn out to be some sort of juju, bringing massive good luck to the kisser.

Mary Ann felt a rush of tenderness for this tall gawky man, with the flop of blondish hair on his forehead and the peeling nose. He had put a jam jar full of wild orchids on the table beside a candle in a beer bottle. He pushed in her camp stool as if he were a footman in a palace, and would tell her nothing until after the first glass of somewhat vinegary wine. Then he talked a blue streak, laughing so much with happiness that Mary Ann hardly took it in. Jim began again, and she understood: he had managed life, he had planned and taken steps and succeeded; he might be inexperienced but this showed he was far from incompetent. 'Crafty,' he kept saying. 'You'll have to watch me carefully, I may turn into a prize crook.'

He came to kneel by her stool, with his arms around her. 'Darling Mary Ann, if all goes well and believe me I'll help it along with both hands, we ought to be free to marry in a very few months. And I feel in my bones that old Harvey will nag the Murchison people into another year. You'll love Billy and Mike, I promise you, and think what it will mean for them to camp on this mountain. We'll have a little village of our own, our tent and theirs and a work tent and an eating tent, oh God in heaven I can hardly wait.'

To his dismay, Mary Ann burst into tears. He couldn't believe it, he could hardly breathe. Not a bowl of cherries, no sunrise rosy future? He was speechless before these incredible daunting tears.

'It won't be soon enough,' Mary Ann said, wiping her cheeks with a paper napkin.

'What?'

So Mary Ann explained that, perhaps not in the eyes of God or man but for practical purposes anyway, they were married already and though she hadn't seen a doctor she calculated she was about three months pregnant.

'My love,' Dr Withers said. 'And you never told me, you carried all that worry around alone? Don't you trust me?'

'I didn't want to make you unhappy.'

'You mean, just be unhappy by yourself? Mary Ann, you're going to have to stop being heroic and looking after everybody else. Darling, don't you want the baby?'

'I want it more than anything in the world.'

'Oh thank God for that. Now everything's fine, no problems, joy on all sides. We'll have *another* tent, a tiny baby-size tent. It's really too good to be true. How do you feel?'

'Sick mostly. But I think a bit better now and pretty much all right by evening.'

'Oh my angel, angel, how *could* you not have told me?'

'Jim, there are problems. Even if we could get married tomorrow which we can't. I don't know how to keep it from my parents; I mean, that we didn't wait.'

'My knees hurt,' Dr Withers said, 'and I still haven't got that sofa. You'll have to stand up.'

He took her in his arms lovingly, and said to the top of her brown head, 'Mary Ann, couldn't we tell them the truth? It's not such a terrible thing, the truth. We love each other and we'll love the baby and there's nothing ugly about how nature works and this is late in the twetnieth century and people don't fall over dead from shock any more when men and women make love without benefit of clergy.'

'I don't know,' Mary Ann murmured against his khaki shirt.

'I do. Leave it to me. You're not to worry about a thing. We'll have a whale of a time on this mountain, and you'll have a perfect baby with two ready-made older brothers and we'll all live happily under canvas forever after or anyhow quite a while. You'll see. I'll manage. Crafty Jim.'

She pulled away from him and looked up that great distance into his face. 'I'll tell you one thing you'll never manage,' Mary Ann said earnestly. 'If you want to marry someone else later on you'll never manage to get my baby away from me.'

By the light of the bonfire Koroga had made, by the light of the kerosene lamp hanging on a pole before the tent, Jim had a vision of how the little brown girl would look when she was old: a little brown woman, square in build, with a very firm chin and a warrior's eyes if anything menaced her loved ones, a tough determined hard-working and fiercely protective little old lady.

He laughed with delight and seized her and hugged her. 'Nothing on earth would make me come between you and your baby. I'm not crazy. I know a lioness when I see one.'

'Drive home with me,' Mary Ann said. 'And use Jane's

room tonight. You can manage Daddy and Mummy in the morning. I do leave it to you.'

There was much talk when Jane and Mary Ann Jenkins left home on Mount Kilimanjaro. All the Europeans had something to say about the surprise departure of the Jenkins girls. In Moshi, they talked at the hotel bar, the post office, the best general store, the petrol station, the bank; up and down the mountain they talked in the farmers' homes when the ladies had a bridge afternoon, at Sunday lunch parties, in matrimonial beds. The young bank manager wished to God these bloody farmers would stop using his bank as a club and stop being such bloody gossips. He was browned off with Africa and would willingly have exchanged his three servants and spacious bungalow for a dingy bedsitter in Earls Court.

Here they were, the regular gang, Henry McIntyre, Arthur Wells, Peter Kinlock, come to collect payday cash for their watu and, lucky for them, a farmer from Meru, Ralph Harrison, come to look enviously at McIntyre's coffee beans and give them all a chance to chew over their bloody gossip again. You'd think this bloody mountain was the only inhabited place on earth and the Jenkins girls the only two living females.

The man from Meru remarked, 'I hear the Jenkins girls have flown the coop. Here today, gone tomorrow.'

The young bank manager groaned silently and waited for the chorus.

'Well, yes,' Henry McIntyre said. 'Jane's gone back to England and good riddance if you ask me. I had a feeling that girl could cause old Bob trouble with the watu, she didn't have the hang of Independence. But Mary Ann's around, on safari somewhere on the other side of the mountain.'

'According to the watu,' said Arthur Wells, 'Jane was whisked off because she'd been hitting the bottle. Houseboy to cook, they didn't know I could hear them, that's the way to pick up the straight gen.'

'I heard worse than that,' Peter Kinlock said. 'Some sort of nasty little African sex deal on one of the Chagga Co-ops, an African got sacked for it, but it seems Jane knew about it for some reason. Tricky thing to be mixed up with. I bet Bob rushed her out for fear the D.C. would want to ask questions.'

This was new news and Henry McIntyre disapproved of it. 'You can't believe everything the watu say. You know how they are, talk, talk, talk their silly heads off. Half the time they're making it up.'

'You know,' Arthur Wells began, as if he hadn't broached the subject often before. 'I'm surprised Dorothy hasn't raised a row about Mary Ann going off with that scientist fella. Dorothy's so prissy you'd think she was running a nunnery not a hotel.'

'Well, for God's sake, Mary Ann's in her thirties. About time she went off with a man.' For once the young bank manager thought Peter Kinlock normally intelligent. 'I've met that scientist fella, can't remember his name. Seemed a nice enough chap, not much to say for himself, but you've got to admit it takes some guts to camp for months on the mountain. He's not like the tourists who have a heart attack if everything isn't just so.'

While the gentlemen were in Moshi attending to business, Mrs McIntyre was giving a bridge afternoon for Mrs Harrison from Meru.

Mrs McIntyre said firmly, 'I hope it's so. Best thing that could happen to Mary Ann and best thing that could happen to Bob and Dorothy if they have any sense.'

'But they're not married, dear,' Mrs Wells said.

Mrs Kinlock said, 'I heard he was getting a divorce, didn't you?'

Mrs McIntyre was senior lady on the mountain and talked when and as she chose. 'Dorothy told me Jane had gone into partnership with a man in London, they're setting up a boutique. Obviously Jane nicked them for the capital. Dorothy couldn't have been more pleased. Really, she and Bob are ludicrous. You'd imagine Jane was about eighteen and Helen of Troy and all the men were panting after her. Dorothy practically said she felt Jane would be safer in a dress shop than on the stage.'

'I didn't notice any men swooning with love for Jane at the hotel,' Mrs Kinlock said. 'She's as cold as an iceberg. Probably wouldn't let a man get near her in case he mussed her hair.'

Mrs Harrison of Meru had been excluded from this purely Kilimanjaro chat, but she had general ideas to contribute. 'You can't count on children for anything any more. I keep warning Ralph that young William will never come home from university and take over our farm. I tell you, we're the last of the settlers.'

'And no doubt one day we'll all end up stabbed to death with pangas,' Mrs McIntyre said.

The ladies laughed merrily.

Bob and Dorothy were happy to be back at work. They agreed that it wasn't very interesting to live in a hotel unless you managed the place, and they had been silly to think they were getting old, people in their sixties weren't old; they must have been suffering an attack of laziness. Again Dorothy raced around, peering, checking, instructing, and Bob returned to the office, the accounts, the bills, the correspondence, and all the new complicated paper work which the government piled on. They did not admit it to each other, but they felt that the hotel ran more smoothly under their supervision, they'd noticed odd looks and odd behaviour in the staff but everyone seemed settled down now, the way they'd always been.

Dorothy was fondly re-reading a postcard, Changing of the Guard at Buckingham Palace on one side and Jane's scrawl on the other. 'Opening great success. Clothes much more fun than singing. Teddy's so talented angelic like younger brother, Love J.'

'More tea, Bob dear? Isn't it wonderful how Jane's fallen on her feet? She's such a clever girl. I always knew she'd be all right. Never caused us a day's trouble.'

'Now, Dorry love.'

'I hate to think anyone can talk about one of our daughters. Yes, I know Jim's a good man and they'll be married but even so, I hate to think what people are saying about Mary Ann.'

'I don't expect they're saying much. People have plenty of worries of their own. And what we don't hear can't hurt us, can it, Dorry? Come on, cheer up, love. You know we've been hoping and longing for a grandchild. You know we have. Think how lucky we are, we've waited for years and now we only have to wait a few more months.'

## :II: IN THE HIGHLANDS

When Luke Hardy took to the bottle, everyone understood.

His wife, Sue, the very picture of health, had keeled over dead while cutting roses in her garden. People heard it was a clot, something like that, one of those things. Luke and Sue were childless; for twenty-six years they lived on Fairview Farm in perfect love. Discussing this sad and sudden death at the Karula Sports Club, a woman said nobody would think to look at them that Luke and Sue were in fact Tristan and Yseult. Not to look at: both short, grey-haired, sun-wrinkled, in their fifties, one lean, one plump. The neighbours, English farmers and their wives from thirty miles around Karula, drove to Fairview to pay condolence visits. They were greeted at the door by Luke's head houseboy who thanked them politely and made excuses for the Bwana. Luke Hardy could not disguise his pain and knew how embarrassing grief is to others.

Luke buried his wife, without benefit of clergy, on a high ridge at the southern perimeter of his farm. They had agreed that the view here was their favourite though it was hard to choose one beauty from so much beauty. After that Luke sat on his verandah, with another spectacular view before him, and started to drink. Fairview Farm went slowly down the drain.

Luke thought a man could drink himself to death at speed but the process proved remarkably long-drawn-out. He applied himself to the task for one year and two months. The head man and the cook stopped coming to the verandah for instructions since the Bwana received them with glassy indifference. Between them they ran the farm and the house to the extent that anything ran. When sober enough, Luke filled time by picking through his collection of books bought at sales after other funerals or when people moved away from the Highlands. The complete works of Robert Louis Stevenson, the complete works of Thomas Carlyle, H. G. Wells' *Outline of History*, Zane Grey, the collected poetry of Robert Browning, Conan Doyle, Agatha Christie, the Koran, Baroness d'Orczy, Jane Austen, on and on, all without interest.

One morning in January, shortly after dawn, Luke was drinking tea laced with whisky while reading Roget's *Thesaurus* when disgust overcame him. He had been insulting Sue. Together they carved Fairview from the bush, with no money behind them. Together they made it a happy prosperous farm, never rich but comfortable for them and their watu. He didn't have it in him to carry on the work alone but that was no reason to destroy it. Sue would hever have thrown away the effort of his lifetime.

Luke got up and shouted for Kimoi, the head houseboy, a man almost as old as he. He wanted a fire built in the boiler outside the bathroom, he was going to wash and shave and eat breakfast and drink much coffee and write a letter which the driver should take to Karula immediately. Kimoi laughed like a lunatic, stoking the boiler. The Bwana had decided not to die. Actually the Bwana had decided to postpone dying; there was business to settle first.

Fortified by coffee, Luke printed the advertisement since his handwriting was none too steady.

BEAUTIFUL FARM FOR SALE. ROTTEN CONDITION DUE TO NEGLECT. FIFTEEN THOUSAND ACRES. UNLIMITED WATER FROM BEST SPRING IN THE HIGHLANDS. TWO THOUSAND HEAD NOTHING SPECIAL CATTLE. DAIRY RANCHING. USED TO AVERAGE FIFTEEN GALLONS CREAM DAILY BUT LESS NOW. ROOF LEAKS OTHERWISE HOUSE SOLID. WILL SELL REASONABLE PRICE TO BUYER I LIKE. DONT WRITE INSPECT IN PERSON. ASK DIRECTIONS KARULA GENERAL STORE LUKE HARDY FAIRVIEW FARM KARULA.

He read this over and thought it an exact statement of the facts. He addressed an envelope to the *Kenya Weekly*

*News*, a periodical subscribed to by all serious cow men.

The neighbours saw the advertisement and wondered to each other how drunk Luke had been when he dreamed it up. It was a real come-on, it made your mouth water; rotten condition, nothing special cows, leaking roof: you could scarcely wait to snap up such a bargain. But anyway, if Luke was making jokes in the *Kenya Weekly News*, he must feel better and would reappear in Karula and start living a normal life.

Luke suffered for a week, watered his whisky, sipped all day instead of swigging, and bellowed orders. The work section of the farm was hopeless but he could spruce up his house and garden for the stream of prospective buyers. The four indoor servants swept, scrubbed, polished, aired everything in sight. Not bad, Luke thought, seeing for the first time in over a year the familiar furnishings. Big red cedar chairs and sofas, with wide arms for drinks and books, and lumpy cretonne cushions; big square tables and straight chairs to match; worn impala and zebra skins on the plank floors; faded brown rep curtains; pressure lamps; book cases; stone fireplace with the obligatory trumpeting elephant in oils above. The two bedrooms were as plain and satisfying. A local carpenter had made it all for the young Hardys, and made it to last.

The garden shamed Luke. How could he have forsaken what Sue slaved over and cherished. The magnolias were dead and the roses and all the soft pretty flowers in the borders around the house. Oleanders and hibiscus survived, as did the podo and pepper trees, the jacaranda and wild fig which framed the view. Luckily golden shower and bougainvillaea and jasmine still bloomed on the rough stone walls of the house. The lawn looked like a hayfield; Sue would have hated that. Luke told the watu to slash the grass; useless to pretend he hadn't let his place fall into ruin.

Every day Luke was shaved, clean, as near sober as possible and waiting. No cars bumped the twenty-three miles over ruts and potholes from Karula to Fairview. Luke couldn't believe it; his feelings were hurt. He was more than half drunk and entirely hostile when a Dodge pick-up turned from the public road into the long driveway. Luke heard the car but did not move. He meant to tell the bastard that Fairview was no longer for sale. In the usual Kenya farm style, the driveway ended at the kitchen door. Kimoi led the visitor around the house to the verandah. Luke had not expected to see a boy; this one wouldn't be a buyer, probably the young dolt ran out of petrol.

'Mr Hardy?'

'Yes.'

'My name's Ian Paynter. I saw your advertisement in the *Kenya Weekly News*.'

'Took your time, didn't you?'

'I'm sorry sir. I only saw it this morning.'

Luke unbent. 'Sit down. Come to look it over for your father?'

'No sir.' Luke couldn't understand the expression on the boy's face.

'You're getting married?' After all he bought this land when he was a boy, with Sue.

'No sir.' My God, Luke thought, what have we here? The chap certainly wasn't making conversation easy. Well then, let's not talk. Silence did not appear to worry the Paynter fella. The Paynter fella sat upright and tense on one of the old verandah chairs which were not built for that position and stared at the view. He must be six feet two and weighed nothing at all. This wasn't the slenderness of youth, this was more like emaciation. Sick for a long time, TB maybe. He had the sort of face young Englishmen have, public school voice, perfectly ordinary young chap, except he didn't seem capable of speech.

Out of this puzzling silence, Ian Paynter said, 'If your farm isn't already sold, sir, I'd like to buy it.'

'You haven't seen it, man, what are you talking about?'

'I've seen this,' Ian Paynter made a small gesture towards the view.

'How old are you?'

'Twenty-five.'

'You're too young to live here alone. The nearest neighbours are five miles away, people called Gale, and I don't much care for them. The ones I like most, the Gordons, live 15 miles the other side of Karula. It's lonely. You'd go crackers. Besides the farm is a mess. You'd have to work your balls off. What do you know about farming anyway? How long have you been out here?'

'A year. I was second assistant to the dairy manager at Ol Ilyopita.'

'George Lavering's place. That's a Rolls Royce compared to here.'

'Mr Hardy,' the boy turned to him and smiled for the first time. The smile came as a shock, revealing a complete set of outsize lustrous false teeth. 'I hope you will sell me your farm. It's exactly what I want.'

Luke Hardy told himself he was a stupid old sot and deserved a kick up the ass. 'How long have you been out here?' What sort of question was that? The boy had been in the war of course; just demobbed before arriving last January. More likely he'd just got out of hospital, ghastly gut wound judging by his skin and bone looks, no doubt infection, poisoned blood, something did in his teeth too. And the nervy way he held himself and the trouble he had to force out a few words at a time, probably recovering from shell shock, plenty of chaps were shaky afterwards, Luke thought, confusing his distant war with the war he had missed, that ended a year and a half ago.

'I'm going to bed,' Luke announced. It was four o'clock on a glittering afternoon. 'Kimoi will look after you. Stay the night. See you in the morning. Talk then.'

Ian Paynter sat alone on the verandah, first refusing Kimoi's offer of tea, then the offer of drink as sunset colours streaked the sky. He was thinking of Fairview and its sozzled owner, Mr Luke Hardy. How can I make him sell it? I must have it, it's the only thing I want. But I can't go through all the talk, I can't explain. Why in God's name do people ask questions?

No, I'm not looking at your farm for my father; my
father is dead, so is my mother, so is my sister Lucy;
everyone's dead except me. It was the war, you see, Mr
Hardy. My sister Lucy was seventeen and riding in a lorry
with a lot of other girls to a dance at some American airforce
base near Aylesbury where we lived. The lorry skidded in
the black-out and overturned and Lucy and one other girl
were killed. My mother went to London for the day to
shop or maybe have some fun, a matinée with friends and
tea at Claridge's, and a buzzbomb hit a building and a piece
of masonry smashed her skull. My father had a heart attack
when he heard, quite natural after two such accidents
wouldn't you think, and that weakened him so he died of
pneumonia. All this happened in England while I was in
Oflag XV B outside Hannover.

No, I'm not getting married, Mr Hardy. I went straight
from Marlborough into the Army and straight from the
Army into Oflag XV B, Dunkirk till the end, five years.
Not much chance to meet girls. I'm not interested, I never
got the hang of them and it's too late now. I loved three
people and they're dead and that's the end of it. No,
Mr Hardy, I won't be lonely. If you'd spent five years in a
room with nine other men, and shared one and a quarter
acres inside barbed wire with three hundred men, you'd see
that being alone in a lot of space is my idea of heaven. I
don't want people. I don't know how to talk to them any
more, I kind of gave it up in those five years. I found the
best way to keep from going round the bend was not to
listen or talk or think or feel, you might say I went to sleep
for the duration.

Perhaps I'll get over it in time, I mean be able to natter
about nothing like other people, but I can't cope now. I
learned that in Aylesbury when I was sent home after we
were liberated. Not to our house, I couldn't look at it, I
stayed with the Mayfields, Paynter and Mayfield, solicitors,
third generation of both families. God how everyone
talked, day and night, squawking like parrots, I didn't
understand any of it. Civilian life in the war. I didn't

understand the soldiers either, when Tom and Larry Mayfield got demobbed and came back. They used to be my best friends. Larry was a gunner, Tom was in the tanks. They talked and laughed until I thought the windows would break. Their war sounded like one glorious leave in Naples and Rome and Brussels and Paris, getting drunk and jokes and girls.

I suppose I wouldn't be here if I hadn't overheard Larry talking to his mother. He said he and Tom were going to visit pals from their outfits because the house was too gloomy with old Ian creeping around like a ghost. I didn't mind leaving, I was glad to, I hated it in Aylesbury where I'd always been happy, people being sorry for me and nagging about my teeth until finally I got these awful choppers which are worse. I remembered some men in the Oflag talking about Kenya, starting a new life there after the war. They said it was big and empty. So I told Mr Mayfield I wanted to go to Kenya and he wangled a job with Sir George Lavering through the old boy network. I didn't imagine I'd like farming but I had to do something and live somewhere. The point is, Mr Hardy, what I've been getting at, is that I like farming better than anything I've ever done, it's wonderful for me, I couldn't begin to tell you how wonderful because now I've got an interest in life, I've got something to think about.

You needn't worry that I won't have enough money to pay for Fairview. I have plenty, being the sole inheritor and our house was pretty valuable and had some good things in it and that's all sold too. I can give you a cheque in the morning, only for God's sake don't ask questions, just leave me alone and sell me the place. I know it's right for me, I know it, and I don't care what shape your farm is in, I haven't anything else to do with my life except work.

Kimoi called him for dinner. The cook had said he wasn't going to wait all night until the strange Bwana tired of sitting on the verandah in the dark. Ian came blinking into the big room, dazzled by the pressure lamp over the dining table. The fire was lit, the table set with sticks of celery and raw carrot in a glass jug, a lump of home-made butter, a home-made loaf on a board, a soup tureen, and a quart bottle of cold beer. Roast beef and roast potatoes, cauliflower, peas and baked apples with thick cream followed. Ian ate like a man starved. He thought this the finest room and the finest food in Kenya. It was extraordinary how contented he felt here in the easy quiet.

At Ol Ilyopita, there were too many people, the European staff, all public school to suit Lady Lavering, all friends, all given to evening drinks and dining in each other's houses. They were jubilant because the war was over, they were alive and where they wanted to be, on the biggest grandest farm in Kenya with agreeable jobs and super perks including polo ponies, two tennis courts, a swimming pool and Lady L's sumptuous parties. They enjoyed themselves at the top of their lungs. Ian was painfully conscious of being a transplanted ghost. They knew Ian had had a beastly war, the worst, and no wonder the poor chap was a bit touched in the head. They treated him with tact like a cripple. Ian saw the reasonableness of their attitude but he hated it. He was not a cripple to himself. He didn't dislike them, he didn't dislike anyone; he simply could not fit in.

His immediate boss, Johnny Leitch, thought well of Ian, who worked hard and was eager to learn but also clearly odd man out in the general chumminess. When Ian thanked him for his teaching and gave notice, saying he meant to buy a small farm, Johnny Leitch said, 'There's no better way to learn than trying it on your own. You can use your digs here as a base if you want, while you're looking around.' The trouble was that Ian had no idea how to look round and was too proud to admit himself helpless from the start. Johnny Leitch showed him the advertisement in the *Kenya Weekly News*, roaring with laughter.

'Luke Hardy's a card, a real old settler. He must have been pissed to the eyes when he sent that in. It's pretty country near Karula. Well, there's your farm, Ian. Whatever you do you couldn't make it worse.'

Ian asked for leave to visit Fairview Farm at once.

Lying in Luke Hardy's guest room bed, Ian thought about accidents. From what little he knew of life, he had decided the whole thing was purely accidental. God was not up there with his eye on the sparrow, busily planning for one and all. There was no plan. People believed they could direct their lives but in fact they were tossed around by accidents. Accidents wiped out his private world and his future, fourth generation in his father's firm and in his father's house. He had not considered that there might also be good accidents, but there were. The first was coming to Africa, the second was coming to Fairview Farm. He began to allow himself hope.

By habit, Ian was up and dressed with the sun. So was Luke Hardy, apparently sober though with slitted eyes and a hoarse voice.

'Show you the early milking,' Luke said. 'Take your car if that's all right, mine's at the workshop.' Where, he did not add, it had been as long as he could remember, perishing of old age and disuse.

In the cool first light, the scene looked so crazy that Ian had to swallow back laughter. Inside a rough circle, fenced with whistling thorn, half naked barefoot Africans sat on stools, sunk in cow dung, and milked the herd while shouting conversation and laughing their heads off. An ox cart dragged milk cans to a dilapidated shed where other talkative Africans worked hand separators. Ian wondered if you could get fatal diseases from germ-laden cream. The watu were plainly astonished to see Luke and greeted him with beaming smiles.

'Haven't been down here much lately,' Luke muttered. 'Might as well stop in at the office.'

Farther along the track, the office occupied one small section of a modest building, cracked cement walls, broken window panes, corroded tin roof. A big African stood in the office door trying to make himself heard above the uproar of a milling jolly mob.

'Simuni,' Luke said. 'Head man. Assigns jobs.'

Here, Luke received an ovation. The mob swirled around him, grinning and shouting Jambo, Bwana, habari. Luke looked embarrassed. He told Simuni to move them off, he wanted to show this Bwana the farm map. Inside the office was a chaos of cobwebs, cigarette butts in dirty tins, loose papers, papers stuck on spikes, ledgers jumbled on shelves and spilled on the floor. The farm map, tacked to the wall, was yellow and fly-specked. Luke began to explain it and gave up; the map was long out of date.

'Africans aren't much good at paperwork,' he said, defensively. 'But Simuni is a good man, trustworthy, doesn't drink.'

He indicated the open door to the next room; Ian glanced in. This was the farm storeroom. Ian could not imagine how the watu ever found anything from salt sacks to nails in such total disorder. Luke was sitting in the Dodge with the scowl of a man ready to pick a fight. He couldn't pick a fight with Paynter who gave him no excuse, no hint of criticism.

'Don't bother to stop,' Luke said as they passed the workshop, which appeared to be a scrap iron dump where three merry Africans prodded in the motor of an antique Bedford lorry.

Luke perked up at the spring. Thick trees, tangled with wild flowering vines, surrounded a large deep transparent pool. The bottom was flat grey pebbles and white sand. The water moved slightly in the current from an unseen source. Ian didn't know what he had expected to see but nothing as lovely as this. A rusty intake pipe and a collapsing pump shed failed to spoil the magic of the place.

'It's really a small version of that spring they've got at Tsavo, Mzima, you know?' Luke said. 'And that supplies all of Mombasa. You can do anything if you've got enough water, water is the most important thing you can have.' Luke seemed to be encouraging himself rather than Ian.

Ian said, 'Yes,' and stood entranced.

Luke sighed. 'Better finish it, take you to the African lines.'

Ian had thought everything a marvellous joke except the spring which was simply marvellous. How or why this farm worked was a mystery, but it did work; the proof being that it fed Luke and his watu. But the African lines were not funny. Rondavels with flaking walls and soggy ruined thatch dotted a large dust patch that stank of garbage and human excrement. Naked black children swarmed around like benign bees, pushing each other to reach Luke. Bwana, Bwana, they shrieked, beside themselves with pleasure. Ian noted their protuberant bellies, their filth, flies nestled in the corners of eyes, noses running yellow slime, scabs and sores. Women, with colourless lengths of cloth wrapped above their breasts, scratched at maize plants, hung rags of clothing to dry on bushes, squatted by blackened cook pots. They too laughed and yelled fond greetings. Mr Hardy had no right to the watu's affection when he let them live like animals.

Driving back to the house, Luke said angrily, 'It wasn't always like this. I wrote in the paper the place was in rotten condition. I told you it was a mess.'

Ian said, 'I don't mind working my balls off.'

Luke did not speak at breakfast and pushed food away while Ian consumed papaw, fried ham and eggs, toast, lime marmalade and coffee with the thick cream that was Luke's livelihood. Luke left him at the table and took a weak whisky and water to the verandah. Ian was not sure whether he should follow; he knew that the morning tour had upset Luke. He could not know that Luke was communing with Sue, blaming himself bitterly.

'I don't see where you put it,' Luke called from the verandah. 'Eating like that and looking like a beanpole. Come on out if you're finished.'

Ian was a chary of smiles, not wanting to expose those tombstone choppers. But in this fresh clear light, the view was so heart-lifting that he smiled all over his face. Africa lay before him and not a human habitation in sight. The land was lion colour shading off to blue green in the distance. It surged upward to trees on the high range in the south, descended in plateaux below him to rise slowly again to a far mountain rim, dropped sharply to a screen of woods on the north.

Moved to speech for once, Ian said, 'I think this must be the most beautiful place in the world.'

Luke grunted. 'Want to see more or have you had enough?'

'I'd like to see everything.'

The farm roads were rivers of dust, a foot deep, more than a foot. The Dodge churned up blinding clouds of it. Hidden beneath the dust, rocks jarred the axles violently. More fences lay draggled on the ground than stood firm on their posts. Unless the dust blew back and obscured the view, everywhere Ian looked was wonder and delight.

Luke had said the bulls were pastured in the southern section. They passed a Masai herder in a squashed felt hat and ancient army overcoat. Luke told Ian to stop. The Masai wore his huge pierced earlobes neatly draped over the tops of his ears, and delicate bead bracelets on his delicate wrists. Luke asked about the bulls; the Masai, pleased to see Luke like all the other farm people, said he knew where the heifers were.

'Go on, we'll find them,' Luke said. 'The herders are Masai. They live in their dung huts off there, south east. Give them some blankets and an old army overcoat from time to time, sack a man if he loses cattle, otherwise leave them alone, that's my system. They've got their own ways.'

'The others?' Ian asked. If you talked you got a mouthful of dust.

'Kipsigis. Good chaps. The house servants are Luos. There's not a single bloody-minded bastard on my farm,' Luke said, again defensive.

On a hill where Luke got out to scan his property for the invisible bulls, Ian inspected a round brick reservoir. The trough that circled it was filled with sludgy water, as much muck as water. He climbed on the trough to peer over the top. The water smelled like a sewer; he thought it might be a graveyard for vultures, bats, snakes if they could make the trip. Obviously no one had emptied and cleaned the tank in living memory.

Luke watched Ian's face for a sign of contempt but there was none. 'I have four of those on the farm,' Luke said. 'They need whitewash with a lot of lime and copper sulphate.'

Ian nodded.

'I can't locate the bulls but there's a nice view at the south if you want to see it.'

After a particularly rough jolt on a buried rock, Luke said, 'Had a bad war, did you?'

Ian was driving slowly, now, with concern for his car, the best he could get, second-hand, 28,000 miles on the meter; had to wait your turn for new vehicles. 'I only had a few days of war, after that I was a P.O.W. in Germany.'

'The whole time?'

'Yes.'

He steeled himself for more questions and for sympathy and blessed Luke for shutting up. The track corkscrewed towards the tree line. The pick-up was about ready to boil.

'Do your parents approve this scheme,' Luke said. 'You buying a farm out here on your own?'

Ian gritted his porcelain teeth; Luke saw the tight muscles in his cheek.

'My parents are dead.' God damn it to hell, why does he ask questions? What business is it of his? Say you'll sell me the farm or say you won't. I'm not here to tell you my life story, I'm here to buy or get out.

'Stop,' Luke said, unnecessarily as the track ended at the trees.

Luke led him to the edge of the ridge.

'It's a pretty good view in my opinion,' Luke said.

Eagles must see the earth like this. Africa went on for ever, in waves of mountains. Ian felt the sky as a presence, alive like the land, another continent spread over them in endless layers of shining blue. He had no words for any of the beauty of this farm, least of all for this.

'Yes, it is,' Ian said.

Luke walked a few yards into the lion grass, where he bent to wrench out handfuls of the tough golden stalks. He beckoned to Ian. At his side, Ian read the headstone, unevenly carved by someone who was not a stonecutter. Susan Elizabeth Grant Hardy, beloved wife of . . .

'I'm not asking you to do anything about it,' Luke said. 'Not keep the bush cut back or anything. I'm just asking you to see it's never disturbed.'

Ian realized that Mr Hardy had finally made up his mind to sell him Fairview.

At lunch, Ian said, 'I'll collect my kit at Ol Ilyopita and be here late tomorrow morning, if that's all right.'

'You haven't asked the price, son. You'll lose your shirt if this is the way you do business.'

Ian permitted himself a guarded smile so as not to flash the full repellent display at Luke.

'How do you know I won't want a hundred thousand pounds?'

Ian let his smile rip; to hell with the teeth.

'I know,' he said.


Luke was on the verandah, with a noticeably darker glass in hand. After seeing the headstone on the mountain, Ian understood why Luke drank and why he abandoned his farm. No drink was available in Oflag XV B but he had wished to die when he lost his family, and he had abandoned his own home without once visiting it again; the emptiness was unbearable. If he were as old as Luke, he wouldn't trouble to live either.

'You must have nipped right along,' Luke said. 'How's your Swahili? Want a noggin before lunch?'

'Beer, please. I think I can make out.' In his spare time, when the other young gentlemen employees at Ol Ilyopita were whooping it up, he memorized word lists, wrote out exercises, and when alone with Africans he practised.

Upcountry Swahili was a patois that even a language dummy like him could learn.

'Good. Seems better to me if you potter around on your own. I've told Simuni you're the new Bwana. Get the feel of it, talk to the watu. I'll be leaving in a week.'

Ian felt a flutter of panic. 'A week, sir?'

'No sense hanging about. We'll have to go to Karula, tomorrow or the day after. Show you the ropes, introduce you around. The station where you'll ship your cream. The post office, you can take over my box. The general store, I've got to pay my bill, you open an account. The bank, we have a little business at the bank, don't we? Sign a deed, get a big fat cheque from you. And the Sports Club. Means two tennis courts.'

'I don't play tennis,' Ian lied. Oh no, people, natter and merriment, all the dumb misery of it.

'Nobody does except the kids when they come back on holiday. The courts look like the craters of the moon. People stop in for a drink after they've finished their errands; gives them energy to drive home for lunch. Meet the neighbours.'

'I'd rather not, sir.'

'What do you mean? Of course you have to meet the neighbours, not all of them, just whoever is in town. You can't skulk into Fairview like a criminal. People would think there's something wrong with you. It's getting much too civilized here but even so neighbours depend on each other in a pinch. And you'll need advice, Paynter. They're experienced farmers.'

Ian decided not to think about it, and was glad to have a free run of the farm. He couldn't very well pry and probe, with Luke distressed beside him.

'Is it all right if I start after lunch, sir?'

'The watu knock off at two thirty; six thirty to two thirty, straight eight hours. We better eat. Kimoi, chakula!'

Ian had a long talk with Simuni, inquiring what rules and routine had governed this farm before Bwana Looki retired to the verandah and the booze. It was clear enough that anarchy now reigned. He feared the watu would resent him as an interloper but Simuni was helpful and friendly. Another reason to be grateful to Luke, who must have spoken on his behalf. When Simuni left for the shameful African lines, Ian started to clear the chaos in the office. He returned to the house at six; Luke was in bed. For two days, with excitement, Ian roamed over the farm and made notes on the order of reconstruction. Aside from Luke's splendid house, everything had to be torn down. A new corrugated tin roof and a few coats of white paint would fix the house. But what if Luke took the furniture with him?

Ian did not know how to approach this matter. 'Unless you want all the furniture,' he began.

Luke, as usual, was drinking his lunch.

'All thrown in, lock, stock and barrel, including one shotgun and one rifle. I won't want any of it at the coast. You'll have plenty to do without furnishing a house. That's woman's work.'

'Thank you very much, sir.' He was overjoyed and hoped Luke could feel his gratitude since he was unable to express it. The atmosphere of the house depended on Luke's excellent things; the house would lose its quality if stripped of them. But now he had to tackle a tricky question and he dreaded offending Luke. 'I thought of doing some building.'

'I daresay.'

'Could you recommend anyone?'

'Going to call in an outside construction man, are you? I made it with my own watu.' Then, remembering the condition of Fairview, Luke was ashamed of his boasting tone. 'George Stevens in Nakuru. He doesn't soil his hands but he has tough Sikh foremen. Be sure you get a definite contract on costs in advance. Otherwise you'll find they've put up a latrine and charged you for the Taj Mahal.'

Latrines happened to be one of Ian's major priorities.

They proceeded to Karula in convoy, Luke ahead in his old Austin, Ian close behind ready to push when the Austin stalled on the boulders and gullies in the road. Luke was taking the Austin to the garage, to charge the battery, tune up the engine, get the old bus fit for the trip to Mombasa. Ian thought with anxiety of Luke in that decrepit car on the long hard journey to the coast. The garage was not reassuring. Behind the petrol pump, vehicles in various states of dismemberment were parked in the workshop, an expanse of oil-stained cement floor under a tin roof supported on flimsy posts. Africans battered away at these cars, shouting comments and advice. Two brave men worked in a pit edged with old railroad tracks to prevent the truck above from sliding down on them. A fat Sikh, the owner, bounced from his box-like office to welcome Luke with protracted handshaking.

'Yes, yes, Bwana Looki, leave all to me, fine as new day after tomorrow,' said the Sikh whom Ian instantly classed as a prize liar in a trade renowned for lying.

Ian had not paid attention to Karula when passing through but Luke now took him round as if they were sightseeing an important city. The station provided no amenities for travellers but was better equipped for freight, the large godown being at present loud with caged chickens and smelling strongly of posho and kerosene. The post office and the bank on the main road, though toy-size, were the only stone buildings. Wooden one-room African dukas and beer parlours lined the two short dusty side streets. The general store looked palatial by contrast, a long narrow shed, painted yellow, with five smeared windows letting in light on a range of merchandise from patent medicines through food stuffs and toys to hardware. The proprietor received them in his office, beneath a photograph of the Aga Khan, and assured Ian it would be his greatest joy to serve him. The remainder of Karula was a sprawl of African shanties and an open fly-ridden market where women sat on the ground by mats displaying small heaps of vegetables and nameless African herbs. Ian saw no cause for Luke to fret about an excess of civilization.

Luke had left the serious business at the bank until last.

He was easing Ian into urban life gently. Though silent as always, Ian behaved all right when presented to the station master and the post master and Ram Singh at the garage and Jivangee at the general store. But Ian froze with Jim Barnes at Barclays. Perhaps the boy became paralysed only in the company of whites. Jim Barnes was visibly put off by Ian's manner. Luke talked to cover Ian's stony silence. Ian had not bothered to ask and Luke had not bothered to say how much he wanted for the sale. Hearing now Luke's price for Fairview and everything in it, Ian was distraught. When papers had been signed and witnessed and the cheque written, Luke, in a temper, hurried Ian out.

'Honestly, Paynter, what bites you?'

'I couldn't say anything in there, Mr Hardy, but it isn't right. It's too little, you're giving me Fairview, I can't take it, I'm not poor, I can afford a decent price.' To date, Luke had not heard Ian speak so long or so fast. He put his hand on Ian's arm, smiling at the unhappy young face above him.

'Listen, son. I know what I'm doing. I don't need more, I haven't anyone to leave it to. I want you to spend your money on Fairview, see? That's all I care about.'

'I will, sir, but all the same this isn't right.'

'It is. Now forget it, will you? We're off to the Club.'

Luke was thinking that Paynter was a good boy, a nice boy, yet with a screw loose somewhere. What ought to have scared Paynter, taking over a large gang of unknown watu, didn't ruffle him but the prospect of meeting a few pleasant neighbours, people of his own kind, obviously scared him stiff. Could Paynter manage Fairview if he had such wacky nerves?

Ian expected the Sports Club to be elegant on the Lavering style and filled with the sleek types who frequented the Laverings. The Karula Sports Club was a tatty little cement building, masked by handsome trees. Mottled brown linoleum covered the floor. A bar, flanked by doors labelled Memsaabs, Bwanas, stretched along one wall. A tinted photograph of the King and a Union Jack had been nailed rather crookedly above the bar. Small wood tables, stained by glass rings and cigarette burns, and kitchen chairs completed the furnishing. Ten people, five of each sex, were comfortably knocking back beer, gin and orange squash in this room where none of them would be caught dead at home in England. They rose, when they saw Luke, and fell upon him with kisses, handshakes, back-slapping and cries of rejoicing. 'Darling Lukie, *what* a treat!' 'Lukie dear, you've *made* the day!' 'How are you old boy, wonderful to see you!' 'You're looking fine, Luke, perfectly fine.'

But he wasn't of course. Luke was the other kind of drunk, the sort that stops eating and shrivels and grows grey-faced and trembly. They were all much more effusive than was their habit, being shocked to find Luke so sick and so old. When they had quieted, Luke made introductions. 'This is Ian Paynter who's just bought Fairview. Mr and Mrs Ethridge. Mr and Mrs Gale. Mr and Mrs Gordon. Mr and Mrs Farrell. Mr and Mrs Brand.' They smiled and shook hands and said cordial things like 'We must get in touch . . . come to lunch soon . . . let us know if there's anything we can do to help.' But they were not interested. They hovered around Luke, who was dismayed to be the centre of attraction. Months of solitude at Fairview had unsuited him for so many voices, so much carry-on. He understood Ian better. Promising falsely to see everyone before he left Karula, tell them his plans, hear the news, yes, sure, I'll appear on the doorstep, Luke extricated himself with Ian in tow.

Safe in the Dodge, Luke took a crumpled handkerchief from the pocket of his crumpled khaki shorts and wiped his forehead. Ian's guarded though knowing smile annoyed him. 'The secretary will send you a membership form and a chit for your dues.'

'Actually, Mr Hardy, I don't want to join.'

'Of course you'll join. If we didn't all pay our dues, how do you think the Club could keep going?'

This was the authentic voice of the old colonialist. The Club must be kept going, not only to satisfy an inborn

English need for clubs but as a symbol of Empire. Ian didn't give a hoot; he would pay his dues, since that was the drill, and never set foot in the place again.

'I'd be glad to drive you, sir.'

'No thanks, I'll go with the lorry.'

'Won't you be awfully early?'

The lorry left at eight in the morning to haul cream churns to the station.

'I have things to attend to,' Luke said. 'And you ought not to waste time. Get on with your job. You'll probably have questions you want to ask before I leave.'

The lorry was as decrepit as the old Austin. Everything about Fairview amazed Ian. Logically, the farm should have ground to a halt long ago.

Luke bought tickets for his cook, Joseph, and Kimoi at the station; they were to sit in the crowded train for most of a day and all of a night but that wouldn't depress them; the train was as good as a beer parlour. What depressed them was the coast, alien territory, alien tribes, but they did not consider refusing to accompany their Bwana into exile.

Luke fumed around Karula in a rage; Ram Singh the old shit didn't have the Austin ready. He had planned a morning call on Helen Gordon and was so late now he could barely make it before lunch.

'About time goddamnit,' Luke said and headed for the Gordons' farm which was called Mastings, a meaningless name, because Charles Gordon's family place in England was called Mastings, also a meaningless name.

Charles Gordon fell in love with Africa while on a shooting safari. To emigrate, he required a wife whom he quickly found, a pretty fair-haired girl, the belle of the previous London season. The parents of the bridal couple regarded this African venture as a foolish fling and expected their children home within months, or else Helen without Charles. The Gordons had now lived in the Highlands for fourteen years. Africa gave Charles everything he really cared about, from trout fishing to stalking elephant. Farming provided camouflage for the sporting life. He talked as if he was a burdened earnest farmer but old Roy Dobson, sixteen years his senior and hired as manager from the beginning, ran the farm. Old Roy, Charles was apt to say, is a priceless chap, one of the best, with the implication that old Roy was not quite one of us.

Helen Gordon liked Roy Dobson more than any man around Karula. Roy had started her on gardening, taught and encouraged her. She built her life on her garden; she was inseparable from it now that Charles had torn her children from her bosom and shipped them home to England. Charles was in a fever lest the war go on so long that his two sons would miss a proper education.

Despite the difference in age, Sue Hardy and Helen Gordon had been close loving friends, bound by their passion for making the earth bloom. Luke turned naturally to Helen for help. He found her, as always, grubbing in the garden, her face streaked with dirt where she had pushed back her sweat-damp hair, her old trousers mud-caked fore and aft.

'Luke! If I hug you, I'll get you filthy, but at least a kiss.'

'You're a pretty girl, Helen.'

'Hardly a pretty girl, darling, not at thirty-four. Lukie, come with me at once. I have to show you my latest. I've made a bosky dell, all spring flowers. In January, that's what I like, so dotty.'

She led him under trellises, down terraces, across immaculate lawns past glowing borders, to a far corner of the garden.

'Charles is furious, he says I'm wasting his precious water. Do you like it? Isn't it a dream? Though I must admit using a sausage tree and mwangwas for shade rather spoils the Old England effect.'

The bosky dell was a small natural bowl with a cunningly contrived imitation natural pool in the centre. Fringing the pool and scattered up the grassy slopes, iris and daffodils, freesia and jonquils, violets, narcissus, fairy bells grew in lovely confusion, as if growing wild. The light fell softly, broken by the African trees.

'Your year's work, Helen? It is a dream.'

'I've sweated blood on moss but I don't think it's going to take. Now come and sit down, behold my rustic bench. I had the carpenter make it as I thought this would be the perfect place for reading poetry, not that I ever sit or read poetry. Tell me your news.'

'I wanted to talk to you about Ian Paynter.'

'The gangly young man you brought to the Club. What's that tic on his face?'

'Tic?'

'Yes, you know the way he keeps loosening and widening his lips.'

Luke laughed. 'I hadn't noticed but I reckon it's his party smile, to stop from showing his teeth.'

'Why, for heaven's sake?'

'They're the size of horse teeth and false. He ought to sue his dentist. Poor chap. I expect his went rotten in that Hun prison camp.'

'Lukie, explain.'

'They shouldn't make war with boys,' Luke said in sudden fierce anger. 'They ought to call up old men like me; let the old men fight their bloody wars. I figure the Huns had Paynter in jail from the age of eighteen to twenty-three, think of it, Helen, the best years of a young man's life when he's just got out from under school and family and feeling his oats, everything is new and exciting, and he can't wait to start. Why not wreck the old men, we've nothing to lose.'

'They did it to your generation too,' Helen said gently.

'Perhaps that's why I feel so sorry for young Paynter. I was lucky, I got in and got out quick.' Second Lieutenant Hardy invalided out with a cushy wound, leaving his right arm permanently shorter and bent and scarred from shoulder to elbow as though by a lion's claw, which didn't hamper him at all. He wore long sleeves. He hadn't missed his youth and the cocky fun of it.

'Anyway, Helen, I wanted to ask you to keep an eye on him.'

'Of course, Lukie. I'll have him to lunch at once, Charles will take him off on his killing sprees . . .'

'No, no, absolutely not. No parties, no fuss. He'll do best on his own at Fairview. Five years like that is enough to bust anyone up but I think there's more.' Luke stopped, feeling he was about to betray a confidence, Ian's voice when he said his parents were dead. 'The point is, he's a bit strange and I don't want people gossiping about him. I know how it gets in a place like this, people start talking and then everyone begins to look at you as if you're queer or contagious.'

'Lukie, you sound positively paternal. He must be a very nice young man. What would you like me to do?'

'Put in a word for him. That's all. See he doesn't get a bad name. And spread the idea that he's been ill or something, hasn't got his strength back, doesn't want a shower of invitations.'

'I'll do my best. Oh Lord, we must run. Charles will give you a drink while I tidy. I've never grasped why Charles foams at the mouth if he's kept waiting for his food.'

The sitting room at Mastings bore no resemblance to Fairview. Chippendale and Queen Anne, family possessions from home, Persian carpets, old Dutch still-lives of dewy fruit, old English rural scenes, flower-filled vases everywhere. Charles Gordon looked at Luke with pity and comprehension and splashed in a drop of soda to dilute the whisky for the sake of good form.

'I cannot understand why Helen is always late,' Charles said. 'Though I suppose I should be thankful she doesn't have her meals sent down to the garden. Have you seen her latest? Pretty soon there won't be water for the stock.'

'How are your boreholes?' Luke needed to drink quietly, and knew Charles enjoyed holding forth on boreholes. Helen interrupted an account of Charles' recent excavations.

'Here I am,' Helen said. 'Bring your drink, Lukie. I

always drink steadily right through lunch.' Iced tea but it
looked enough like whisky to avoid shaming dear Luke,
and the houseboy filled glasses without being told.

'We've been talking about Ian Paynter, Charles.'

'Well, Luke, I hope you got a good price for Fairview
since you wanted to sell it, but my God what a monkey the
watu will make of that young chap. You know how sly
they are. They'll see he's green as grass and pull all their
tricks on him.'

'He seems to do all right with them.'

'Naturally, at the beginning. He's the new Bwana. But
in a couple of weeks, they'll be coming to him for money,
moaning about funerals, sick totos, I can hear it now, and
then asking for leave, more funerals, more sick totos.
They'll drive him up the wall. A young chap with no
experience can't run a farm like Fairview. They come out
from home thinking there's nothing to it but we jolly well
know better.'

Helen smiled; her great big booby couldn't run a
chicken coop without Roy's guiding hand. Luke drank.

'I give him a year,' Charles said, interested now in a plate
full of delicious lasagne verde. Except for tardiness at
meals, Helen was a highly satisfactory wife. She had taught
herself to cook and then taught that surly old ape in the
kitchen. 'One year,' Charles said, chewing contentedly.
'Then he'll go broke and Fairview will be on the market
again.'

Helen saw that this wounded and worried Luke. 'Come
off it, Charles,' she said abruptly. 'You met the man once
for a minute. How do you know he won't turn out to be
the best farmer in the whole Karula district?'

Luke gazed at her with affection and began on his third
whisky. She thought it wise to give Ian Paynter a rest.
Charles might decide to put on his farmer act and list all
the ways Ian Paynter could mishandle Fairview.

'What are your plans, Lukie? Where are you going?'

'I'll stay with Billy Blake, you remember him, he used to
farm on the Kinangop. Moved to the coast about four

years ago, high blood pressure, some place the other side of Kilifi creek. He'll lend me a bed until I find a furnished house.'

'But Lukie, nothing grows at the awful coast. Nothing except bananas and mangoes. You'll die of boredom. What will you do?'

'Drink,' Luke said. 'With a clear conscience.'

Joseph and Kimoi had been driven off in the lorry with their iron cots, bedding, pots and pans and cardboard suitcases loaded behind. They looked like men on the way to prison. Luke was leaving two servants for Ian. Mwangi, Luke explained, was as good a cook as old Joseph but Joseph's jealousy held him down to assistant and substitute when Joseph was on leave. Kimoi trained Beda and Beda was a perfectly capable houseboy. In case Ian wanted more servants; Ian interrupted to say he would never need more. Now Luke was ready to depart. He took only four worn suitcases as salvage from his entire adult life. Ian felt like bursting into tears which would disgrace him, Luke, Marlborough and the British Empire. Mwangi and Beda stood at the kitchen door weeping without shame.

Luke had not foreseen the anguish of this moment. It was as if Sue died a second time. He wanted to hurry away from the sight of Fairview and the pain of homesickness. Ian closed the door of the old Austin.

'Thank you for everything, sir.'

'Take care of the place, Paynter. Take care of it and find someone responsible to leave it to.'

'Leave it to?'

'You aren't immortal, you know. A place like this,' Luke said, with difficulty, 'a place like this deserves looking after.'

The Austin backfired and creaked down the drive. Ian watched its dust trail rising into the tall double row of eucalyptus that Luke and Sue had planted long ago. He watched until he could see no further sign of Luke. Depressed and aimless, he wandered on to the verandah, thinking he would take a look at his property before facing the tedious chore of sorting out the office. Some kind of miracle happened there in the morning sun. He saw no visions, heard no divine voice. The miracle was how he suddenly felt so happy, happier than he'd ever hoped to be again. He had a reason for living: fifty African families and land and stock and a house and garden to look after. And there was this wonderful feeling in him, like coming home.

The watu were bewildered by their new master, Bwana Panda. They had never seen a European, naked to the waist, sweating as they did, wield a pick and shovel alongside them. Bwanas kept clean and gave orders. They had never seen anyone, black or white, enjoying work like this Bwana. If he wasn't racing over the farm, pitching in on all the jobs, he was racing to Nakuru. Each time he went, more lorries full of cement timber roofing piping bricks fence wire machinery arrived at the farm, as well as more outside workmen to be hounded by that Sikh boss. There was no peace; everyone was running around as if in the middle of a forest fire.

When it rained for a week in March, the watu counted on a rest. Nobody wanted to get soaked and chilled, you couldn't be expected to work in the rain. Bwana Panda worked in the rain, soaked and chilled, driving them and himself. What's a little water, he said; dig drainage ditches along the roads while the ground is loose, pry out the rocks, get trenches ready for new piping, put up fence posts. Hurry, hurry, hurry. This wasn't the life they had known.

But Bwana Panda was not a bad man, by which they meant bad-tempered, their only standard for judging Europeans. He never shouted at them. Ian knew from the Oflag how it eats into a man's soul to be shouted at and unable to shout back. The watu gave him a nickname, as they did to all Europeans. They called him Soft Voice. It was a compliment.

Though Soft Voice was constantly crazily on the move, the watu had seen him stop his small truck and stand beside it for a moment in silence. They discussed this act and agreed that Soft Voice was praying. His God commanded him to stop anywhere, any time, and stare at Africa, praying. Ian looked at the land, mile after empty beautiful mile, stretched out to the smooth receding mountains and said to himself: I'm free, *I'm free*.

The African bush telegraph operated with its usual efficiency. Karula was also an information centre. Ram Singh at the garage and Jivangee at the general store were subtle gossips with connections in Nakuru. There was a steady flow of news about Ian and Fairview Farm. Paynter had built new large rondavels for his watu and piped in water to standing taps. Every rondavel had a latrine. Moreover, Paynter gave his watu domestic furnishings, iron cots and kapok mattresses, wood tables and chairs, buckets and cook pots, blankets and coarse towels, and a regular ration of blue soap. He had dressed the labourers in new overalls and wellingtons and thrown in yards of cloth for the women and children. This was unheard of, a dangerous precedent. If you spoiled the watu, they asked for more and worked less.

Reports filtered in about projects for a stone dairy with a sixteen unit milking parlour and milking machines to run off a new generator, a new pump and pump house at the spring, a rebuilt and richly equipped workshop, a new office and a storeroom like the Nakuru Star Hardware Emporium, the Public Works bulldozer to clear new farm tracks, and miles of fencing. Drivers from other farms saw the new Fairview Chevrolet lorry at the station and Ram Singh said Bwana Panetah had put his name down for a new Ford pick-up to haul his endless purchases from Nakuru. Everyone knew that Paynter was spending money like water and getting little back. Gopal the station master confided to Mark Ethridge, whence the word went round, that Bwana Panetah was shipping less cream than Bwana Looki had in his declining years. Anybody could tart up a farm but that was not the same as making it pay. Charles

Gordon's opinion became general: Paynter would go bankrupt within a year and Fairview be back on the market.

No one had the straight gen from the horse's mouth because Ian only went to Karula early on Friday mornings to collect cash for payday and his mail. If any of the farmers met him, by chance, Ian answered questions in monosyllables. Sam Brand observed that Paynter always behaved like a man in need of a pee, twitching and wriggling until he could get away. The Memsaabs said that if Ian happened to spot one of them in the distance, he fled. This terror or distaste caused Rose Farrell to ask Maggie Ethridge if she thought Ian was queer.

They were shopping in the general store.

'Just a minute,' Mrs Ethridge said, checking her list. 'Don't tell me you're out of Gentlemen's Relish again, Mr Jivanjee. Oh well, never mind. How do you mean, Rose? Queer-homo or plain queer?'

'I don't know. I can't decide.'

Dick Gale, gnawed by curiosity, dropped in at Fairview Farm uninvited. He did not find Ian, which was all to the good. Beda said the Bwana was cleaning a reservoir. 'Himself?' Mr Gale asked. Beda said oh yes, Bwana Panda worked with the men on everything. 'He comes to this house at night, seven o'clock, eight o'clock, eat, sleep, wake up, go, work, come back eat quick, go, work, come back, eat quick, go, work. Not like Bwana Looki.' Dick Gale had a snoop round and a chat with Simuni who looked harassed.

Mr Gale's audience at the Sports Club next day was spellbound. 'The man's off his rocker. Can you believe it, Simuni told me he's putting up a pig palace and he doesn't own a single sow. There's an army of builders swarming over Fairview, but the same old mingy herd, from what I could see. Luke was always a lazy farmer, but Paynter must be mad. His watu seem pretty fed up, I mean no one works like that, fourteen hours a day.'

'He's a boor,' Mrs Farrell said. 'Sending everyone the same note — so sorry, I have to be in Nakuru. As if Nakuru was Calcutta. A child of two would have better manners. He won't be invited to our house again.'

'I bet George Stevens is swindling the pants off him,' Charles Gordon said with some satisfaction. 'If he asked advice, any of us could save him a lot of money and mistakes.'

Ah Lukie, Helen Gordon thought, they're all miffed, the men and the women, because your Paynter boy doesn't want them or need them. How can I keep my promise to speak up for him?

'I think he looks like Gary Cooper,' Helen said out of the blue.

This was greeted with shouts of laughter.

'I do,' Helen insisted. 'Nice and shy and with a golden heart, like Gary Cooper. He never says anything but Yes Ma'am or No Sir and everyone suspects him because he's a loner but in the end he gets the girl and they make him Sheriff. Come on, Charles, we'll be late for lunch.'

They were wafted out on waves of merriment which was better than pointless spite. How well Luke understood the neighbours or perhaps the human species though, apart from elephants, the animal species didn't seem full of Christian charity either. She longed to get back to her garden.

The Africans kept headline news to themselves. Though tireless chatterers, they could be secretive when they wished. All the watu around Karula knew that Bwana Panda had quelled a mutiny six months after he took over Fairview.

At first, Ian's watu could hardly believe their good luck. Fine houses, more goods and chattels than ever owned before, clothes, double rations of tea and sugar and posho, kuni and charcoal, and those large bars of soap. Soft Voice even laid out a big new shamba for the women, and gave them seed. Instead of scratching at a few plants of their own, they were to cultivate the shamba in turn and share the produce. The women were doubtful of this innovation until the shamba sprouted a glut of cabbages and beans, potatoes and tomatoes, maize and onions, more than enough for all. The men were paid regularly once a week instead of irregularly maybe once a month. Soft Voice evidently had a soft heart.

The watu were happy until Soft Voice expected them to earn his gifts. After hours, Soft Voice wanted them to tear down their old houses; for what reason; they had moved to new quarters. Soft Voice ordered this same kind of useless work all over the farm. They were sick of hearing Soft Voice say 'Safi', clean – clean this, clean that, make it clean, keep it clean. Every week, he inspected their village, sharp-eyed for taka-taka, dirty papers, empty bottles, and stern about latrines. Bwana Looki was easy-going; he let them live as they liked. Simuni was their proper overseer; Bwana Looki didn't interfere with Simuni; he also let them work as they liked.

They took their comforts for granted now and told each other life was better in the old days when a man had time to down tools and rest and laugh with his friends. They began to dawdle and loaf and malinger. They were sullen and complaining. Ian saw this at once with despair.

At the Lavering estate as a newcomer to Kenya, Ian was quickly taught the European doctrine on Africans. The watu were lazy and filthy and ungrateful. It was senseless to try to change them or improve their lives. This didn't mean the watu were wicked, it simply meant that they were shiftless children and should be treated accordingly with a firm hand. Left to themselves they would do nothing except get drunk and screw their women. Firmness was all they understood.

Ian rejected this doctrine. He had been treated as inferior; flea-ridden, half starved, dirty, ragged and helpless while his jailers were clean, well-fed and powerful. All men were not equal, of course, but all men had a right to respect. He meant to trust his watu, assure their needs, and explain the purpose of their work. He talked to every man on every job, pointing out that their joint task was to make Fairview

efficient. Dirt and disorder were not efficient. When the
farm operated as he planned and showed a profit, their
wages would rise. He should have saved his breath. The
watu were determined to prove the European doctrine
correct.

Ian knew what he had to do and he hated it. Make
examples, he thought with bitterness, like the goddamned
despicable bloody Germans. In one week Ian sacked a
Masai herder who had neglected to report a sick cow, three
men who were smoking and telling stories instead of
cleaning a reservoir, and the gardener who was watering
Ian's roses in the heat of the day. Ian gave them all twenty-
four hours to get off the farm. The watu were impressed,
and especially by the way Soft Voice shouted at the gardener. His face was pale with rage, he swore at the man.

No one heard what went on at the Masai encampment
but in the African lines there was female wailing. The
wives knew they would never live so well on any other
farm. A revolt against the men flared among the women.
They screamed and nagged; if their men were *bure* and
*shenzi* and lost their jobs, they would leave them. Punishment worked like a charm.

It worked on Ian like an illness. He slept badly and lost
his appetite. He couldn't rest, he walked up and down,
sitting room to verandah, back and forth, trying to understand why he had come to this ugly relation with the watu.
He had to talk to someone or jump out of his skin so he
wrote a letter to Luke which he knew he would tear up.
Dear Mr Hardy; I thought I got on well with the watu, I
liked them and I thought they liked me. I know I'm a
deadweight with other people and I even know what they
think of me because I overheard that too, Mrs Mayfield
telling Larry I had an inferiority complex from being a
P.O.W. Out here I didn't care what people thought, I could
keep out of their way and I felt easy with the watu and I was
happy because I'd found the right life for me. I wanted
them to live and work in decent conditions and I wanted
Fairview to look the way it should. That's all I've been

working for. You've got to admit Fairview was a shambles and the watu lived in a pigsty. But they loved you and now they treat me as if I wanted to cheat them instead of help them and I feel they hate me. They've made me see I can't get on with anyone. I'm a misfit wherever I am.

He tore the letter up; apart from being shameful, a good cry on Mr Hardy's shoulder would not help. The full truth was worse. The watu could defeat him. The watu could drive him from his home. If the only way to run Fairview Farm was by bullying and fear, he couldn't do it. He couldn't live like that.

Cold and unsmiling, Ian went on with the work; no more jolly chat, no more stripping off his shirt to give a hand and an example. Simuni received flat orders; inspecting the jobs from his pick-up, Ian made flat corrections. The watu were subdued; everyone worked as directed. Ian wondered how long he could stand this atmosphere, harsh master, obedient slaves. Slowly, the climate of the farm changed. The watu worked without that air of cringing; they smiled and greeted him amiably. Jambo Bwana habari. Ian assumed they had made their choice: work and be rewarded, otherwise get kicked off the farm. He was wrong. They had simply become accustomed to the new regime and the new Bwana who would tolerate no nonsense and now kept his distance as a Bwana should. Fairview hummed along cheerfully, Bwana Looki and the old ways forgotten.

Ian still liked the watu but they had disappointed him. They did not respond to trust, they responded to a firm hand. A firm hand need not be cruel. He could live on these terms, accepting the barriers set up by the watu. He felt lonelier but compensated by the work; week by week he saw his dreams for Fairview coming true.

He dealt with the men all day long and could not have worked with them except on terms of liking, however altered. He saw the women once a week and they repelled him with their shrieking laughter and their hideous bodies, black blubber swelling out to huge bottoms. But these repellent women produced the best totos he had ever seen, round-eyed, chubby, fur-topped, fending for themselves as soon as they could waddle. In childhood, they grew thin and swift and lovely as gazelles. More food, good housing, soap, enforced hygiene had transformed these totos. The totos loved the new Bwana. When Ian inspected the African lines, they rushed to meet him. He brought them toffees, he let them clamber over him, patting and hugging, he played with them, he carried the smallest in his arms. With them there were no barriers.

The watu were amazed by the Bwana's devotion to their children. They mulled over this clear but mysterious fact and decided that Soft Voice felt about their totos as he felt about his roses. No one understood his feeling for the roses either.

Ian had made a trip to Nairobi to buy the plants at a nursery. The names meant nothing to him, Golden Dawn, President Hoover, Madame Butterfly, Picture: they were roses and roses had been his mother's favourite. Ian's roses were set out in two rectangular beds, like infantry platoons, on the rough lawn in front of his verandah. To protect them from the sun, they were hidden under little thatch roofs with straw packed around their roots. Perhaps they didn't look like much but they were there and occasionally Ian cut a few and put them in a beer mug in his sitting room. The roses mattered to him. His mother was buried in the churchyard in Aylesbury. He felt that his roses kept something of her alive and with him.

Coming out of the post office, Ian saw Helen Gordon in tears by the wall of mail boxes. He could not pass without a word yet could not think what word to say to an unknown woman in unknown trouble. He stood near her, silent and awkward until she looked up.

'It's Luke. He's dead. Read it.' She gave Ian a telegram. LUKE DIED LAST NIGHT IN HIS SLEEP DOCTOR SAYS HEART ATTACK HE LOOKED PEACEFUL WHAT SHALL I DO BLAKE.

Ian felt a pain that was as sharp as it was unexpected, for himself not Luke. He had written to Luke a week ago inviting him to Fairview to see how he had spent his money, how he had kept his promise. In the year of work, he imagined Luke approving, he counted on that, he wanted desperately to show what he had done and talk about it and be praised. Now there was no one who would care. He had thought of Luke as somehow his partner and his friend because they both loved Fairview.

'I can't bear to think of Lukie dying there alone,' Helen said.

'He wouldn't mind that. He couldn't bear living alone.'

Helen brushed at her tears, too absorbed in grief to notice that Ian had spoken to her for the first time.

'But he had so many friends, we all loved him.'

'It's not the same thing.' He had friends too, long ago in Aylesbury. If only he could have shown Luke Fairview, if only that, just once, for both their sakes.

'This Mr Blake,' Ian said. 'Does he mean what to do with the body?'

Helen flinched. 'Yes, I suppose so.'

'He ought to be buried at Fairview, beside his wife. He ought to have the same headstone, only saying beloved husband of, instead of beloved wife.'

'You really are a very nice man just as Luke said.'

Instantly Ian was thrown back into himself and became a mumbler, anxious to flee.

'I'll have the place ready. And I'd like to pay for it all, whatever there is. I owe Mr Hardy a lot.'

Four days later the funeral cortège arrived at Fairview, six cars and the coffin in the Gordon pick-up. Helen made a blanket of rose geraniums to cover the coffin. The pick-up looked like a florist's van with all the sheafs and wreaths and bouquets contributed by the neighbours. The neighbours had doubled up, since you wanted company badly when going to a funeral. Beda faced this crowd and delivered his speech in agitated English.

'Bwana Panda say you follow his driver, please come

after here for food and drinking. Bwana Panda sorry he must go Nakuru.'

Mrs Ethridge laughed.

Mrs Gale said, 'I don't think it's funny.'

Mrs Farrell said, 'I think it's the absolute limit.'

Helen Gordon slipped away from the indignation meeting. Walking around the house, she saw that Ian had obviously planted the seeds in the borders packet by packet. Pansies grew beside hollyhock, lavender next to dahlias, asters clumped by gladioli. The lawn was coarse Kikuyu grass but well mowed with the hideous rose beds in the centre. Poor old boy, Helen thought, he's tried hard. Sue would think it touching, the feeling was right even if the result was an eyesore. Helen returned to hear Sam Brand saying, 'Look, he didn't invite us to a party. He offered a place to bury Luke so let's get on with it, shall we?'

They piled into the cars, following Ian's pick-up. Ian had detailed two men, in clean overalls, with ropes and shovels for the manual labour. On the way to the gravesite everyone craned and peered, rather shamefaced, to see what Ian had been doing out here alone. They pulled themselves together on the mountain, forgetting Ian, while Sam Brand read parts of the funeral service. Though Luke was not a churchgoer or believer, they had agreed he wouldn't mind if they left out the Resurrection and so on, and kept the factual bits about being born of a woman cometh up and is cut down.

No one stopped at the house for food and drink. The Farrells and the Brands and the Gordons were silent driving back to Karula in the Gordons' estate car. Helen prepared to give them hell if they began to complain of Ian's manners. Luke's little burial ground was turfed and fenced in, with morning glories twining around the white slats of the fence. As a gardener, she knew this work was recent and she knew whose work it was.

Charles Gordon broke the silence. 'Whatever one thinks about him, I have to hand it to Paynter. He's made Fairview better than it ever was. He's really done a bang-up job. Luke would appreciate that.'

These were lush years for the farmers in Kenya. Britain needed all the food it could get; the African weather did nothing drastic; no epidemics of disease or insects blighted the animals or the crops. The farms boomed, none more than Fairview. Ian sold off the lacklustre cattle inherited from Luke and bought pedigreed Friesian bulls to serve his high grade shorthorn cows. Now he had two lorries making two daily trips to Karula station, hauling whole milk as well as cream. He filled what Dick Gale had called his pig palace with large white sows and shipped baconers to the Uplands factory. He acquired sheep because he liked the look of them nibbling away on the slopes north of his house, but soon the sheep proved so fertile that he was sending lambs to the Nairobi market. His own vegetable garden and chickens also overproduced and Mr Jivangee at the general store was pleased to take the surplus. The watu were not slow to see that profits for Fairview meant profit for them, as their wages rose; they settled down into a reliable work force.

Fairview was coining money. Ian did not care about money; he would have been satisfied if the farm broke even. But money was the sure proof of success and he coveted success for Fairview. This success had a soothing effect on Ian. He gained weight and forgot his teeth for weeks at a time until he forgot them entirely. Though not by nature a roistering type, he smiled when he wanted to. He felt equal to other men, in work at least. He could talk farming with confidence and knew that his peers, the Karula farmers, accepted him as one of them. He was still clumsy with the Memsaabs but no longer bolted on sight and managed polite if brief conversations. The Memsaabs were used to him and besides had him taped ever since Simon Farrell said that Paynter couldn't help it if he was a misogynist. 'I never believed they really existed,' Simon Farrell said. 'But obviously that's what Paynter is. Poor fellow, he doesn't know what he's missing.' There was nothing personal in being a misogynist so the Memsaabs stopped scolding about Ian's manners.

Ian celebrated his twenty-ninth birthday with an extra whisky. He lay on the sofa by the fire, balancing the glass on his stomach, and thought of Fairview. Five years ago he had been a hopeless ghost in Aylesbury. Now he was a man with a mission and the mission filled his days and would fill the rest of his life. Time didn't cure the old sorrow that remained like an ache in his bones. When he imagined his parents and Lucy here with him, he was close to tears; his father taking over the business end, proud as he was to see this small industry galloping along; his mother making a beautiful garden; Lucy gay and noisy in the house, riding beside him in the pick-up, loving the land, mad about the totos. It was useless to cry for what might have been. He missed three people, no others could take their place. Without them, he knew he would always be alone but alone in this peaceful room on this marvellous farm. That was the way accident had shaped his life. He didn't have the happiness he would have chosen; he had a different happiness and enough to keep him going.

Except for Ian, all the Europeans knew that Miss Grace Davis has arrived in Karula. Miss Davis came from England to teach spelling, grammar, penmanship, composition and reading to small girls at a small boarding school, Heather Hill, outside the town. Advance news of a young woman fresh from a fashionable school at home secretly worried most of the Memsaabs. They foresaw a peach complexion, the latest hair-do, and the sort of smart clothes bought in a city for country wear. Africa was unfair to European women, as the Memsaabs frequently said. The sun struck straight down from the equatorial sky and ruined their skin. The men's faces were like cordoba leather, which was becoming, but the Memsaabs finally looked like withered apples or, if they fled the sun, grey-white mushrooms. Their figures did not survive too well either, growing stout like Mrs Ethridge or skinny like Mrs Gale. The exceptions were Helen Gordon who exercised by gardening and preserved her skin by magic, and Rose Farrell who exercised relentlessly in her bedroom, watched her diet, creamed her face and bought the best clothes she could find in the best shops in Nairobi, but was the most worried Memsaab in the area due to Simon's wandering eye.

Women who feel they have lost or are losing their looks tend to be nervous about their husbands. Miss Davis posed no threat to anyone and was therefore an instant hit with the Memsaabs. She was invited to all the farms and to the Karula Sports Club; she met everyone, she went everywhere. The Memsaabs were bursting with cordiality. Almost at once they seemed to know the story of Miss Davis' life. She had been engaged to a wonderful man, a bomber or fighter pilot, in the R.A.F. or the American Airforce, who was shot down in flames over Berlin or Hamburg or some other place. The wives passed this sad tale on to the husbands.

'You must be getting barmy, Rose,' Simon Farrell said. 'Do you mean to tell me that any pilot, and they were the glamour boys and in a hurry too, would go for those specs, that awful crinkly mud-coloured hair, and that body. I can't look at her without thinking of a Dover sole.'

'Eight years ago, perhaps ten years, she might have been very pretty,' Rose said, delighted.

'Balls. All you can say about her face is that she has the usual number of features and none are actually deformed.'

Mark Ethridge said, 'Well, Maggie, since men are known to copulate with sheep, I am ready to believe anything. Though I'd rather have a nice warm soft sheep than Miss Davis any day.'

The wives soon tired of Miss Davis. She had an affected voice, she was so ladylike you wanted to kick her, and she gushed. 'Drowns you in syrup,' Mrs Gale observed. Miss Davis, they agreed, was a typical spinster schoolmistress and fine for the children but they had done their duty and that was that.

During her popular period, Miss Davis met Ian Paynter at the Karula Sports Club. She had no idea that this was a unique occasion. It was a Friday before Christmas and Ian had been doing business with Simon Farrell in the bank, relative to a sale of heifers. Simon Farrell said, 'Come and have a drink at the club, Ian, Christmas cheer and all that.' When Ian began to mutter excuses, Simon Farrell said crossly, 'Oh stop being such a blushing violet, nobody's going to eat you.' Ian's war victim act had gone on long enough; Ian was a mental hypochondriac. Simon Farrell had had a whizz of a war, chasing the Wops out of Ethiopia, but thought that good or bad wars were ancient history.

Goaded and indignant, Ian followed in his brand new cherished Landrover, a Christmas present to himself. The club room looked even nastier decorated with artificial holly and mistletoe. Miss Davis was sitting with Mrs Farrell. Pink gin for Mrs Farrell, orange squash for Miss Davis. Miss Davis wore a blue linen dress and looked like a hospital nurse in uniform. As a favour to Helen Gordon, Mrs Farrell had collected Miss Davis at Heather Hill, which was on her way to Karula. Mrs Farrell was now thinking that the claims of friendship and motherhood were both excessive. She was bored rigid by Miss Davis. She had been buttering up Miss Davis on behalf of Jenny, her ten-year-old daughter, but this was her last effort and Helen Gordon could jolly well drive an extra eight miles in future.

As soon as she saw the men, Mrs Farrell said, 'Simon, you have time for a very quick one, you know I've got a mob of little girls to lunch.' Before Simon could protest, his wife gave him a fierce wink. She was in such a hurry to leave that she didn't remark on Ian's presence. 'You'll take care of Miss Davis until Helen gets here, won't you Ian?' Mrs Farrell said, beating a fast retreat.

This was much worse than Ian had expected. He could already feel the silence that would lie between him and a woman he had never even seen before. He asked if she'd have another drink and Miss Davis thanked him for more orange squash while he downed a strong gin and french.

But then, to his amazement, there were no silences; Miss Davis chattered and he only had to say Yes or No, and with two big gins under his belt and this easy conversation he found he was quite enjoying himself. Miss Davis had ascertained cleverly that there was no Mrs Paynter. Just as cleverly, she led Ian to invite her for lunch at his farm the next day. Ian gathered that this was how Miss Davis lived; on weekends and during holidays she lunched around the countryside.

When Helen Gordon arrived to pick up Miss Davis, she couldn't believe her eyes. 'Why, Ian,' she said in a wondering voice and Ian immediately became all stumbling feet and stammers. On the way back to Mastings, Helen Gordon said, 'You're a wizard, Miss Davis. You must be the first woman Ian's ever talked to. He's so shy it's like a disease. The men say he's perfectly normal with them, but he has St Vitus' dance with the ladies. I think he's sweet though I can hardly get a word out of him. Oh, he's about twenty-nine or thirty. Yes, he lives alone at Fairview and he's made it clear to all of us that the last thing he wants is company. He's in love with his farm, he doesn't need anything else, and I'm convinced he's going to be the best farmer around Karula. A born bachelor, I'd say; what Charles calls more steer than bull.'

With her eyes on the road, Helen didn't see the prim tightening of Miss Davis' mouth. How long can I dish up this babble, Helen thought, and how on earth will we get through lunch?

'Not that he's unattractive,' Helen went on. 'Except for those teeth. No, his family doesn't come out to visit. I don't know anything about them but Lady Lavering is such a cracking snob that she wouldn't let old George hire anyone who hadn't been properly vetted. Oh yes, Ian worked for the Laverings before he settled here.'

Miss Davis was restfully silent during lunch. Helen sent Miss Davis back to Heather Hill with the driver; one personally escorted trip was all politeness required.

'You see, Charles, you didn't have to raise such a hellish

row. It wasn't that bad. Poor thing, I do feel sorry for her, she's so wildly unappealing.'

Ian was stunned by his invitation. In almost four years, four years next month, he hadn't asked anybody to Fairview, and was greatly relieved when the Memsaabs stopped inviting him. Miss Davis seemed to think that he would naturally have people for lunch and this assumption was flattering though he couldn't explain why. Miss Davis' lack of looks was an advantage. Ian didn't see her as a woman. She was a nice person who gave him the happy impression of being easy to talk to. He didn't know about women or think about them; they did not exist in his life.

All the twenty-three bumping miles home, Ian fretted over food. What to give Miss Davis? He was both nervous and elated. He never planned meals, that was Mwangi's business; but for this special event he would make suggestions. Friendly, nice, about his age; roast chicken with bread sauce, mashed potatoes, peas, brussel sprouts, tinned fruit salad with cream and a bunch of roses on the table.

Grace Davis had always harboured great expectations. The mystery was why, exactly, on what basis, for what reason she entertained so many hopes for so long. Her father had risen from a shoe clerk, bowed forever over female feet, to part owner and still active salesman in a small shoe store in Lincoln. Her mother, by temperament a mouse, became a mouse ravaged by childbearing and housework. Her three sisters and two brothers, as plain as she was, had burrowed warm holes in the world. Grace despised them all.

She chose to be a teacher since not much training was required and a teacher was several cuts above trade, especially her father's trade. Grace learned enough to teach young children, whom she did not care for; more importantly, she learned a refined accent and finicky manners. Her origins had nothing to do with her. She felt herself born to be a lady, her hands alone proved it; the hands of an aristocrat.

Grace was just twenty-two when the war began. For a girl whose sole ambition was to marry a gentleman, the war came as a boon. Aside from all else, war is a giant game of musical chairs. Men are seized from their homes and shunted around the world, men without women. In England, plain girls were finding mates right and left among displaced Poles, Dutchmen, Frenchmen, Americans. Lonely men without women were not a bit sure they would have time to seek their true loves. Grace could not understand why she was passed over.

She had been rejected by the F.A.N.Y.s because of her near-sighted eyes. Her occupation as a teacher saved her from factory work. She volunteered for every job that brought her close to men; the canteen at the station, the N.A.A.F.I. club, the local hospitality committee. She struggled to be where she could be met, appreciated, invited out, proposed to. But she was never invited out, let alone proposed to.

She did not deceive herself that she was pretty, but girls less pretty were walking out on a soldier's arm, or better still on an officer's arm. She was not misshapen, she was not old, heaven knew she was eager to please. Perhaps determination to get a wedding ring and no nonsense beforehand is something men can sense or smell; and if the virtuous girl isn't much to look at, why waste time trying to beat down her defences. Perhaps the men of all nations could not take Grace's refinement. Perhaps it was her voice. Even when Grace was using it hopefully to charm and compliment, her voice had a thin built-in whine.

There had never been a hero fiancé, shot down in flames above a German city. Leaving Lincoln, after the war, twenty-eight years old and bitterly conscious of spinsterhood, Grace invented the fiancé, Robert, over bedtime cocoa with the geography and history mistress at a girls' boarding school near Southampton. She was terrified by her story after it emerged in dim outline; she lay awake that night wondering if it could be checked and she prosecuted for libel, defamation of character, false pretences. The story

remained fixed in its bare form of love requited and death
the tragic end. Grace took strength from this myth and
soon believed it. She had been loved; a blissful married
future in America was destroyed by anti-aircraft fire.

St Mary's, outside Southampton, was no academic or
social pinnacle but for a while it seemed perfection to
Grace. She had left for ever the insufferable vulgarity of her
home. Next to the games mistress, Grace was the youngest
teacher in the school. After a few years, she saw her elders
as crotchety old maids, and her future like theirs. Knitting,
tea parties, sensible brogues. When Grace read the advertisement in the personal column of *The Times*, offering a post
for a qualified English mistress in Kenya, she wrote a letter
of application that night and held her breath in hope.

St Mary's didn't teach much but it was a cosy little school
and the old maids were fond of their girls. As a teacher,
Miss Davis' work could not be faulted; but the children
hated her. She discouraged them and disciplined them with
sarcasm; she was unsmiling. Even by St Mary's standards,
it was alarming to see how badly the girls got on in Miss
Davis' classes; and more alarming, for Miss Heyworth the
headmistress, to see the mulish faces of the girls after an
hour with Miss Davis. Miss Heyworth dreaded scenes or
any trouble. She had reached the hand-wringing stage over
her nightly camomile tea. 'I can't sack her, Hetty,' Miss
Heyworth said to Miss Burton, her second in command. 'I
have no grounds. What if she kicks up a rumpus? What am
I to do? She makes the girls miserable; it's all wrong.' Miss
Heyworth wrote a fulsome recommendation and thanked
the Lord for providing Heather Hill in Kenya.

The Misses Ferne, who owned and ran Heather Hill,
were astounded and delighted to receive the letter from
Miss Davis. They knew that anyone who could read and
write was adequate but the parents of their pupils insisted
on trained teachers from England. One letter to an academic
employment agency in London had brought a lowering
answer: salary too small, and where was Karula, and what
was the scholarship rating of Heather Hill? In desperation,

the Misses Ferne launched their need like a bottle on the sea, addressed to *The Times*. And got Miss Davis, whose photograph looked suitable, and whose present employer recommended her warmly. Miss Davis explained that she was leaving the congenial environment of St Mary's because she must live in a warmer climate; she'd had serious problems with her chest the last three winters.

Beneath that healthy but flat chest, excitement began to bubble. Miss Davis was careful of money, a prudent saver. She splurged now on clothes: nothing in her life or the English weather had previously called for cotton frocks in lovely pastel colours, and two evening gowns, one of blue taffeta, one of yellow chiffon. These alluring garments were for the ship and though Miss Davis adored them she felt uncomfortably naked with her white thin arms and so much of her bosom exposed. She sailed early in September, to be ready for the October term; and was giddy with hope as she walked up the gangway of the B.I. liner.

The ship added tightness to Miss Davis' narrow lips. There were deck games and dances and card parties, but the shipboard company divided into two worlds: welded old couples and the flirting young. The purser danced with Miss Davis once and was seen wiping his forehead afterwards. Miss Davis dressed proudly for dinner every night, alternating between hard blue and vicious yellow, and sat alone to drink coffee and listen to the band in the lounge. Every night she wept in her inside stateroom. Some of the old couples made friendly gestures and were rebuffed; Grace Davis was afraid of age now.

Karula was like the ship. There seemed to be no single people of either sex except the five spinster teachers at Heather Hill and boys and girls too young for wedlock. Evidently people could not live alone in this vast silent country; any partner was better than none. The African day was beautiful and sparkling and so was the night, but the night oppressed. The Africans shut themselves in their huts, closing doors and windows and sleeping in a huddled consoling fug. The Europeans shut themselves in their houses with the lamps lit and played their gramophones and talked or quarrelled or read together, holding the night at bay.

Miss Davis, lunching around the countryside, decided that even those couples who snarled at each other were as tightly attached as Siamese twins. At any rate, the climate was an improvement over Lincoln or Southampton, and a teacher here was not treated as a genteel hired hand but as a member of the community in equal social standing.

Ian Paynter did not appear as an answer to prayer because Miss Davis did not go in for such revealing prayers. She told herself that Ian was a dear and dreadfully lonely and she must do everything she could to be kind to him. She was thirty-three years old, with hope still, hope again, hope undefeated despite all the years of failure.

Miss Davis began to exclaim the minute they turned into the driveway under the arching eucalyptus.

'But it's heavenly!' Miss Davis said. 'It's much the most beautiful farm I've seen!'

'The view!' Miss Davis said.

'The roses!' Miss Davis said.

'What a divine house!' Miss Davis said. 'It's so full of *character!*'

'Goodness, you've done wonders!' Miss Davis said. 'In less than four years, all this! It must be a model farm, isn't it?'

'Do you mean to say you plan such superb menus yourself?' Miss Davis said. 'I always thought men living alone didn't mind what they ate. Too delicious, I haven't had anything like it since I came to Kenya. Well, I would love some more; I'm making an absolute pig of myself but I can't help it.'

'Oh it all looks so different!' Miss Davis said. 'I didn't see how people could bear to put the Africans in those terrible dirty huts. But yours really look pretty enough to live in oneself.'

'They're positively edible, those babies,' Miss Davis said.

'Such dear little funny black faces. And the way they follow you around! They *worship* you!'

Ian asked Miss Davis to come again on Sunday next week, if it wouldn't bore her. He'd like to show her his cattle, his shambas, his pigs and chickens and workshop and dairy. Friendly, nice, about his age: and so easy to talk to. Miss Davis decided to invest most of her remaining savings in a second-hand car. With her own car she could drop in from time to time for tea; much nicer when you didn't have to arrange about transport. She bought the car within a week at Nakuru, an old Morris which listed slightly to the right.

'Poor little Morrie,' Miss Davis said. 'It's got a limp from climbing all these hills.' Ian thought that funny, the sort of thing Lucy might say.

Ian would come home, soaked by the erratic rain of that winter, to find Miss Davis curled up on the sofa, saying, 'I hope you don't mind. It was so gloomy at school. I thought I'd just drive up and beg a cup of tea.'

'I'm delighted,' he said, meaning it. 'Give me a minute to change.' He shouted to Beda to bring tea and raced through his bath and thought how agreeable this was, someone to talk to at the end of the afternoon. He couldn't of course knock off work so early as a regular thing. Normally he would dash in for tea and dry clothes and dash out again to oversee the last milking and catch up on paperwork. But as a surprise and special treat, Grace's visits were lovely and it was sporting of her to make the trip in such weather.

Sunday had become a fixed engagement; Ian never knew how but certainly didn't object.

'See you next Sunday,' Miss Davis would call gaily as she drove off in her Morris. Once, Miss Davis suggested staying on for dinner but Ian would not hear of it. If your car broke down at night on the appalling roads, either you were a competent mechanic or you slept on the back seat. It took Miss Davis three months to steer Ian into an invitation for the weekend: arrive Saturday afternoon and have the whole of Sunday to themselves. If she wouldn't mind the walk, Ian said, he knew a pretty spot at the top of the farm for a picnic. Ian did not consider gossip, being pure in heart. Miss Davis had already considered and devised a plausible lie about meeting friends from England at the Lake Hotel in Naivasha.

Any risk was worth it. Ian must become used to seeing her at all hours, dependent on her presence in his house. Miss Davis was not in a hurry. Her contract with the Misses Ferne ran until the end of the school year late in June, and it was only April now. Besides Ian never went to Nairobi or Mombasa or anywhere that he might meet other women.

Mrs Ethridge had a chat with Mrs Farrell in front of the post office, among the dusty farm cars and the shoving Africans.

'Seems Miss Davis has got off with Ian Paynter,' Mrs Ethridge said. 'Can you beat it?'

'Poor brute,' Mrs Farrell said.

Mrs Ethridge giggled. 'Mark says it gives him a cold sweat even to think of Miss Davis in bed.'

'Bed's not everything,' said Mrs Farrell, who had surmounted Simon's various infidelities.

Mrs Ethridge was prematurely grey and overweight and drank too much but she knew what she liked. 'Maybe not everything,' said Mrs Ethridge. 'But quite a lot.'

At the petrol pump, Mark Ethridge had a thoughtful discussion with Charles Gordon about tyres, then gave him the latest bulletin on Miss Davis and Ian Paynter.

'My God,' said Charles Gordon. 'He must be barking mad.'

'He's got his head screwed on right when it comes to farming. But if he falls for that piece of old rope I'll think he's the biggest clot from here to the Zambezi.'

'He's an odd chap, isn't he?' Charles Gordon said. 'I don't mean queer or anything like that but you know what I mean.'

For many reasons Grace did not speak of her life, past or present. Instead she listened. Ian saw that he had hungered for company without knowing it. He was starved for praise, starved for concern, and needed to talk about Fairview as a lover needs to talk. With Grace, he felt almost as if he were talking to his mother again, sure that she wanted to hear, was never bored, and shared his enthusiasm. Words poured from him, he could tell Grace all he had done and all he planned to do. As soon as the profits justified it, he meant to clear a thousand acres for arable land; he foresaw waving wheat fields, barley, oats, lucerne, his pasture enriched by sowing better grasses. He dreamed aloud of overhead irrigation. He showed her, as if showing art works, the catalogue pictures of combine harvesters, tractors, seed drills, road scrapers. Grace applauded his past achievements and his future schemes and said he was wonderful, wonderful, wonderful. Ian ate it up.

At first, he refused Grace's generous offers of assistance. She was run ragged during the week at school and deserved a rest at Fairview. But he was always behind on paperwork and Grace said she loved helping him with the cattle records and the muster roll books and the accounts. Coming from the same background as Ian's in a small English town, Grace said, she had always thought of farmers teetering on the edge of bankruptcy but here they were, with their heads together over the big dining table, seeing in clear figures just how well Fairview paid.

Ian never spoke to Grace of Oflag XV B. He blotted out that memory except when it overwhelmed him in nightmares. On the third of the now regular weekend visits, he told Grace about his family. Grace said nothing but put her hand on his and Ian saw tears in her eyes. Then she said quietly, 'I am alone too.' That was another bond of another kind. Hard enough for him, a man, how much worse for a woman, with no one to care for her, no home as a refuge. That night Ian began to feel pity for Grace and the tenderness of pity.

Yet it did not occur to Ian to think of Grace as a woman who could be a wife. He thought of Grace with gratitude as his friend, someone like him too old for that romantic part of life and uninterested as he was. They were lucky to have found this companionship; they were both content in it. Years ago as a schoolboy before the war, Ian had imagined that he would meet a beautiful Aylesbury girl one day and fall in love with her and marry her in the same church where his parents were married: a nice boy's standard dream of the future. It had not been an urgent dream and was long forgotten, lost with the rest of his past.

The precepts of his school and family on the subject of sex were daunting; Ian had no urge to go forth and sin. He was a virgin when he joined up and on the rare days of leave from his training camp he went safely home. In France there was neither time nor opportunity for an experience which he didn't anyway crave. He still had a known future then which included the beautiful Aylesbury girl, virgin like himself.

After that there was Oflag XV B. The other nine men in his room were married or engaged; they wrote their weekly permitted letter card to these girls, they read their mail in longing silence. They talked of their wives and fiancées but not of sex, perhaps from discretion, perhaps from being too hungry to yearn beyond food. Something that had not waked in Ian stayed dormant. He wasn't suppressing desires, he did not feel them. And when all the people he loved died, the concept of loving died too. He was still a virgin, without sexual curiosity or need. The idea of marriage never crossed his mind.

The idea of marriage never left Grace's mind. Sex was the horrid part and she avoided thinking of it. She saw marriage as wifeliness and constantly demonstrated her talent in this role. She sewed buttons on Ian's shirts and darned his socks. On Saturday afternoons she made goodies for Ian, crusted apple pies and sponge cakes and oatmeal cookies and caramel custards. She bought Mr Jivangee's best fake cut glass flower vases and filled the house with bouquets from Ian's garden. She tidied his clothes in drawers and cupboards and arranged his bills and accounts and records in admirable order. Ian said, 'I don't know what I'd do without you.' Grace held her breath, but nothing came of it.

Stretched on separate sofas after Sunday lunch, digesting and reading, Grace murmured, 'Oh how I wish I could stay here always.'

'I wish you could,' Ian said absently and turned a page. It was now May.

By June, Grace had dark circles under her nearsighted eyes. Her voice not only whined but lashed at the unfortunate girls in her charge. She was smoking heavily and often had to clasp her hands to hide their trembling. The Misses Ferne, though fluttery and not very bright, had observed exactly what Miss Heyworth observed before them. They might not be able to lure another trained teacher from England but a pleasant amateur from Kenya would be better than Miss Davis. Their Kenya girls were more high-spirited than the inmates of St Mary's had been. They protested to their parents.

'She's an old cow,' Jenny Farrell informed her mother. 'No, she's a damn old bitch, that's what she is.'

Grace knew that her next year's contract should already have been discussed. She also knew that the Memsaabs had been watching her throw her cap, as if it were a hand grenade, at Ian Paynter. She felt rejected, mocked, isolated and terrified; and time was running out. All or nothing, this Saturday night.

Ian's best hour was before dinner over drinks; he became annoyingly sleepy afterwards, having been up and on the go from five thirty in the morning. Grace had taken on the service of drinks and learned to swallow gin without making a face when Ian remarked that he wished she'd join him, he felt like an old boozer drinking alone. Two whiskies were Ian's evening ration. Grace said she was a bit weary, let's have another. Ian's drinks were strong while hers were mainly water. Grace had worked on her face and hair and left off her spectacles. She was wearing a new long loose housecoat from the Asian tailor in Karula.

'I've got to make up my mind,' Grace said.

Ian looked interested.

'I don't think I can bear another year at Heather Hill. All work and almost no pay and it's so frightfully boring.'

Ian now looked sympathetic.

'I've had a good offer from Roedean. I have to let them know this week. Of course one dreads the English weather but on the other hand.'

'Oh no,' Ian said, startled.

'Well, what shall I do?' Grace peered across at the man who was a brown blur on the opposite sofa.

'You can't go,' Ian said.

'You'd miss me?'

'Grace, you know I would. I can't imagine . . .'

'All I've cared about was the time with you. Working with you, trying to help you, being here with you.'

Ian looked touched. Grace waited. In vain. She didn't know what she felt: despair, fury, for God's sake the man was like an ox, slow, slow, slow, didn't anything jell in his brain; she wanted to weep and hit him.

'I can't throw up a good job in England. I really can't. I have to think of the future. Unless . . .'

'Unless?' Ian asked.

'Unless *you* were my job.' Grace was now peering at her hands, clenched in her lap and trembling uncontrollably.

'You mean?' Ian said; actually he did not understand.

'We've been like partners for a long time,' Grace murmured. 'I hope you've been as happy as I . . . you see, Ian,' and here it was, all or nothing. 'I love you.'

The silence seemed to Grace endless, hours of it. She dared not raise her eyes, besides she could not have seen Ian's expression unless she put on her spectacles.

'I can't believe it,' Ian said at last. Impossible to decipher his voice; it sounded dazed.

Silence again. Grace felt cold and on the verge of hysteria; her head ached.

'You mean you'd stay with me, live with me here?' Still that bewildered tone.

Grace nodded, unable to speak.

'We're not young.' A note of doubt had crept in.

'Two people alone,' Grace said hurriedly. 'Keeping each other company always.'

Another silence. The pain in her head was blinding; her hands were ice cold but wet.

'We could get married!' Ian said with an air of discovery. 'Between us, we'd make Fairview the best farm in Kenya!'

Now Grace raised her head, smiling tenderly.

'Married!' Ian cried and bounded across the room to kneel by her sofa. 'Grace, what a brilliant idea, I'd never have thought of it.'

Ian took one of her ice cold hands and kissed it. He did not think of kissing her on the mouth; he had never kissed Lucy or his mother like that. Grace rested her other freezing hand on Ian's hair, blinking away tears due as much to relief as to migraine. Close beside her, Ian was no longer a brown blur but his features remained indistinct. Grace could imagine him as she had so often imagined the man that never was, the passionate pilot on his knees begging and imploring her to become his wife . . .

Ian ate while Grace talked ways and means. The church at Nakuru, so much nicer than the tin-roofed cement chapel in Karula. Let's see, we'll invite the Misses Ferne of course and the Gordons and the Ethridges and the Farrells and the Gales and the Brands and the Parkinsons and the Barnes and the Ogilvies and . . . The wedding breakfast at the Nakuru Hotel, surely they can manage a proper cake. Immediately after the end of term, first week in July would be best. Lovely if Ian had a ring of his mother's, did he, such a joy to wear his ring, she could hardly wait to tell everyone, wasn't it thrilling. Ian smiled and nodded; he seemed to have no opinions of his own.

Grace sent notes announcing the engagement and the wedding date. She added that Ian would have written too but you know how he works himself to the bone, scarcely a minute to breathe.

Rose Farrell showed this letter to her husband at lunch. 'I thought you said he was a misogynist?'

'Well, my God, if this doesn't prove it, what does? No normal man would regard Miss Davis as a woman.'

Helen Gordon said, 'Oh Charles, do you think Eddy and Alan will suddenly tell us they're going to marry some absolutely horrendous girl?'

'Considering that Eddy is in his first year at Eton and Alan's still in preparatory school, I hardly see the need to have a fit now. I'm not going to spoil my dinner just because Ian Paynter is off his chump.'

Mrs Gale said, 'Do you suppose she'll want to be neighbourly, Dick? Popping in for a cuppa and a nice matronly chat? I'd go out of my mind.'

Mark Ethridge said, 'My heart bleeds for that poor sod and I don't care to talk about it.'

'Better to marry than to burn,' Sam Brand said, 'If I am quoting St Paul correctly. In some cases, any fool would choose burning.'

When the great day came, the farmers grumbled furiously about dressing up and besides it was as jolly as going to a hanging. The wives would not hear of defections. The prevailing sentiment seemed to be that they had to rally round Ian in his hour of need but at the same time Ian wanted his head examined. The congregation, assembled in town suits and hats, listened with varying expressions to that noteworthy phrase in the marriage ceremony: with my body I thee worship. At the Nakuru Hotel, toasts were drunk with grim cheerfulness. The champagne was not very good and also not very cold. The hotel dining room smelled of hotel cooking. Everyone ate cake and spoke heartily to the bride and groom, and in lowered tones to each other.

Rose Farrell sauntered over to Helen Gordon and said, 'Your hat's even worse than mine, I'm pleased to see. Wouldn't it be a good thing if the new Mrs Paynter had a dear friend to advise her never never to wear yellow?'

'I think we should all stop being mean. She looks

radiantly happy. Really. And happiness improves people. Who knows, it may be a wonderful marriage.'

Mark Ethridge joined them. 'I've done my best with this champagne but it isn't having any effect. The bridegroom looks to me as if he'd been poleaxed. And he hasn't said a word from beginning to end except "I do".'

Coming in on this remark, Mrs Gale said, 'The bride makes up for that. If only they could change around like Jack Sprat and his wife, if you see what I mean.'

Helen said, 'We must break this up. Come on now, shoulder to the wheel. Let's try to make it merrier for Ian.'

As soon as was decent, the entire company returned to Karula. A pouring unseasonal rain had not helped and Grace was cross about damage to her new shoes, dress and hat, but Ian was delighted, thinking of his pasture. The rain was really the best part of the day. There had been no question of a honeymoon; Ian could not possibly leave Fairview.

Ian had told Beda to make up the guest room and shift his clothes, so the drawers and cupboards in the master bedroom would be empty for the Memsaab. Naturally he gave Grace the best room. He had hardly seen Grace since the night they agreed to marry. She said the end of term was hectic and she had all her packing to do and she had the sense to keep to herself the fuss of the wedding preparations and her intense elation. To Ian, this marriage was a sensible arrangement for them to work together at Fairview, companions as before. But Grace had been unlike herself at the awful wedding party, clinging to his arm, holding his hand, smiling at him in a new embarrassing way; and he had also been shaken by the same words in the marriage service that so impressed the congregation. Now while Grace unpacked, he lounged around the house disoriented and filled with foreboding. Surely Grace did not expect . . . they should have discussed this before.

After a light supper, the newlyweds said in the same breath, 'You must be dead tired,' and laughed a little and went to bed, with perfect accord, in separate rooms. That's all right then, Ian thought. He rather missed waking to the view from the front bedroom but would soon get used to the change.

For a week, Grace was busy dominating Mwangi and Beda. In a week they knew who was boss. But Grace started to worry because Ian showed no intention of claiming his marital rights and she wondered whether an unconsummated marriage was actually legal. She remembered something about Roman Catholics, a wisp of information from a newspaper: unconsummated marriages could be annulled, something like that. Inwardly shuddering, she held Ian's hand as they reached her bedroom door.

'Ian dear?' A rising note, a smile, a special look.

Ian got the message. He couldn't speak and his stomach clenched in nausea. Too late now to say this was no part of the agreement. Grace would be mortally hurt if he refused and how could he when there she was, gleaming at him. He undressed slowly and went to her room, well buttoned and tied in his pyjamas, to find Grace well covered in her nightdress. He turned down the pressure lamp and slid into his own bed which felt strange and hostile, with a rigid woman filling half the space. The disastrous failure left them both hot from shame and limp from fatigue. Grace blamed Ian silently and with fury. It was a man's place to know how to handle this. Of course a man should keep himself pure for his wife, just as a girl should for her husband, but that was meant for young people and a man of Ian's age ought somewhere to have learned whatever you had to know. She dreaded the next attempt but instinct told her that she must persevere, in her own best interests.

The second attempt was even worse, since both now knew what indignities to expect. Ian rose in the dark room from the disordered bed. He wanted a bath and a strong drink, he wanted to be a hundred miles from here. But more than anything else he wanted never to go through this again as long as he lived. He didn't care what Grace felt.

'I'm sorry, Grace. There's been a bad misunderstanding and it's my fault. I should have said something before. But this isn't on, I'm very sorry. You are of course free to get a divorce. I only wish I'd had better sense sooner and I apologize.'

Grace, though numb with disgust over the proceedings, was galvanized by the word 'divorce'. She sat up in bed, collecting her wits quickly, and said, 'Oh Ian dear, what a stupid muddle. I thought *you* wanted it. I'm so sorry, do forgive me. You know what I love is living here and being with you and working with you. I don't want anything else ever. Divorce, my goodness what an idea. We're going to be happy exactly the way we were before.'

So that took care of that, except for hidden and confused emotions. Grace hoarded her contempt for Ian, he wasn't a real man; a real man would have known how to take her in his arms and teach her love. Deep beneath this righteous sense of being cheated lay doubt too painful for words. No man had wanted her; perhaps another woman would have known how to teach Ian. Ian was relieved by the way Grace ignored what had happened. But he felt a lingering sadness: if he had grown up normally, slowly – he knew he was slow – learning about girls through Lucy's friends, he might have met the beautiful Aylesbury girl, at the right age, and loved her entirely as a man loved a woman.

Now that this sordid mess was disposed of, Grace got down to the real business of life.

'Ian, I'll have to do the house over from top to bottom.'

Ian was drinking beer in one of the old comfortable chairs on the verandah, waiting for lunch. The glass wobbled in his hand.

'But Grace, you said . . .' He remembered all she had said, she never stopped saying it's such a *homey* house, it's so right for this country, it's so welcoming, so lived-in, it has such character.

'Oh of course, Ian, it was fine for a man living alone. But not for a married couple. You don't suppose Mrs Gordon or Mrs Farrell live in such a primitive place. I assure you they have civilized houses like a country house in England.'

He didn't want an English country house and he was shattered. But the house was the Memsaab's province and he couldn't deprive Grace of any more rights.

'I'll need money,' Grace said. She meant to sound casual and sounded mistreated. This was a test point.

'That's all right, I'll fix it at the bank, a joint account. You know as much about the farm finances as I do. You know what the farm needs. Otherwise you can do what you like.'

Grace was his wife and he wanted her to be happy. Grace was now free to shop in Nakuru and Nairobi, hire work-men, boss and buy. Unfortunately she seemed more exhausted and outdone than happy.

'My God, how can they be such fools!' Grace cried, showing Ian a chest of drawers that was painted shut. 'You have to stand over them every second and even so they can't do anything properly.'

'Look at these curtains!' Grace cried, showing Ian cur-tains that hung eight inches from the floor. 'The Asians are as hopeless as the Africans. I told Patel the exact measurements six times if I told him once.'

'You won't believe it!' Grace cried, 'I've been to Karula again to that idiot carpenter. Never ready, never ready. The idiot just smiles and says "bado". I could choke him.'

'I will *not* accept these sofa covers!' Grace cried.' 'Lalji will have to do them again, that's all.'

'It's enough to drive you crazy!' Grace cried. 'No one in this country can get *anything* right.'

Ian said mildly, 'I think everything looks fine, Grace,' and she flew at him.

'It does *not*. It's disgraceful. You're far too soft. I will not pay for such shoddy work.'

Grace's trials and tribulations were the stuff of all con-versation. Ian began to cringe from her voice, the drilling quality of the whine. The poor girl was strained of course;

she wasn't used to Africa; she wanted everything to be like England which was impossible. She'd learn to make-do as everyone did and stop fussing. Beda looked hunted, cleaning up after the untidy workmen with the Memsaab snapping at his heels. Ian prayed the house would soon be finished to Grace's satisfaction.

You couldn't sit here or touch there and the rooms smelled of paint and were cluttered with the new bits and pieces Grace bought. He used to put his drink on the wide arm of a wooden chair or on the floor but those big chairs were gone and a spindly table stood by an upholstered settee and he'd been ticked off sharply after he knocked the table over twice. He had to think carefully and move carefully lest he damage Grace's handiwork.

At last the house was done, not to Grace's satisfaction, but near enough; or perhaps she was worn out and defeated. Ian said he thought the bright yellow brocade curtains in the sitting room were very pretty and so were the chintz slip covers of parakeets and hibiscus flowers. Grace was sweet to get the mail-order shower stall for him and the large cupboard for his bedroom. He did not say that the room looked absurd, like a nursery, with the old brown wood furniture painted red and curtains of gambolling red and white lambs. He didn't care. He only wanted peace and an end to Grace's nervy complaints.

'Well, it's a home,' Grace said, surveying her achievement. 'We don't have to be ashamed of it at any rate.'

Ashamed? He felt as hurt as if Grace had insulted an old friend. Though Grace said this stuff was only fit to burn, he saved all Luke's things in a partitioned section of the workshop out of respect for Luke and the past. You didn't throw on the junk heap furniture that had served well for more than thirty years. Perhaps Luke's house was unsuitable for a married couple but that was no reason to speak of it with contempt.

Grace quickly defined her share of the work. She was responsible for whatever concerned money and for the house. She attended diligently to bills, statements, and accounts ledgers in her bedroom at an ample new desk. Nothing would persuade her to work in the farm office, surrounded by Africans. Of necessity she had to deal with Mwangi and Beda, who at least understood English, but there she drew the line. Ian must absolutely forbid Africans to come to the back door when they wanted home doctoring; tell them to go to the office with their loathsome ailments. Healthy Africans smelled bad enough, sick Africans smelled to high heaven. Ian's suggestion that she take over the inspection of the African lines was grotesque. Poke at their huts and latrines and garbage dumps, with African brats swarming over her? And she wasn't going to let Ian bore her blind with tales of pregnant cows and the foibles of his generator. Farming was Ian's job and deadly, except that it paid.

Grace was now ready to entertain.

'I have so much hospitality to repay, Ian. I'll invite people here on Sundays. They'll love seeing my house.'

'If that's what you want, Grace, but I'm no use at parties.'

'You just pass round the drinks. The women do the talking anyway.'

Grace did the talking. Ian hoped the Gordons and the Farrells were interested to hear the story of every nail, tin of paint, yard of cloth, for they were treated to a play by play account of Grace's struggle against the stupidity and incompetence of Africans, not that Asians were a great deal better. The party broke up right after coffee, with Grace saying, 'Surely you're staying for tea?' She had baked a special cake; when she was a teacher, lunching around the countryside, she always stayed for tea.

'I have to keep an eye on the new gardener,' Mrs Gordon murmured. 'He drowns things.'

'Trouble with the main pump,' Mr Gordon said, backing her up. 'You're damned lucky with your spring, Ian. My boreholes are a curse.'

'I must get home to Jenny,' Mrs Farrell said, 'I promised to give tea to a horde of her chums.'

Mr Farrell was past speech. Grace and Ian waved goodbye and Grace led the way back to the verandah where she flopped into a new canvas chair, looking sulky.

'That was very pleasant,' Ian said tentatively. At least the ordeal was behind him.

'I thought I'd die with shame over Beda.'

'Why? What did he do?'

'Didn't you see the way he stacked plates, like in a cheap café? And the way he passed the pineapple flan on the wrong side to Mrs Gordon and Mrs Farrell?'

'Did he?'

'And he looks so disgusting. Mrs Gordon's houseboy wears a hat, you know, one of those Arab things, and a white jacket. Beda looked as if he'd slept in his clothes, not even clean, and he keeps grinning at one's guests as if they were *his* friends.'

The whine was razor sharp. Ian's heart sank. Beda had worked here for almost fifteen years. Beda's great quality was cheerfulness.

'You could buy him a tarboosh and a jacket,' Ian said.

'He'll never learn. He's got bad habits, he's sloppy and lazy and that grin is just plain cheeky.'

Ian surprised himself by a life-saving idea. 'Why don't you get another houseboy, for serving at table? With two of us and the house so new and everything, we really need an extra servant. Beda can go on with the cleaning and you find someone to train for parties.'

'They're backward apes, these upcountry natives. Perhaps I could find a boy in Nairobi.'

So Beda was safe and the first of a series of houseboys, with red tarboosh and white jacket, entered the Paynters' lives. They came and went, not pleasing Grace, but changing the atmosphere of the home. They quarrelled with either Beda or Mwangi, they upset the fixed routine by which Africans do their work and which makes their work bearable. Beda's grin disappeared.

All the Sunday luncheons were the same; Grace talked and everyone left promptly after coffee. In return for hospitality, they were asked to other people's Sunday luncheons though these were smaller affairs, just themselves and their hosts, with the hostess saying she'd not been able to lay hands on a soul, people were at the coast or fretting over farm problems or playing polo or off on safari or ill. Gradually no one was free to come to Fairview Farm on Sundays; nor were there invitations to leave Fairview Farm.

Ian felt this creeping ostracism as an absence of pain. It was disloyal to be embarrassed by your wife. He was ashamed of Grace and for her, and ashamed to be ashamed. He couldn't understand the change that had come over her, from the contented friend before marriage to this restless garrulous woman. Driving around the farm, Ian no longer stopped to look with a lifted heart at the shape and sweep of the land. He was curt with the watu, grown nervy from life with Grace and his failure to understand her. More and more, Ian remembered his mother and father, their smiling affection, their gaiety together, an unspoken tenderness that spread around them and made their home serene. His mother had been a beautiful Aylesbury girl.

Grace saw the melting away of invitations as proof of jealousy and her triumph. The Paynter farm was the most successful, the Paynter house the most elegant: the neighbours were green with envy. She didn't like them anyway, she had only wanted to exhibit her surroundings and herself as Memsaab.

Grace now turned her attention to the garden. People talked about Helen Gordon's garden as if gardening were some sort of art but Grace believed Helen Gordon had fooled them from pure vanity, it was her way of showing off. All you had to do was tell the gardener what you wanted. Grace set out to reform the borders around the house, the vines on the walls, and the pots and hanging baskets on the verandah. Ian left before Grace got up in the morning, returned for a quick breakfast and a quick lunch, came back at dark, and resolutely ignored signs of destruction. One day he arrived for lunch and saw the rose beds dug up. Sun poured down on the exposed roots. The roses looked like a massacre.

Holding himself very still, Ian said, 'What are you doing, Grace?'

'They're too silly planted out like that,' Grace said. 'Like a public park. I'm going to move them into the borders.'

'You should have asked me.'

'Now Ian,' Grace said, her voice raising to its steeliest whine. 'I wish you wouldn't interfere. I don't tell you how to manage the cows.'

'They will die,' Ian said.

'Nonsense.'

Ian did not wait to hear more. He drove the Landrover recklessly, jarring along the roads with dust like a comet's tail behind. He had no idea where he was going, he wasn't thinking, he saw nothing except the uprooted roses. He waked from this vision when he found he was in Nakuru, running out of petrol. With the tank filled, Ian sat in the car until the African attendant asked him to move, another Bwana was waiting. He didn't know what he wanted, except to be away from Grace. South of Nakuru, the great lake offered sanctuary. He drove as far as the narrowing track allowed and left the Landrover. On foot, in silence, Africa was given back to him.

Through the fever trees, he saw grazing zebra and tommy. A tiny dikdik leapt away almost under his feet. Above him, a tribe of vervet monkeys rollicked. Walking carefully, he came to the lake edge but his presence disturbed a legion of flamingos who rose, like a pink scarf thrown against the sky, and settled to feed farther along the shore. He sat cross-legged and still, watching ibis and egret and heron and hearing the lovely babble of birds. Where the land curved into the flat water to the north, giraffes were nibbling at the tops of acacias.

The land around the lake was not as beautiful as his land, too enclosed in rocky jagged hillsides. But it enclosed wonders, flashes of colour in the trees, tits and starlings and hoopoes and sunbirds, the pink fields of flamingos, a sudden glimpse of curved horns and the sheen of impala. He hadn't lost the capacity for joy, because he felt it now as a sense of thanksgiving. If only he could stay forever, cross-legged and marvelling, at the edge of Lake Nakuru.

He hardly remembered his mother's face; she had blue eyes and smooth hair, a gentle mirage, not a face. But he remembered her voice and it sounded like music in his mind, always low, soft, loving. His mother and roses. The roses he had planted and grown and cherished. His mother and his roses. After eight months of marriage, Ian knew he had made a fatal mistake and was imprisoned in it. Of his own accord, like a man doomed, he had destroyed his freedom and built his private Oflag. He thought of himself with despair. He was a misfit and a failure. But Fairview Farm was not a failure. He had a purpose in life, quite apart from the catastrophe of his marriage. For the sake of his farm, he would protect himself in the old known way. He would detach himself from Grace as he had learned to detach himself from Oflag XV B.

Grace was waiting, with anxiety under her anger.

'What on earth is the matter with you, Ian?' But already he had started to be deaf to that voice. 'Behaving like a baby in a tantrum! I never heard of such nonsense! What do you suppose the servants think? The Bwana rushing out of the house without luncheon. Coming back late for dinner. All because of a few roses. I won't stand for such behaviour!'

Ian ate without speaking. Grace's complaints and arguments beat against his silence and ceased. She was afraid now though she could not name her fear. Divorce? On what grounds? Rose beds? It was laughable, it was ridiculous. If Ian wanted to sulk, she would show him who could sulk longer. Her mouth narrowed; she tossed her head; her spectacles flashed in the light of the pressure lamp hanging above the table. Ian ignored these signs of temper; he was thinking methodically of a better way to sterilize his ten gallon churns.

Grace soon decided the gardener was a moron. She told

him what to do, using Beda as interpreter, and he made a complete mess. The wretched flowers wilted and died or looked even scruffier in their new arrangement. She lost interest before she had time to tamper with the vines on the house or the flowering shrubs or finish the borders. Half the borders remained as Ian had planted them; half, with bald patches, showed Grace's intervention. The gardener went on with the watering and mowed the grass. Whatever Grace had not killed survived as before. There were no more roses.

The Mau Mau Rebellion, the Emergency, which caused such horror throughout Kenya, proved a blessing to the Paynters.

Grace had never let a day pass without stating, in detail, how Africans got on her nerves. Now irritation turned into terror. The Africans were mad, were monsters, they were murdering Europeans like savages, cutting off heads, hands, one dared not think of it. She demanded police dogs to guard the house at night. Ian refused. Alsatians had patrolled the high barbed wire fences of Oflag XV B. Grace whined and whined, beside herself with fear. Ian was out of his mind, she kept saying, they could be killed in their beds; they must have bars on the windows. She could have bars on the windows of her room; Ian would not allow any other windows to be barred, none that he saw. And there were no weapons, Grace shrilled, did he want her to be hacked to pieces?

'You can take the shotgun to your room at night.'

'I don't know how to use it,' Grace wailed.

'You don't have to know. Just raise it and pull the trigger. Deadly at close range. Be careful you don't fire it by mistake at Beda when he's bringing your morning tea.'

Grace wept. She was supremely ugly when she wept.

Ian said, 'Grace, go to Nairobi, for God's sake. Stay in a hotel with a lot of other people. There's no danger there, none here really, but you can't go on like this. Stay in Nairobi until it quiets down.'

'What about the book-keeping?' Grace said.

Ian laughed then, merrily, showing all his false teeth.

Grace found a gem of a hotel, the Dorset, the nearest thing to a Bayswater Residential. Altogether charming, she wrote Ian, such an attractive room with ornamental iron grille work on the windows, and two comfy chairs and a small table if she wanted to take tea by herself, and a very pretty colour scheme, cherry pink and baby blue and a bit of mauve. The permanent guests were delightful, well bred, mostly retired or civil servants. They sat at their own tables in the spotless dining room and were served by trained respectful servants, but talked to each other cosily from table to table.

She had met an angelic older woman, Mrs Milbank, widow of one of the top men in Mackenzie King, and a Miss Greene who was Secretary at the hospital and a Miss Ball who worked in a government office; they made a bridge four. She had taken up needlepoint and was stitching away on darling patterns for footstools at Fairview. The shops were lovely, all the little things one needed, and a tiny bookstore with a lending library, the latest novels from England. Sometimes she went with Mrs Milbank to the pictures in the afternoon though she wouldn't budge at night but the hotel was very gay and lively, always someone to talk to or play cards with. She hoped Ian wasn't too lonely and advised him to be careful.

Ian was not careful. If his watu went crazy and decided to slit his throat, then they would. He saw no reason for them to do so and certainly wasn't going to take precautions. He hated the whole thing, he wanted no part of it and he wasn't on anybody's side except the victims. After there had been enough killing all round, enough Oflags for Africans, enough general misery and waste and ruin, the British politicians would give the African politicians whatever they asked for; it worked like that every time. He detested the lot of them but since he could do nothing to save this beautiful country he meant to withdraw and save Fairview.

When a young British officer from the Kenya Police Reserve came to Fairview for a routine check on African staff, Ian went to meet him before he could get out of his car. Ian said stiffly, 'There are no Kikuyu on this farm. I vouch for the others. They've worked here for years, they're family men, not lunatics. My herders and I are all over the place all the time, we'd know if any strangers moved in. Besides this isn't Mau Mau territory. We won't have any trouble at Fairview and the best way to see that the work goes on sensibly is to leave us alone.'

He didn't offer a drink or future hospitality, like all the other farmers who welcomed their compatriots and their protection. The young officer, much put out by Ian's manner, made inquiries and learned that Ian was known locally as an odd fellow and a hermit by choice. No doubt, the young officer said, he'll be more cordial if the Mau Mau attack him, more cordial or dead.

Ian's watu were terrified by the news that flowed over the bush telegraph. Mau Mau murder victims were mostly African; European soldiers took Africans away and locked them in camps for no reason; there were rumours of torture. They knew Ian had protected them. Ian thought he was probably being foolish but it seemed as if the watu were now at last as fond of him as they had been of Luke.

In Karula on Fridays, Ian listened with sorrow to his neighbours telling each other horror stories. Simon Farrell had shipped his wife and daughter home to England. The Ethridges barricaded themselves at night in the style Grace had wanted. Helen Gordon said she wasn't going to abandon her garden just because some insane Kikuyus were drinking blood and swearing oaths. All carried handguns in their cars and slept with them at their bedsides. The farmers pointed out that war was straightforward, why didn't the bastards fight honestly, this way was indecent, you didn't know who the enemy was or where, any African could be a killer. Even your own servants after all you'd done for them. Obviously no one was happy.

Except Ian. Since Grace had gone he was happy again, a free man. He ordered Luke's furniture to be brought from the workshop and Grace's twiddly junk stored there instead. The house felt like its old self, happy too. Beda and Mwangi sang and gossiped at their work. Fairview was all right; Fairview had declared a separate peace.

Beda and Mwangi were as shocked as Ian when Grace returned suddenly after three months' absence, calling, 'Ian, come here, look what I've got.'

That voice again, spoiling the pleasure of his midday beer. He walked sadly to the kitchen door.

'I knew you wouldn't mind,' Grace said. 'Morrie was on his last legs.'

A new blue Volkswagen shone through recent dust.

'I left Nairobi practically at dawn and drove like the wind,' Grace said. 'It's safe if you go fast on the roads in daylight. I can only stay two hours, I must get back before dark. But you never answer my questions and I know how careless you are about business. I decided I had to come and make sure everything is in order.'

Ian brightened at the news of her departure but nerved himself for a scene when Grace saw the house. To his astonishment she said, 'Quite right, Ian. No sense using my good things when I'm not here.'

Ian hurried to the farm office to collect the papers and ledgers Grace wanted. She ate a snack lunch at her desk, having no time for talk.

'You've done splendidly, Ian, to keep things going in these dreadful times. But you are careless about money. Have everything ready for me, I'll pop in once a month and go over the books and take the chits back to Nairobi and send out the bills from there. Really, you needn't bother with the accounts. I can manage easily.'

Ian scarcely had a chance to speak before Grace whisked off in her blue car. He could bear a few hours once a month, especially since Grace would be too busy to trouble with him or the house.

On these blessedly brief visits, Ian began to notice that
Nairobi agreed with Grace. He had the vague impression
that she looked better and was more amiable. Grace saw
herself, with ravishment, as a new woman. Mrs Milbank
was responsible. Mrs Milbank's hairdresser cut Grace's
shapeless crinkly hair short and dyed it so that it resembled
a cap of some unknown auburn fur. Mabel, the beautician,
prescribed a peach-toned foundation, a touch of rouge,
blending powder, and showed Grace how to draw an
outline around her narrow lips with a red crayon and fill
in a wider softer mouth. Mabel said specs were no reason
for a girl not to make the best of her eyes. Grace became
adept with mascara and eye shadow. Mrs Milbank and
Mabel together had the real brain wave: specs with pale
blue tinted lenses so Grace would seem to be wearing
stylish sunglasses. Finally, Mrs Milbank led Grace to a
lingerie shop where Grace was introduced to the wonders of
modern technology, a padded brassière.

New clothes completed the transformation. Feminine,
floating, fragile, all shades of peach as advised by Mrs
Milbank. 'Peach is your colour, dear,' Mrs Milbank said.
'You haven't done yourself justice. I can see you've been
too busy taking care of your husband but an attractive
woman should never neglect herself.'

Grace did nothing to correct the assumptions of her
darling friends at the Dorset. Somehow the idea had grown
that Grace's was a war-time marriage to a man rather older
who'd been turned into a neurotic recluse by his dreadful
experiences in a German prison camp. Grace was the ideal
of a devoted wife and of course her husband adored her,
but still life must have been hard for her all those years
alone on an upcountry farm. It was a joy to see the dear girl
bloom before their eyes, so sweet in her manner, the
youngest resident and everyone's pet. The older gentlemen
were in the habit of saying, 'How's our pretty Mrs Paynter
tonight?' The slightly less old gentlemen were more
reserved in their gallantry but Grace sensed their admiration.
Her middle-aged lady-friends were charmed by Grace's

thoughtful little gifts and her deference and her pleasure in their company. At the Dorset, the whine almost vanished from Grace's voice.

Grace had waited in vain for Ian to speak of her appearance. Her pilot would have told her he had to fall in love all over again with a bewitching new woman. Her pilot would have noticed each small detail, from the pearls in her ears to the high-heeled sandals, and kissed her saying she looked her true irresistible self. Ian was blind, deaf and dumb. She burned with anger against the cold unnatural man who cared for nothing and noticed nothing except his farm. Her lifelong belief that a wedding ring guaranteed happiness had been crushed by Ian in less than two years of marriage. He could never make any woman happy. His wedding ring only guaranteed release from genteel poverty and rasping work but Fairview was as dull as any boarding school. Now, for the first time, she knew what happiness meant. She had everything she'd always wanted: this chic pretty person in the mirror, this delicious city life surrounded by doting friends, and the status of a married woman. Yet how much better to be a widow, all the advantages without the fearful drawback of Ian and Fairview looming ahead.

Partly because he knew all the totos and partly because he had to account for any new face or new absence, Ian spotted the little greyish, big-eyed creature at once.

'Ndola,' Ian said, 'Where did you get this baby suddenly?'

Ndola was an old man in his fifties who cleaned the dairy; his wife Sita was an old woman with breasts like leather saddle bags.

'It is the child of my daughter. The one who works in the house of Asians in Kericho.'

'She looks sick,' Ian said.

'Yes.' And if she died, Ndola thought, it would be as well. His daughter would never bring in bride money; she was sixteen and any man could have her. This would not be the last child dumped on him. If a child came, you fed it. A sick child died.

Ian studied this wizened infant who did not cry, whose face looked strangely and pitifully wise, and said, 'Tomorrow morning I will take your wife and the baby to Karula to the doctor.'

Dr Parkinson was the Europeans' doctor, a kind bumbling man who grew show dahlias and loved bridge and felt that people either survived Africa or didn't. He held out little hope for this speck of black humanity. The child seemed to have been semi-starved from birth. Ndola's wife had no information about the first three months of the baby Zena's life but imagined that her whorish lazy daughter had not bothered to feed the child and brought it to Fairview when she saw it was going to die. It was not good to be near a death; someone might talk lies and the police would say you killed the baby yourself. Dr Parkinson doubted whether Ndola's wife would take the trouble to mix a formula but gave Ian the ingredients and the instructions.

Driving back to Fairview with the baby so bravely silent on Sita's lap, Ian came to a decision.

'Sita, you know the house for the man with the hat?' The imported houseboy, gussied up in tarboosh and white jacket, was a joke to the watu. The last of these passing servants had long since left Fairview but the rondavel, built for him, remained empty alongside the two small rondavels used by Beda and Mwangi. These round huts with their pointed thatch roofs stood forty yards behind the main house, screened out by a high cypress hedge.

'Yes, Bwana.'

'I want you and Ndola and the baby to move into that house. Ndola can weed the lawn, he will be a gardener. You will take care of the baby and I will see you every day when I finish my work.'

Ian was determined that this child should live. Perhaps because he was revolted by all the needless dying in the country. Perhaps from some sort of pride; the children on his farm did not die, they flourished like everything else growing here. In his kitchen Ian showed Mwangi and Beda and Sita how to prepare the first bottle. Now they had seen what they must do; no one was to forget; their most important job was to feed the baby Zena as the Daktari ordered. He would punish negligence.

Grace never knew that the unused servant's rondavel now housed a couple of old African farm labourers and a baby slowly fattening. Ian had been perfectly understood when he told Beda it was better not to worry the Memsaab with the problem of the sick child. Dr Parkinson watched the baby's recovery with interest. He wondered why Ian was so involved with little Zena but it wasn't his business and he did not gossip about his patients. The baby was nine months old when he tickled it professionally and it waved its now plump legs and arms and laughed. Dr Parkinson and Ian laughed too.

'We're a pair of sentimental fools,' Dr Parkinson said. 'She's all right now, old boy. No need to bring her in unless something goes wrong. Cod liver oil. Takes care of everything. We'd die flat out if we had half the things Africans have. Very tough people. The old woman can look after the child. You've done your bit.'

The watu were mystified by the Bwana's concern for the baby Zena. The women had seen Sita's daughter arrive one morning on the farm lorry when it returned from Karula station. The driver had a busy arm around her; he stopped to let her off at the African lines before parking the lorry at the workshop. The next morning he took her back to Karula. They remembered that girl, she'd been a whore from the age of thirteen. They also remembered that Bwana Soft Voice had never spent a night away from Fairview nor travelled further than Nakuru or nearby cattle sales. He could not have flown on wings to Kericho to find the slut girl and make the baby. They talked and talked and finally concluded that Zena was like Bwana Looki's big brown dog with the squashed face, in the old days; Zena was Bwana Soft Voice's pet. Nobody wanted the child so she was lucky that Bwana Soft Voice had his peculiar notions.

Every morning after breakfast and every evening when
the dairy was cleared and his office locked, Ian visited the
rondavel behind his house. Zena knew his voice. The large
solemn eyes watched until he came close; the delicate little
hand curled around his forefinger; the baby smiled. You're
better than roses, you are, Ian thought and then thought he
really must be round the bend, what in hell did he mean by
such an idea? Zena was fifteen months old when the
Emergency officially ended.

Grace put off her return, writing that she was obliged to
stay on a few weeks in Nairobi to see the dentist. Ian
quickly wrote back, urging her not to hurry home. For two
years and four months, they had enjoyed an ideal married
life, apart. Neither of them considered the obvious solution. Had anyone suggested separation to Grace, she would
have rejected the thought with fury. People would say Ian
threw her out, she was a failure as a wife. Separation was as
shameful as divorce. And she would have died rather than
admit to her Dorset friends that Ian was not at all the
worshipping husband they imagined.

Ian's view was simple. He married Grace of his own free
will. She gave him no just cause to break a contract. It
would be unfair and dishonourable to deprive her of a
home. If Grace had a family the situation might be different, but she had nowhere to go. He told himself to buck
up, grin and bear it, and it wasn't so bad. He felt at home
with himself so it didn't matter how he felt with Grace.

Grace could no longer spoil his delight in his farm and
his life. From the moment he watched the sun lift over the
rim of the mountains to the moment he stood on the
verandah in the cold night air for a last look at the stars, he
was conscious of happiness. Too much time had been lost
during the bloody Emergency; again George Stevens'
workmen were imported to construct a second dairy,
overhead piping, all the dreams Grace had listened to with
concealed boredom long ago. More rondavels were built
for more farm labourers, Kipsigis recruited by Simuni so

that peace would reign among the watu and hopefully he would not be hiring drones. The men cleared arable land while he hurried to cattle sales, in search of grade stock for an increased herd. This intense growth of Fairview was joyful in itself but he had an extra private miraculous joy in Zena.

Zena had arrived wrapped in a scrap of dirty blanket. She was then wrapped in bathtowels from the house until Ian caught on to the idea of clothing. He drove to Nakuru and found a shop where he asked for all the clothing a baby would need, at various stages, until it was two years old. He came back with a small mountain of infant wear, a chest of drawers, a crib and a plastic tub. On a later trip he bought floor matting and an iron stove for Ndola's hut. These luxuries, unknown in any rondavel, were due to his fear of Zena catching cold in the wet season. Every Friday, he brought gifts from Karula for Zena. Every evening, he played with the tiny girl like a kitten to make her laugh. Since he tickled her with kisses, she had learned to kiss him too. Ndola and Sita, silent and dry and old, observed these goings-on without comment. They lived more comfortably and had more money because Bwana Soft Voice was foolish in the head.

But there was one foolishness which so shocked Ndola that he always left the hut, even in rain, to smoke outside; no man should behave like Bwana Soft Voice. Ian thought Sita rough and slapdash over Zena's bath. He rebuked Sita, but Sita was stubborn; she had washed her own children like this and resented the unnecessary work of washing Zena every night. The baby looked miserable under Sita's hands. Ian pushed Sita away and bathed the baby himself. This was probably the happiest single act of his life. It became a nightly game, soapy splashing and baby laughter, and the perfect end of the day.

After Ian tucked Zena in and kissed her goodnight, he walked back down the drive where he had left the Land-rover out of sight of the house and drove noisily home, amused by this deception. He had not planned to keep

Zena secret from Grace; there was no reason to hide her. But he realized he loved Zena too much to let Grace intrude. He could hear Grace's voice questioning, bossing, arguing, jeering. No. Zena was entirely his; their life behind the cypress hedge belonged to them alone.

Immediately upon her return, Grace had said, 'Well, it's nice to be home. I'll have this dreadful stuff moved out tomorrow and my good things brought back.'

'Leave my big chair here.'

Grace opened her mouth to say this was absurd and would ruin the looks of the room. Something in Ian's face warned her not to.

Next morning, she said, 'I do hate eating breakfast on the verandah, it's too cold. And eight thirty in the morning. It was so lovely at the Dorset, ringing for breakfast in bed whenever I woke up.'

'Why don't you fix that with Beda? I intend to eat here, I like seeing the view.'

He could hardly conceal his satisfaction over this new arrangement. Fifteen quiet minutes to bolt eggs and bacon and fifteen minutes with Zena.

That evening when Ian came home from the visit behind the cypress hedge, Grace said, 'Ian, for God's sake, where did you store my things? They're an absolute mess, dirty, spotted, you might as well have kept them in the pigsty.'

Ian, unhearing, went to take his bath and change. Alone he'd worn pyjamas and dressing gown; he sighed as he put on fresh khakis. He settled by the fire with his book and his whisky. He had become fond of Jane Austen. The evening routine was a half hour with Jane Austen and two whiskies before dinner. Grace stood in front of him, furious.

'Ian!'

He was absorbed in *Emma*. Grace snatched the book from his hands.

'Ian, how dare you treat me like this?'

'What?'

'Oh nothing. You pay more attention to your sheep. Or

the watu. Much more attention to the damned watu when you know they hate us.'

'Sorry, did you say something?'

'Yes, I did. I said my good things are completely ruined. I'll have to start again from scratch.'

'All right. You can do what you like except I won't have any new servants. Beda and Mwangi were fine through the Emergency and I don't want uproar in the house. And you are not to touch the garden. I've made it the way I like and I will look after it. And my chair stays here. Otherwise, go ahead. May I have my book, please?'

Grace, dazed by receiving instead of giving orders, changed her tactics.

'I'll need to go to Nairobi a lot, to find the right things. I hope you won't mind.'

'Not a bit. Why don't you go every week? You might keep your room at the Dorset.'

'Oh no, that won't be necessary.' She had prepared for an argument; his swift agreement alarmed her.

Ian thought this an unexpected piece of luck. Perhaps she would be away several days a week, perhaps more. And when here, he calculated that out of sixteen waking hours he only had to see Grace for two hours and see was not the same as hear. When you got down to it, he didn't actually have to see her; she would be around, that was all, not much more of a nuisance than the tasteless rubbish she'd buy.

Though Ian had been inattentive and boring enough before she went away, Grace found Ian changed and worse. He wasn't surly as he had been after the ridiculous fuss about the roses, nor nasty as he was when they quarrelled over the Mau Mau. He wasn't anything; that was the point. He behaved as if she weren't there. She would be making conversation at dinner like a civilized human being and Ian would finish his meal, leave the table, go to his chair and start reading. She bought a new radio in Nairobi and played it loudly in the evenings, read the novels she brought back from the lending library, stitched at needlepoint and lived for her frequent trips to the Dorset and the lovely chats and shopping and the pictures and bridge with her darling friends.

She knew she was a good wife, a real helpmate, Ian had absolutely no cause for complaint, he ought to be wildly grateful for all her work on his accounts and letters and bills and statements, she took an enormous burden from him. And she always asked if there was anything he wanted from Nairobi and searched for hardware and spare parts in the ugly remote industrial section, tiring herself to death for him. She tended his clothes, she kept his house pretty, she couldn't think of a woman who did more for a man. But she was anxious.

Something strange had happened to Ian; he was too happy, happier than she'd ever seen him. And he was always so encouraging about her departures. Yes indeed, what a good idea to go off to Malindi when her friend Miss Ball had a holiday. If Miss Greene wouldn't go alone but was dying to drive to Tanganyika and stay in that famous hotel on the side of Kilimanjaro, of course Grace must keep her company. It's called Travellers' Rest, she'd said, and I'm afraid it's frightfully expensive. Not to worry, and since it was such a long journey why didn't she stay ten days or a fortnight. All Grace's trips to Nairobi were welcomed. Ian never asked how long she would be away. Grace took with her uneasily the memory of Ian's smile when he said goodbye.

Though Mrs Milbank was her dearest friend and an older woman, Grace could not ask advice. She longed to fling herself on Mrs Milbank's motherly bosom and weep out her grievances and her confusion. He has never given me a present, never remembered my birthday or our wedding day, never taken me for an outing not even to the cinema in Nakuru, never paid me a compliment not even now when everyone says I look so pretty and attractive, never thanked me for all I do to manage our finances, he isn't human that's all. He doesn't see me or hear me or talk to me and he goes around as if he hadn't a care in the world and he was perfectly happy and I could drop dead right in front of him and he wouldn't notice enough to get me buried. No, no, she could not breathe a word of her trouble to anyone. She had a special standing at the Dorset as a woman loved, and loved by quite a wealthy man. She wasn't going to endanger her one happiness, her position at the Dorset.

Grace's uncertainty grew, month by month, though she could find no reason for this sensation of doubt. She began to study Ian for a clue which would explain his calm separate happiness. She had wondered if he met another woman at cattle sales but gave up that suspicion because of timing; he went and he came back. He was gone on Friday mornings in Karula just as long as it took to drive to and fro and stop at the bank and post office. Though she really dreaded it, she made a few sorties around the farm, to see whether he might have left Fairview without her knowing; but Ian was always to be found in some revolting place among cows or pigs or Africans. Thinking it over she decided she'd become a ninny from nerves; the very idea of Ian and a woman was ludicrous as who should know better.

One Friday she happened to be standing by the kitchen window when Ian came home for lunch. The rear seat of the Landrover was loaded with parcels and bundles but Ian never bought anything for himself, his clothes were embarrassing, as if he hadn't a penny to his name.

She called, 'Ian, I do hope you've got yourself some new clothes.'

Ian was surprised to see her there; normally Grace summoned Mwangi to her presence. The period of baking goodies was long past.

'No. Presents for totos.'

'Oh, Ian really, don't you spoil them enough, what a way to waste money.'

'The totos are my greatest pleasure,' Ian said flatly. 'And what I spend on them is none of your business.'

Thank God he'd had the instinct not to speak of Zena.

All day, when he was at work, Zena would have been at the mercy of that voice and those prying eyes and the meanness of Grace's nature. He had no talent for lying and was proud that he had instantly said 'totos'. Grace knew he had always been fond of the totos, plural, though he felt a bit guilty now because he was merely a walking toffee shop for the totos and the presents went to Zena at dusk. He couldn't be fair and equitable, he'd never counted the totos, they seemed to be born in litters. The truth was simply that his own child came first.

Grace puzzled over those presents for the totos. No gifts for her of course but anything to please the totos. She could picture Ian playing Santa Claus with the screeching, runny-nosed, smelly African brats clambering over him. But it seemed an implausible clue. For two weeks, she spied on Ian's Friday return from Karula, peering out of his back bedroom window. The Landrover was regularly loaded. After lunch, Ian drove towards the African lines.

'Beda,' Grace said. 'How long has the Bwana been taking presents to the totos?'

Blank-faced, Beda said, 'I do not know, Memsaab.'

That was a mistake, one should never question servants. Grace checked a month of Fridays and concluded this must be it. Though grotesque for anyone else, it would be typical of Ian, the man disgusted by women, to have a passion for children. She gnawed at this thought. She remembered her first and only visit to the African lines when she had seen Ian covered with totos, while she did her best to keep clear of those grubby grabbing hands. She hadn't considered it, she had forgotten.

'The totos are my greatest pleasure.' My God. The man couldn't start a child but craved children. What difference did it make? Let him be a joke Daddy to a hundred black totos. He couldn't divorce her because she was childless, she hadn't refused his conjugal rights, he was unable to consummate their union. This was ridiculous, there was nothing Ian could do against her. She would ignore his abominable manners, she didn't intend to lose the advan-

tages of marriage. He wouldn't dare go into a divorce
court and say . . . oh no, she was getting sick from imagin-
ings. Anxiety festered and finally led to a cautious talk with
Mrs Milbank.

'If only we had children,' Grace sighed. 'We never
mention it but I sense that Ian would love a son to leave the
farm to.'

Mrs Milbank offered a plate of small sandwiches provided
by the hotel at tea-time and filled Grace's cup. They were
having a private tea and chat in Mrs Milbank's room at the
Dorset, sitting on the two stiff pink brocaded chairs on
either side of the little tea table. Mrs Milbank thought of
Grace's flat lean body, but her own was everywhere plump,
with a large bosom, large hips, and just as barren.

'My dear, I know exactly how you feel,' Mrs Milbank
said. 'It was our one sorrow. Of course when I was young
like you, times were different.'

'How do you mean?'

'Well, in those days, no one adopted children, it wasn't
done. But now everyone seems to be doing it. My niece
Marjorie, the one in Wiltshire, has three sweet adopted
kiddies. It's quite usual, I understand many people adopt
children even when they have their own.'

Grace looked thoughtful.

'If I weren't so old,' Mrs Milbank said, 'I'd really consider adopting a little girl now. Our Vicar has been trying
to place the most adorable baby. I told him he'd have no
trouble at home but out here people seem so selfish. It's
quite a problem because dear Mr Braithewaite is getting
on and his wife's not strong. A darling blue-eyed baby girl
with blonde curls. The child was simply chucked on the
Braithewaites, I don't know how, the Vicar would never
betray a confidence. I imagine it's the baby of a British
soldier and one of the European typist girls. We saw enough
of them billing and cooing together.'

Mrs Milbank glanced at Grace who looked more
thoughtful.

'It would be wonderful if you took the baby, dear. I

mean you have everything, a devoted husband, a beautiful home, plenty of money. And I feel it would make all the difference to you because you must be a bit lonely out there on the farm. If you don't mind my saying so, I think it might help your husband, bring him out of himself more, give him a new interest in life. And of course a child does bind people even closer together. Besides, I know how kind-hearted you are and it would be an act of real Christian charity.'

Grace was shaken by the suddenness of this idea. Her brain clicked like an adding machine. If she had guessed right, and she knew she was right, Ian was queer about children and using the totos as an outlet for his paternal feelings. Everyone said men always preferred their daughters; she could see Ian wouldn't want a boy from nowhere to carry his name but a girl was another matter. Instead of rushing off to spoil a horde of dirty African kids, he could pet and cuddle a clean pretty little white girl at home. He'd have to stop acting like a deaf-mute; the house wouldn't be ominously silent with a child in it. And as angelic Mrs Milbank said, a child binds people together; Ian couldn't work up some furtive scheme to get rid of her if they were parents. This might be a heaven-sent answer, startling though it first seemed. At any rate, she had nothing to lose by taking a look.

So Mrs Milbank, who had introduced Grace to a beauty salon, now introduced Grace to motherhood. She arranged a visit to the Vicar's house and Grace was enraptured by the pretty baby. Grace had never liked the children she once taught but this was different. A cuddly sweet baby of her own, a lovely child to dress up and show off; she imagined the picture and the words: young Mrs Paynter and her beautiful little girl. The least Ian could do was agree; it was entirely his fault that she hadn't become pregnant.

Ndola's daughter, the wayward sixteen-year-old, had coupled with her Asian employer or the employer's son or any stray Asian, for Zena was half-breed. Her hair was soft brown fluff, her skin copper-coloured, her large eyes almond-shaped, not African round, her nose and lips finely formed. As a cattle breeder, Ian thought it a pity that Africans and Asians were not more warmly disposed to each other. Mixing the races produced a fabulous child.

Zena was now at the golden age of two. She called her grandparents Ndola and Sita having heard no other names. She called Ian Baba. Ndola and Sita, old and tired, not unkind but not interested, did not trouble to explain that Ian was Bwana the master, not Baba the father. Zena obeyed her grandparents without question, as caretakers. They had little to say to each other, less to her; she grew up in quietness, knowing she must not get under foot and must play by herself except for the few romping morning minutes and the evening hour with Ian. She ran on fat little legs to Ian's outstretched arms, while Ndola grunted distaste for this daily foolishness of pats and kisses.

'You're a beauty, that's what you are,' Ian said.

'Bootee?'

'Yes, Baba's beauty.'

'Baba's bootee.'

He had carried her away from the rondavels to watch the fading sunset colours. They had a pattern for their hour.

'Now tell me what you see in the sky.'

'Red, awringe, grin, blue, *peenk!*'

'Very good. Shall we read our book?'

A devotee of farm catalogues, Ian had guessed there must be catalogues for everything and became a collector of toy catalogues. Aside from the teddy bear and rag doll, the big rubber ball and train to pull on a string, bucket and spade for her small sandbox, the plastic fish and frog to join her bath, Ian gave Zena alphabet blocks, chunky wood puzzles requiring her to fit pieces to form straight lines of colour, round pegs for round holes, square pegs for square holes, a big abacus with coloured beads and piles of picture books. They read these together, she poring over the pictures and watching words. She knew the stories by heart as he did with less enthusiasm. He was sure Zena would have learned to read to herself by the time she was four.

His child was beautiful and brilliant and healthy. Dr Parkinson kept saying, 'Ian, you really needn't bring her in for check-ups; she's about the healthiest child I know.' But Ian seized his chance every few months when Grace was away, to make sure. Any neighbours, seeing Ian and an old African woman and a toto on the road or at Dr Parkinson's, would think nothing of it. They all chauffeured the watu on errands of charity, it was a permanent part of the job.

Zena's delightful fingers had just pushed the last abacus bead for tonight's lesson. 'Twelf!'

'You're my clever girl too, you know that?'

'Clevah gul?'

'Yes, but I reckon we better not say that too much.'

'Not too much,' Zena said solemnly.

She could say anything she liked and as often as she liked, she couldn't possibly talk too much for him. Her voice sounded like music: low, soft, loving.


The drought was the worst in years. Most of last night and most of today he had been at Dick Gale's farm with a lorry-load of his watu, digging wide deep firebreaks against the fire that could be seen in the dark like a frightening long red snake sliding sideways down the mountains. He smelled smoke everywhere and dreaded just one African careless with a cigarette; the dry grass would practically explode. There was also a plague of cattle thieving on the farms in the neighbourhood and one of his herders had been rushed to Gilgil hospital with a spear wound in the stomach, delivered by a fellow Masai, those rotten *morani*, adolescent alleged warriors with ochre pigtails, bloody cattle thieves. His driver brought back from Karula rumours of an outbreak of foot and mouth disease around Thomson's Falls. Trouble always came like this, in bunches, and would be survived, but he was tired and took a third drink when Grace offered it, without noticing.

Grace remembered how a third drink had served her long ago. She broached the subject timidly but warmed up as she went along. At first Ian did not listen. Then words percolated past his trained deafness: baby girl, adoption. He began to listen with care and astonishment. He thought he knew Grace through and through and knew her to be lazy, selfish, interested only in money and what it bought her, a small-minded egotist playing the role of lady of the manor. She certainly didn't yearn for sex, she'd had plenty of time to hook on to a man if that was what she wanted. He had even hoped, when he saw how she dolled herself up and painted her face, that a man lurked in the offing and would carry her away with his blessing. Could this woman have one sincere and natural need? God, what a day. This on top of all else.

'Well,' Ian said.

'She's absolutely adorable, Ian, I know you'd love her.'

Grace waited in silence, remembering with anger bordering on hatred how she had waited before for this slow stupid man to take in an idea. Again her hands trembled and her head ached. She had lost the power to command Ian, she wanted to beat him but could do nothing except wait. Without his permission, young Mrs Paynter would not have her beautiful little daughter.

Ian thought about Zena. He had a child, he didn't want another. Grace had nothing, no work, no love of the land, no company. He wondered whether being a mother would make her happier and nicer. Or would it make her more shrill and complaining? He had no right to refuse, because of Zena. Comical, he thought, Mr and Mrs Paynter with their brown and white daughters.

'We haven't much room,' Ian said. Justice be damned if an adopted child meant sharing Grace's room.

'She'd sleep with me,' Grace said eagerly. 'But I don't know where to put the ayah.'

'What's the use of an ayah? If you don't mean to look after the child yourself, why adopt her?'

'Yes of course, Ian, you're quite right.'

'How old is she?'

'Fourteen months.'

'Well, Grace, if you take this on, it will be your show entirely. I have more on my plate than I can manage. There'll be legal things to attend to, there'll be all kinds of things. If you're sure you can cope by yourself, it's okay with me.'

'Oh Ian! I knew you'd agree. A baby will be such a lovely common interest for us.'

He also didn't want a common interest. An interest for Grace would be quite enough. He foresaw pitfalls by the dozen but was too tired to think about it.

'You know the funniest sweetest thing, Ian. Those dear old Braithewaites haven't given the baby a name. They felt it was wrong; her new parents ought to choose. They just call her baby. She's too young to notice naturally. I've thought of a divine name for her; Mr Braithewaite can christen her.'

'Oh?'

'Joy,' Grace said. 'Isn't it lovely?'

'Fine,' Ian said and stopped listening.

Grace was gone for a month and a half. She wrote to Ian, reporting progress. She spent most of every day at the Braithewaites, learning from the ayah how to take care of little Joy. She had seen a lawyer. She was getting adoption papers and arranging to have Joy put on her passport. She had shipped baby furniture to Karula station. She was so sorry Ian couldn't leave the farm to come to the christening party. All too soon, the blue Volkswagen appeared on the long driveway with a baby in a carry-cot lashed to the front seat. Grace unpacked, while bossing Beda on furniture placement. 'The baby's bed *there*, can't you see?' She had prettied Joy in a ruffly little dress and was ready with the child in her arms, making an adorable picture, when Ian came back for lunch.

'Give Daddy a kiss, darling,' Grace said.

The baby recoiled from the strange man and began to cry.

'There, there, my angel,' Grace said. 'It's your farm smell, Ian. I should have waited until you've had a shower.'

Ian had long since realized that Grace was lazy. She worked in short bursts of frenzy on anything that concerned her, house furnishing, farm accounts, but otherwise passed her days with novels, cosmetics, the radio, solitaire, embroidery, if possible reclining. Now her working day began at six in the morning and ended twelve hours later, though Ian often heard the baby wail and Grace moving around her room in the night. She and Joy had breakfasted before Ian returned from his early morning chores. While he ate alone on the verandah, Grace washed and dressed the baby and herself, a slow process which sounded cheerful enough judging by Grace's crooning and baby gabble and laughter. At lunch, Joy was fed in a high chair alongside Grace. Grace talked only to the baby.

'Just another spoonful for Mummy, darling. There's my good little girl.'

The baby moved her head aside, spat out food, and cried. Grace seemed intent on stuffing the child until she choked.

'Maybe she doesn't want to eat so much, Grace, maybe she doesn't need all that.'

'Since when have you become an authority on the care and feeding of infants?' Grace said, with fury.

Soon Grace announced that one thirty was too late for Joy's lunch; she ought to eat at noon.

'Fine,' Ian said.

'I haven't time to arrange two luncheons.'

'You and Joy eat when you want to. Mwangi will warm something up for me. I can't change the hours of the farm work.'

Ian was very quiet when he came home for his lunch-time shower and his warmed-over meal; Grace and Joy were asleep. In the evenings for an hour Grace described every detail of Joy's day and went to bed at eight thirty. Ian didn't believe Grace could keep it up; he waited for torrents of regret and blame. Grace was haggard, thin as a stick, but never complained or never of Joy. Though Ian steadfastly unheard her conversation, words sifted past his defences. Joy had picked a flower and given it to her, wasn't that adorable . . . Joy tipped her plate on the floor at lunch and really and truly said 'bad', wasn't it divine . . . The basic words were divine and adorable.

The divine adorable baby, however, did not look well; she was pale and puffed, simply too fat, and given to colds. If Joy sneezed, Grace foresaw bronchial pneumonia. If Joy threw up, Grace imagined cholera or appendicitis. If Joy slept restlessly sweatily, Grace knew it was the onset of polio. Grace sent Beda on his bicycle to tell Ian that Dr Parkinson must come at once.

After the third of these visits, Dr Parkinson drove to the farm office, closed the door behind him and said, 'Ian, I want to talk to you.'

'Right.'

'I have many patients and some of them are actually quite ill. It's a forty-six-mile round trip for me, to visit a child who is not ill. She is kept out of the sun because your wife has some mad idea that her skin will be ruined for life. She is overfed, and bundled up like an Eskimo. There is nothing the matter with Joy except her mother. I find it difficult to talk to your wife. I don't think I've ever seen a woman like her. You'd imagine that Joy was the first baby on earth. But I will not come here again unless you send the driver with a note of your own; then I'll know it's serious. Meantime, here's a book to give to your wife. Tell her to read it, believe it and obey it.'

He handed Ian a paperback with a coloured picture of a bonny babe on the cover.

'By a fella named Spock,' Dr Parkinson said. 'American but sound. I hope he can persuade your wife to be sensible, I certainly can't.'

'It won't do any good but I'll try.'

'How's Zena?'

'Fine, better every day.'

'Quite a contrast, isn't it?'

'You bet,' Ian said fervently. They smiled at each other.

Ian hesitated for three nights. Yes, he was sorry for poor snivelling Joy but scenes with Grace were such a terrible bore. As he knew, Grace took any suggestion as an insult to her mothercraft and snarled into the attack like a she-wolf. He didn't think Grace could actually kill the child with over-care, but he ought to make an effort to get Grace off old Parkinson's back. Braced for rage, he said, 'Grace, I couldn't have learned farming without books; raising children must be something on that order. Dr Parkinson left this for you. He said it was a sort of guide book.'

Grace did not hurl the book in the fire, abuse him for interfering and flounce from the room. Perhaps she was too exhausted. What would be the end of it? Grace in the Nairobi hospital with a nervous breakdown and the baby back at the Braithewaites with an ayah? Ian resigned himself to some kind of howling crisis but instead Grace grew almost rational. Either Dr Spock or experience had convinced her that the baby was not in imminent peril of death. The playpen was moved from the sitting room to the lawn. At least Joy would be exposed to a few hours of the morning sun.

Grace lived in terror that she would mishandle the helpless beautiful baby whose existence depended on her alone. If only dearest Joy could say what she wanted and how she felt. Grace hovered over the child as always but began to trust her ability to protect the little angel. Whenever the baby said Mama, and waved her fat arms as Grace drowned her in kisses, Grace's heart turned over. That breathless melting exalted sensation was her first experience of love.

Once, mistakenly, she believed that a wedding ring would secure happiness. Again, mistakenly, she believed that the delightful Dorset was everything she craved. She might have lived and died without knowing herself defrauded of love. Through loving this tiny person she had at last found true happiness. She lost the hunger of needing for herself; she wanted whatever her child needed. She no longer suffered from the monotony and isolation of Fairview and the

presence of a dull withdrawn abnormal man. Fairview was
a good healthy place for her baby.

This new emotion was of a power Grace could hardly
understand. At night in her room, she stood over the baby's
crib with tears of gratitude running down her cheeks. She
kneeled by her child and prayed God to keep Joy always
safe and well.

Since her return from glamorous Nairobi after the Emergency, Grace had abandoned housekeeping. She saw no
point in a futile effort to order and plan interesting meals.
Mwangi was a mule and Ian did not care what he ate. The
house ran itself. Presumably Mwangi told the lorry driver
what to collect for the kitchen. If she had to live at the back
of beyond, at least she would spare herself annoying tasks.
The drive to Karula was uncomfortable and she had no
desire to meet the other farm wives.

But Joy loved outings and Grace loved to show off her
bewitching two-year-old daughter. The farm mechanic
rigged up a sort of seat belt and several mornings each week
Grace drove the child to the Karula general store to buy
sweets and toys and be seen. The other farm wives, shopping list in hand, were besieged by Grace and her conversation. Yes, Joy's very advanced for her age. Yes, isn't
it a pretty frock, friends in Nairobi get them for me. Yes,
everyone says her eyes are exceptionally beautiful.

The wives thought Grace was batty. What did Mrs
Paynter mean, appearing in Karula dressed as for a garden
party with her infant done up like a chocolate box, bows
all over. And how frightfully bad for the child to be stuffed
with toffees and put through tricks like a poodle. 'Kiss the
nice lady darling.'

Rose Farrell and Helen Gordon fled together from one
of these visitations.

'Walk with me, Helen. I have to buy plimsolls for Jenny.
God knows what she does with them, she can't eat them.
I think there must be a huge plimsoll racket going on at
Tanamuru Girls School.'

'How's Jenny liking it?'

'Fine. Not that she'll ever be a shining light of intellect but her manners are improved. Speaking of manners, I thought our Grace had hit rock bottom at those grisly Sunday lunches but she's surpassing herself with that unfortunate child.'

'She's hard to take all right. Still, she can't help being so stupid. And I really believe she adores the baby. It's something in her favour. I'm positive she never gave a hoot in hell for poor Ian.'

'The child's pretty anyway.'

'You know who's lucky?'

'Who?'

'The ugly baby of her own that Grace didn't have. She'd have been a fiend to it.'

At the age of three, Joy had already learned how to control her mother. She could always get what she wanted. She had only to cry or feign sickness or snuggle and kiss and say, 'Mummy, Mummy I love you best,' words she had picked up from Grace. Joy did not try to conquer Daddy. She scarcely saw Ian except on Sunday afternoons when he might be reading on the verandah. Daddy was no use to her.

Daddy observed Joy's slyness with pity and irritation. Poor beast, he thought, spoiled rotten, trained from the cradle to be a pain in the arse that everyone's going to hate. Joy inherited from her unknown parents her large blue eyes, her golden curls and her neat short nose, but had acquired Grace's whining voice. Having been assured that she was delicate, Joy also acquired the habit of complaint and a petulant expression. She could not amuse herself for a minute and demanded constant attention. She was quickly bored. 'I'm tired of that game, Mummy, play a new game.' On Sunday afternoons when he might have been with his lovely unspoilt clever little girl, he had to sit around and listen to Joy, who drove him up the wall, until the late milking made an excuse to sneak behind the cypress hedge.

Karula soon palled. 'I'm tired of that old place, Mummy. I want to go to Nairobi. Please Mummy, please Mummy.' Joy knew all about Nairobi; it was full of shops with pretty dresses for pretty little girls and toys for good little girls. Grace longed to show Joy to her Dorset friends; they were the ones who would truly appreciate her treasure.

At dinner, Grace said, 'I wonder if the drive to Nairobi would be too much for Joy, too tiring?'

'I don't see why.' By some mysterious inner antenna, Ian heard Grace when she said something to benefit him.

'My dentist ought to look at her teeth.'

'Grace, you deserve a holiday, you really do. You haven't left Fairview for what? Nearly two years?' It seemed forever.

'Twenty-three months,' Grace said. 'I measure time by Joy's growing.'

'Why don't you take Joy to Nairobi for a few weeks? There must be a garden at the hotel where she could play. Other children too. And you'd have your friends in the evening.'

In Nairobi, Grace felt that her life had reached a state of ultimate perfection, happiness piled on happiness. Mrs Milbank and Miss Greene and Miss Ball and the Braithewaites were dazzled by Joy's charm and beauty. They hadn't words enough to praise Grace's gift for motherhood. And Joy adored Nairobi. Grace had taught her to fear everything on the farm, from the Africans who were dirty and smelly and nasty to the land which was full of bad things like insects and snakes and wild animals and not a nice place for a little girl to wander. Joy was not the least frightened of traffic in Nairobi, nor of strange people in the hotel. She ran about the Dorset being pretty and petted. She loved window shopping with Mummy and the session at the beauty salon, where her curls were cut and fancily arranged. But Joy did not take to the few other children who happened to be staying at the Dorset. They were rude; they said 'shut up' when she told them how to play.

'Go out in the garden with those nice children, dear.'

'No Mummy, no, I want to play with you.'

Grace thought this divine; in any case, Joy always did what she wanted. On the way home, Grace promised that they would have a holiday in Nairobi every month. Ian dimly heard how strangers had stopped in the street to admire Joy, how the whole Dorset was enslaved by Joy, and more of the same, but came alert when Grace said, 'I very foolishly promised I'd take Joy back every month because she was so happy at the Dorset, but now I've said it I'll have to do it, won't I, Ian? One must never break a promise to a child. I've made arrangements with the hotel for a special rate; it really won't be expensive.'

'As long as you don't eat into what I need for the farm.' Anything that got Grace and Joy away from Fairview was cheap at the price, but he thought it a wise tactic to seem somewhat grudging about money. If Grace knew how he blessed her absence she might not leave so readily.

Grace had given him one valuable idea which wasn't an excess in six years of marriage: a seat belt for Zena. The farm mechanic fixed a device of canvas straps to cross Zena's thighs and chest. For a week each month, Ian could safely take Zena with him in the Landrover on his long bumpy morning drives over the farm. He had daydreamed this endlessly but the daydream was set in future time, Zena older, and for some reason unexplained by the daydream, Grace removed from Fairview. He hadn't hoped to have such joy so soon. Zena was speechless with excitement, her eyes enormous and her eyesight, Ian discovered, an African heritage. This was another of the many mysteries about Africans, they saw farther and faster than anyone when interested, saw nothing when bored.

'Baba, *look! Horses!*' Zena's picture-book culture.

'No, zebras. See the stripes?' He had not seen them, a small herd grazing in the sun far away.

'Where are they coming from?'

'I don't know. I don't know how long they'll stay either or where they're going. They're wild animals, they're free, they go where they want.' Well, with limits, but ecological lore would have to wait.

'Beauty?'

'Yes indeed.'

The Landrover lurched and bounced on the farm roads; Zena gurgled with laughter. Worth it, to Ian, if she did nothing more than laugh. She had so little chance for laughter, growing up with the silent old people; that always worried him.

'Baba *look!* What is it?'

'Baboons. You see the baby baboons on the backs of their mothers?'

'Wild animals?'

'Yes.'

'Nice. Funny. Not beauty?'

'No, not beautiful but I love to see them. If we're lucky we'll see some wild animals every day. If there were no fences they'd be roaming all over the farm. I must have fences for the cattle though I wish I didn't. But the whole farm isn't fenced and anyway they get past the fences. This is what I love most, every day, if I can see wild animals here.'

'I love most too.'

Zena saw them all, when they were there to see, and saw them first. Ostriches running like mad dowagers along the fences, eagles sitting on fence posts, tommy leaping away from the noise of the Landrover; distant giraffe. One morning she spotted elephants, the great travellers, moving slowly among the trees near Luke's burial ground. He stopped the Landrover to gaze at those wonderful beasts.

'They're not afraid of anything,' Ian said. 'Except men. They are good and kind to each other and very clever.'

'Why are they afraid of men?'

'Because men shoot them. Can you see their heads?' Maybe she could; he saw only their enormous grey shapes.

'Yes, they have big teeth on the side.'

'Tusks, baby. They're made of ivory and ivory is worth a lot of money, so men shoot them.'

'You, Baba?' She was clearly distressed.

'No, never.' Not that the watu, who feared the tembo, didn't beg him to call the game warden and have them shot. He'd let them knock down anything on the farm rather than harm them.

'It's a *very* fine day if we see elephants, Zena. It doesn't happen often.'

The watu grew used to the small brown girl in the Landrover with the Bwana. Bwana Looki, in the old days, took his big brown dog everywhere with him. Zena was accompanying him in his work and Ian explained the work as they went. Baba, does the milking machine hurt the cows when it pulls? No, not at all. What is that man doing, Baba? That man is Alhamisi and he is a mechanic, he fixes machines when they break. He is fixing the pump and by God's grace he will succeed or else I will have to get a fundi, a man who knows everything about pumps, to come from Nakuru. What does the pump do? It pushes water to many places on the farm so that we can all have water to drink, the people and the animals and the shambas. Nothing can live without water. Baba, does the big pig make all those toto pigs at the same time? Yes. How? A brief factual description of animal sex sufficed, neither of them being much interested.

The watu were not surprised to see Soft Voice stand by his Landrover, holding the child's hand, while together they stared at Africa. Soft Voice was teaching Zena his religion but a new act of prayer had been added; Soft Voice lifted the child in his arms and pointed to the sky. Mungo, God, they told each other. Ian was showing Zena the clouds, cirrus and cumulus, sharing his wonder in the African sky. He was giving her all he had, his world, and knew it was a great deal for a four-year-old to understand, but month after month Zena learned with intelligence and love, as taught.

Zena had always been a smiling child and Ian could not doubt her happiness and still he worried. His little girl was growing up in isolation; children needed other children. Without much hope, he told Sita to walk the mile to the

African lines where she could chatter with the other women and Zena play with the totos. Zena returned in tears, she didn't understand the totos' games, they pointed and stared and shouted at her. She was of course a foreigner, she wasn't their colour, she lived a separate different life. Sita complained that her legs ached and it was *bure* anyway.

'I play with Bobby and Betty,' Zena said.

Ian loathed Bobby and Betty, golden-haired twins, hero figures of the first book Zena had read to herself. In his opinion, a more miserable pair of anaemic prigs had never existed but they were engraved on Zena's heart, her imaginary friends. She spent her days with them, she talked to them and about them; Ian was kept abreast of their activities and had to admit that they became less dismal as they developed in Zena's imagination. With love and the best intentions, he had put his child into a sort of prison. He seemed to have a special talent for prisons. Zena's extended back from the cypress hedge through a long stretch of leleshwa and lion grass to the fence at the public road. He made it as amusing as he could, with a swing and a pet lamb, which Zena named Mary, and toys and books, but he raged that he could only take Zena out on parole, by Grace's tacit permission.

When Grace began one of her devious conversations, Ian realized she was about to do him a tremendous favour. Living at this altitude all year round was bad for a child, Grace said, Joy ought to go to the coast for her health. Ian gave his usual falsely grudging consent. That was the first of the journeys to Malindi and lasted two weeks but, as Grace pointed out, she couldn't break her permanent promise of a week in Nairobi. Malindi, Nyali, Bamburi; all for Joy's health. Soon Grace said that Joy ought to see the sights of East Africa as part of her education; it was absurd for the child to miss Kilimanjaro which was world famous, a splendidly long holiday at Travellers' Rest, and Mount Kenya, another long holiday in Nyeri with Miss Ball who was interested in the tree ferns, and Treetops, once visited by the Queen. Cannily, Ian said that Joy looked much healthier after the trips to the coast, having judged that this was what Grace and Joy liked best. By skilful manoeuvring, he could get them off the farm for two sure months in the winter and for joint vacations with the Dorset clique and the guaranteed week in Nairobi at the least.

Ian left supervision of the late milking to Simuni, giving himself afternoon hours with Zena as well as the morning Landrover rides. Always proficient in the use of catalogues, Ian had found a correspondence school course for home teaching by parents stranded in outposts of civilization. They studied together. Unless he was making a muck of the grading system Zena was far ahead of her years. Since Grace did after all come home as a shackle on his freedom, Zena learned to prepare her lessons alone because Baba could not always spend so much time helping her. She didn't mind solitary homework, having Bobby and Betty for fellow pupils. Ian wished he had never given Zena that book, she should have started by reading the adventures of young devils instead of the mealy-mouthed inanities of the bloodless twins. He was stuck with Bobby and Betty and it would be cruel to criticize the child's only friends. But his little girl was too gentle, too docile, too quiet; she needed real lively children. In the back of his mind lay the dread that he was turning Zena into a misfit like himself, unable through lack of experience to join in the normal life of ordinary people.

When Grace and Joy were taking their long holiday at the coast, he could have brought Zena to live with him in the house. Ian thought of this with a yearning like hunger pains but decided that shuffling Zena back and forth from a European house to an African rondavel would badly dislocate the child. And besides, no: except for his old chair, the house was Grace's, tasteless and tainted by Grace. Considering the impression made on Zena by gruesome Bobby and Betty, it would be a major mistake if she got the notion that this house was the way a house should look. Everything on his farm was right and good for nourishing Zena's mind, but not Grace's house.

He was forced to deny himself a real life with Zena while Grace and Joy lived as they chose, returning to Fairview only because Daddy meant money and keeping up the pretence of a happy home. He was paying with pain for the inconceivable error of his marriage but Zena was paying too, unfairly, wickedly, though the child didn't yet know it. He would never be free of Grace and Joy for the simple reason that no one else would ever want them. Zena was the loser which he could not bear. He got drunk one night, mixing bitterness with whisky, and flailed around Grace's sitting room, kicking twee tables and hurling fringed sofa cushions at china ornaments, shouting 'Till death us do part', and ended the night in tears to wake with a gruelling hangover and Zena still alone behind the cypress hedge.

Joy was equally isolated though neither she nor Grace noticed this. They lived in flawless harmony based on Joy getting what she wanted and Grace's adoring subservience. While Zena learned how to manage a farm, Joy learned how to manage hotels and the adults in them. Ian thought Joy was a hellish child, Grace's perfect product, but there was hope in the future because Grace would send Joy to boarding school, driven by snobbery to copy the local ladies. The girls at boarding school would either whip Joy into shape or murder her. For Zena there was no future like that, nothing to save her from an unnatural childhood.

Obviously, Joy and Zena should have been playing with each other since infancy, the reasonable solution for both children. He didn't see how he could have engineered it, knowing Grace's sentiments about all skin that wasn't one hundred per cent white. Grace might have softened after eleven years in Kenya, might even be secretly concerned over Joy's loneliness and surely Joy, born here, couldn't be a confirmed racist by the age of seven. More and more troubled by Zena's solitude, Ian invented and discarded and invented fresh schemes for bringing the little girls together. Away from Grace, Joy must have some human childish instincts, he couldn't utterly condemn a seven-year-old, and Zena would improve her.

This wavering idea was killed dead by Joy, lately returned from a grand hotel near Mombasa and accustomed to grand hotel service. Joy's presence at the dinner table was a recent hardship, a wretched half hour when Joy showed off her clothes and her grown-up manners. Beda was by no means the sort of servant Grace and Joy approved, but it was not his fault that Joy suddenly flung out her arm, to exhibit new silver bangles, and knocked a bowl of fruit salad from his hands. The bowl crashed to the table, spilling half its juicy contents on Joy's lap. She sprang up, shaking her dress, shouting, 'Look what you've done, *you stupid black baboon!*'

Beda stood as though frozen. Grace made angry clucking sounds and hurried to wipe Joy's dress.

Ian said, 'Apologize to Beda, Joy.'

Grace and Joy stopped their annoyed cleaning operation and stared at Ian.

'You heard me, Joy. Apologize to Beda.'

'Mummy!' Joy wailed; tears spurted from her eyes. Grace put a protective arm around her angel.

'How dare you, Ian? How dare you speak to the child like that? Of course she won't apologize. It's one of her best dresses.'

'Joy,' Ian said, his voice even and icy. 'Apologize to Beda.'

Joy was now wailing loudly, her face hidden against Grace's skirt.

'*Ian!* I will not tolerate such behaviour. *You* apologize to Joy!'

'She will either apologize to Beda or go to her room and stay there until she does so,' Ian said, his voice unchanged.

'Darling, go to your room now, you wouldn't want to stay with your dress all wet and sticky. Mummy will be along in a minute.'

'Beda,' Ian said. 'I apologize for Joy and Joy will apologize later. We won't need anything more.'

Beda, still frozen, closed the kitchen door carefully behind him.

'Now Ian,' Grace began, her eyes fiery, her voice a drilling whine.

Ian got up from the table.

'You are never to speak to the child like that, do you hear me Ian? And she's certainly not going to apologize to a clumsy stupid servant.'

'Joy will not leave her room until she can lower herself to an apology. Otherwise you can both leave the house. You're perfectly free to go at any time.'

He sat in his chair by the fire, seemingly undisturbed, seemingly deep in *The French Revolution*, and mocked himself for a fool, a real fool, a dangerous fool. In his idiot folly, he might have suggested that Zena play with that sickening child. There was no hope for Joy, deformed for good, and he didn't care. No doubt she and Grace would find plenty of company to their taste. But there was also no hope for Zena; she'd have to go on playing happily with Bobby and Betty, the little ghosts who proved that his child belonged nowhere.


'It's the Socialists!' Grace cried. 'Naturally they don't mind what happens to people like us! The Africans will take their pangas and murder us all!'

Grace had returned from Nairobi, hysterical with Dorset prophecies. The British Government had promised Kenya Independence next year. Whites would be ruled by blacks, as if blacks could manage the water works, the post, the trains, the electricity; name anything you could think of and imagine the hopeless botch they'd make. Quite aside from killing whites whenever they liked, and whites having to call them Bwana.

'You must sell the farm!' Grace shrilled. 'Ian, you *must*. We have to get out while we can. The Ethridges are moving to South Africa, you know that, don't you? I hear the Farrells are going back to England. People in Nairobi and Mombasa and everywhere upcountry are selling out while there's still time. None of us will be safe. It's too dangerous, it's terrible, life won't be possible here, I can't risk Joy.'

'Rubbish,' Ian said, turning a page of the *Kenya Weekly News*. The tone of Grace's voice, her wild eyes reminded him of the maddening early days of the Mau Mau rebellion. He didn't think he could bear this nagging idiocy a second time.

'I insist,' Grace said. 'I absolutely insist.'

'I don't give a damn who rules this country, I don't give a damn what happens to the water works or the mail or the trains or anything. Worst comes to the worst, Fairview can be self-sufficient. I'm staying here, this is my place. Besides which, I don't believe for a minute that Africans will butcher whites. No reason for it, once they've got what they want. I don't mind calling them Bwana. Why not?'

'You don't care what happens to Joy and me! And you haven't any pride, you'd lick the Africans' feet if that helped Fairview. You'll get on all right, it won't make any difference to you when we're all insulted and pushed around and probably in jail if not dead. You're a nigger lover!'

Ian rose from his chair and stood tall above her, his face rigid with distaste.

'That kind of gutter language may be acceptable among your friends, but don't ever use those words in front of me again. Never, do you understand?'

Ian stalked out to the verandah. Clean fresh air. How was he going to live with this odious woman under the new regime? She would whine about African outrages day and night, her usual contempt again turning into hate and fear. He found Grace huddled by the fire in tears.

'I'm thinking of Joy,' Grace said. 'I'm afraid for Joy.'

He always ended by being sorry for Grace. He didn't forgive her, he pitied her. She was so unattractive and so wrong-headed; he always ended by thinking how awful it would be to be Grace.

'Joy will be fine. Listen, Grace, talk to Helen Gordon

not those scared Nairobi people. You'll get a different
angle. And the Farrells aren't leaving because they're
spooked; they're leaving because Simon inherited a house
and stable from an uncle in Oxfordshire; they're horse
crazy, that's all.'

'Oh Helen Gordon,' Grace said, sniffling. 'Why does
everybody act as if Helen Gordon was so special? She's
ridiculous. They could shoot her husband and burn down
her house and she'd stay, just as long as she could keep her
garden.'

There was nothing to do about Grace except not listen.
Grace now drove to Karula every afternoon, feeding her
fears on rumours in the general store and at the Sports
Club. At dinner, she repeated these rumours accusingly to
Ian's serene deafness.

Joy was bored with her doll's house under the jacaranda
tree. Before that she had been bored with the beads she
strung for necklaces and with her paint-box and colouring
books. Mummy had stopped taking her to Karula, she said
the daily drive was too tiring. Mummy said, 'You're my
darling big girl now. Play by yourself for a little while.
Mummy wants to rest.' She considered waking Mummy
from her nap but she was cross with Mummy.

At morning lessons Mummy said sharply, 'Pay attention,
Joy, you're not trying.' Her feelings were hurt and she
cried and Mummy comforted her but also said they would
work again after tea. Joy hated morning lessons; they were
a bore too; everything at Fairview was a bore. She had
learned the word from Grace.

Joy always obeyed Mummy about staying on the lawn
to play; she had no desire to explore the hidden dangerous
world of the Africans. But today, from spite and idleness,
she decided to creep to the cypress hedge. She could run
home to safety if there were snakes and nasty people. It
was Mummy's fault for leaving her alone with nothing to
do. Joy tiptoed behind the house and across to the hedge.
She peeked around the corner and saw a brown girl on a

swing. As there were no visible snakes or horrid Africans, she came closer.

'Who are you?' Joy said.

Zena had her back turned but jumped from the swing to face a girl who looked exactly like Betty, a beautiful pink and white girl with a blue bow in her golden hair and a blue and white polka-dotted dress and white sandals. A real Betty had come to play with her. She was so excited she could only stare in admiration. Beda and Mwangi spoke of this toto, the Memsaab's child, but Zena had never seen her. The cypress hedge was an impassable frontier. Sita said that the Memsaab lived on the other side and would beat Zena if she caught her.

'Who are you? Can't you talk English?'

'Zena,' with a warm smile.

'How old are you?'

'Nine.'

'What are you doing here?'

'I live here.'

Joy was not smiling. Zena wore a faded, patched pink dress, too small for her, which Joy recognized.

'Where did you get my dress?'

'Beda gave it to me.'

Grace had thrown it out. Beda brought everything Grace threw away to Zena. Fortunately Zena was the smaller child.

'You can't wear my dress.'

Zena said nothing.

'Where did you get that swing?'

'Baba gave it to me.'

'Who's Baba?'

Zena did not know how to answer. Why was the beautiful white girl looking at her with angry eyes and speaking in an angry voice?

'You heard me,' Joy said. 'Answer when I talk to you. Who's Baba?'

'The Bwana,' Zena said helplessly.

Joy thought about this but couldn't decide what it meant.

'Show me your house,' Joy said. Zena led her to a ron-davel and Joy started to go in but drew back. Africans were smelly and dirty, as Mummy said. From the doorway, Joy saw rough wooden shelves with toys neatly arranged on them.

'Show me your toys.'

Obediently, Zena brought her toys from the rondavel and laid them on the table outside her grandparents' hut. Inside, Sita woke and stayed silent, listening. Mwangi and Beda and Ndola had walked together to the Asian duka on the road, this was the afternoon free time.

Joy studied the surprising collection of toys which were as good as her own. She knew it was not right for an African child to have anything like hers.

'You stole them,' Joy said.

'No! Baba gave them to me.' Tears began to leak from Zena's large brown eyes.

'Baba,' Joy said mockingly. 'You stole them. I'm going to show them to my Mummy.'

Joy collected as many of the toys as she could carry, a large flaxen-haired doll, a bag of glass marbles, a big rubber ball, the prettiest things she saw, and marched off beyond the cypress hedge. She had no intention of showing them to Mummy. She hid the toys in the doll's house, and was playing there peacefully when Mummy called her for tea.

Zena sat on the ground and wept. She knew what stealing was; Sita had not neglected her basic education. The police came for totos who stole. Joy had taken her best beloved doll, Betty, who closed her eyes to sleep, and her jewels, and the ball she and Baba played with.

Sita came out of the hut and said, 'Stop crying.'

'Why did she say I stole my toys and take them away?'

'I don't know. She can do anything she wants.'

Joy had discovered a fascinating occupation for the empty afternoons. She waited impatiently for Mummy to finish lunch and lie down in their room. Zena wasn't like the children she met in hotels who were rude and told her to go away and wouldn't play as she wanted. Zena was

better to play with than Mummy or Mummy's friends, all
kinds of new games she had never tried before. If Zena did
not do what she ordered, quickly, she pinched Zena who
cried and obeyed. Joy was specially fond of games in which
she was the Queen, meting out punishment to Zena, the
villain or slave. Zena did a lot of kneeling and begging for
mercy as the Queen commanded, though her head was often
cut off anyway.

Zena cried at night and woke to fear the coming afternoon. Sita had no sympathy for these tears and warned
Zena not to tell Baba because that would bring more
trouble for everyone. Abandoned by the only people who
could protect her, Zena took to hiding like a hunted animal.
She crouched behind a leleshwa bush and fled into the tall
grass as soon as Joy appeared. She expected Joy to run
after her and waited shivering to be trapped. But Joy did
not follow. Zena stayed silent and motionless in the thick
scrub. It was hard to keep so still and she never knew
when Joy might creep up and pounce on her. She didn't
feel safe until Sita called, 'She's gone. Come back now.' But
it would start again tomorrow, it would never end. She
wept at night in despair; Baba didn't love her. If he loved
her, he would save her.

For once Joy couldn't run to Mummy to get what she
wanted. She dared not brave snakes and wild animals and
dared not shout to Zena in case Mummy heard and found
her in this forbidden territory. Zena was a pig and a black
baboon and she would really punish her, not play punish,
when she caught her. She couldn't think of any way to
reach Zena until Sita came yawning from her hut.

From Beda and Mwangi, Sita knew how the Memsaab
ruled the house and spoiled her toto and how the Bwana
allowed this as if afraid of the Memsaab. She didn't want a
dispute with the Memsaab and the chance of losing the
best rondavel on the farm. Though the white toto broke or
stole all Zena's toys, she didn't actually injure Zena and
Zena would have to get used to this sooner or later;
Europeans were the masters. Sita never emerged from her

hut until sure that the Memsaab's toto had left them in peace. Today she was fooled by the quiet; instead of stamping around and muttering threats, Joy stood glaring at the wilderness that hid Zena.

Joy was well aware of her power. Sita, being African, had to obey her. She ordered Sita to fetch Zena and Sita walked slowly into the bush, looking for the unhappy child. Joy slapped Zena hard for her attempts at escape.

'You do what I tell you or my Mummy will send you away from here,' Joy said.

That would be worse than all Joy's torments; she would never see Baba again.

Grace lay on her bed in the afternoons, trying to distract herself with novels and calm herself with aspirin, while her nerves felt like taut wires and she was eaten by fears of the future. Ian's selfishness was monstrous, criminal. On her worst days, she imagined Joy stripped and flung about like a rag doll by brutal laughing Africans. After Independence, no British soldiers would protect them against the murderous Africans. Her only comfort was Joy who was so gay and bright and such a darling considerate child, unlike Ian who had no consideration for anyone. To shame Ian by showing him this difference, she said, 'I'm always astonished by Joy's thoughtfulness. A little girl of eight but *she* worries about me. Today she said, "You need your afternoon nap, Mummy, you work so hard." I wish you had a tenth of her concern. But oh no, you don't care, you'll let us stay here to be attacked . . .' Before Ian stopped listening, he wondered vaguely what tricks Joy was up to now.

Sita, wanting no trouble, tacked an old piece of cloth over the bare toy shelves. After Joy's first looting visit, Zena hid her books under her bed so that as usual Baba and she spent their evening hour studying and reading together. Ian saw nothing strange but something was very wrong. Instead of running to meet him with laughter and kisses, Zena cowered in a corner of the hut and waited for him to hold out his arms. Zena stopped working by herself in the afternoons, she had no samples of writing and finished arithmetic lessons to show him. When he asked for her notebooks, she shook her head and would not look at him. She read in a whisper, stumbling over words she had read easily before, close to tears. He was alarmed by this change and bewildered. What had happened? The child seemed afraid. He held her on his lap, reading to her, and her slender little body was stiff as if he had become a stranger.

Ian called Sita out of the rondavel and said, 'What have you been doing to Zena? She was never like this before. Have you been beating her? Tell me the truth.'

Sita said stonily, 'Not me.'

'Ndola?'

'Not Ndola.'

Ian found a moment to question Beda and Mwangi. 'Not me,' Beda said. 'Not me,' Mwangi said. 'Then who?' Ian asked. 'Don't lie to me. I know someone is frightening Zena.' He was up against the wooden faces of Africans who are unwilling to speak. They shrugged, all of them. When he asked Zena gently, rocking her in his arms, she buried her face against his chest and wept. The child only became almost her normal happy self during their week's holiday, when Grace and Joy were in Nairobi.

Ian took Zena to Dr Parkinson, having decided Zena must be ill, parasites maybe, one of the invisible African wasting diseases. Dr Parkinson reported bruises and scratches, nothing special. Zena could have got those playing in the bush. Yes, he agreed the child seemed different, nervous, perhaps the Africans were filling her with stories of evil spirits and black magic, upsetting her that way. Ian tried a new line of questioning and again Sita, Ndola, Beda and Mwangi said 'not me' and looked at him with the same wooden faces.

The rains put an end to Joy's interesting afternoons. Mummy said she would catch cold and must stay indoors, not that she wanted to get soaked and dirtied by the mud in the servants' quarters. She missed Zena, Zena was a good playmate who did as she was told. There was nothing to do in the long dull afternoons and Mummy went to their room with a book and left her alone to be bored. Grace was reading when Joy stood by the bedroom door and said, 'I *hate* it here!'

'Now, angel, we'll be going to the coast soon.'

'I hate it here. I don't want to live here. I want children to play with.'

Grace felt this as a knife wound. She knew it had to come, but so soon, so soon? Already she was not everything to Joy as Joy was to her. Before the prospect of Independence drove out all other fears, Grace had blocked from her mind the torturing thought of boarding school and her loneliness, separated from Joy.

Joy pouted and scuffed her feet.

'There's a girl here to play with.'

'Here? You mean an African? Oh darling, what a foolish idea, you wouldn't want to play with an African.'

Joy pouted more, hung her head, twisted her body.

'Where did you see her?' Grace asked.

Joy had not expected questions. She had never been scolded but she sensed trouble.

'In back,' Joy said sullenly.

'Beda's child or Mwangi's probably. Oh no, angel, they come from horrid dirty huts on a reservation somewhere.'

The wives of Beda and Mwangi, with assorted children, drifted in for visits when they saw fit and drifted off. Grace objected to this long ago. Ian said it was the custom, and he couldn't change it, and Grace didn't have to see the visitors. She would speak to Ian about this tonight, and sharply. Up to now during the day, on her specific orders, Beda and Mwangi kept their children in the African lines where they belonged.

'Not Beda's,' Joy said.

'Then Mwangi's, darling; it's the same thing.'

'No!' Joy shouted, furious with Mummy.

'Well darling, nobody else lives out there. Now be

Mummy's good little girl and forget that silly idea. We'll play a lovely game together.'

'She's Baba's child,' Joy said.

'Who's Baba?'

'The Bwana.'

Joy had an active imagination and often made up stories, using words she did not understand. The child had no notion of what she'd said, of course.

'Let's play Snap,' Grace suggested. 'You find the cards and we'll play right here, nice and snuggly on the bed.'

Joy liked Snap, which she always won, and forgot Zena.

If Joy's story was true, Ian was giving in to the Africans even before Independence. Soon they would be all over the place, squatting and spitting in her garden. The blacks weren't rulers yet and her authority must be enforced: African children were forbidden to wander near the house where they might spread their disgusting diseases to Joy. But Joy should not be brought into it. After the unforgettable and unforgivable incident with Beda, she could see Ian taking the Africans' side, saying Joy had no business behind the house, blaming and upsetting Joy not the servants. She would find out for herself before Ian came home as if Joy had not alerted her. Grace quietly set her watch an hour ahead.

'Heavens, look at the time, darling. It's such a nasty wet night, wouldn't you love a picnic in bed? With the radio and whipped cream on your cocoa and delicious lemon pie?'

Joy was devouring lemon pie, the radio at full blast, when Grace took a torch and walked through the drizzle to the cypress hedge. She saw a lighted rondavel and approached the open door. Ian was sitting on a low stool, his back leaned comfortably against the wall. From beyond the doorway Grace smelled the African stench. Ian looked at home in this squalid place, smiling and easy. He held a small brown girl on his lap, stroking her hair while she read to him. When the child stopped, Ian lifted her up, hugged her close and kissed her cheek. 'You're Baba's clever little one. That was *very* good. Better every day. Tomorrow I'm going to bring you special presents from Karula as a prize for working so well.'

Grace turned and walked silently back to the house. She stood inside the verandah door, with the torch in her hand, too shocked to think or move. Then the meaning of what she had seen poured over her; she felt as if she were on fire, burning with hate, choked, gasping for air, burning. She stumbled towards Ian's room, the gunsafe, the shotgun, you don't have to know, just raise it and pull the trigger, deadly at close range, dead, dead, before he could bring his filth into her house. The noise of the radio stopped her at Ian's door. Joy terrified, Joy alone when they took her away. Oh God, no, I'm mad, I must think. Her legs were shaking, she leaned on chairs and tables, making her way back to the sofa by the fireplace.

Zena's sickness, whatever it was, had disappeared as inexplicably as it came. Perhaps she was quieter and less ready to laugh but she wasn't a baby any more that he could tickle and bounce on his knees. He had been desperately worried, knowing his child was unhappy and unable to help because he didn't understand. But it was all right now, the best sign being that Zena studied again in the afternoons and prepared her homework to show him and was eager to learn. And soon they would be alone, with Grace and Joy at the coast; he'd have the time he needed to play with her and cheer her up. Ian walked through the kitchen, whistling, and headed for his door not noticing Grace at the far end of the sitting room.

*Whistling*. He came here from that, whistling. The weakness left her, she sprang to her feet, powered by hate. She wanted to tear at his face with her nails, she wanted to scream at this monster, but was obliged to whisper. The radio still blared but Joy might not be asleep and voices carried, she could not risk Joy hearing.

'You are unspeakable,' Grace hissed. Ian turned to look at her with astonishment. 'There aren't any words for you, such filth, such vileness. That's what you were doing during the Emergency. No wonder you wouldn't leave here, you were sleeping with your African whore. And you keep your half-breed bastard right behind my house, where Joy could see her, where Joy *did* see her. How dare you live under the same roof with us? I wish I could kill you. You hear me? I wish I could kill you! *You nigger-lover!*'

Ian was transfixed. He stared at this familiar plain face, distorted by hate, he listened to the voice that he also knew too well, now whispering with a fury he had never heard anywhere, and he made no sense of it. It was too sudden. He opened his bedroom door and undressed and took his bath as usual. Lying in the hot water, he untangled what Grace had said, and understood what she meant, though he couldn't imagine how she reached this crazy conclusion. He felt nothing at all; whatever Grace thought was a matter of indifference. He had actually heard Grace say that she wished she could kill him, and he believed her, and he felt nothing. She might have been complaining of the weather.

Ian returned to the sitting room in clean shirt and khakis and mixed a whisky and soda at the drinks tray. He saw no reason to discuss Grace's lunatic accusation. Grace took this cool silence as the final outrage. The revolting beast expected her to accept what he had done?

'You listen to me, Ian Paynter,' Grace whispered. 'I will get a divorce and I will take every penny you have. You can live with your whore then, like an African, just like them, in a dirty rondavel, that's all you're fit for.'

'Divorce?' Ian began, dimly, to see a miracle solution to his life. He had to speak with caution and prevent himself from smiling.

'You heard me. Everyone in the country will know about you. You won't have a shred of reputation, every decent person will despise you, you won't be the big Bwana of Fairview, you'll be an outcast, you and your black whore and your bastard.'

'For a divorce,' Ian said mildly, 'You need proof.

You'll have to find the woman first and then you'll have to find witnesses who have seen me with her. Just seeing isn't enough. They have to prove I was in bed with her. Do you think you can swing that?'

'Beda and Mwangi,' Grace said with loathing. 'They'll have seen you.'

'There's no woman out there, and Beda and Mwangi have seen nothing.'

'You mean you went away from the farm? Oh it's too horrible and disgusting to talk about. I can't bear to look at you. You make me sick. Being in the same room with you makes me feel dirty, covered with slime. Anyway there's your bastard, she's out there, I saw her.'

'You have to prove she's my child, don't you? Your word against mine. You'll never find any witnesses.'

Grace felt the sweat on her forehead, she was dizzy and shivering, she swallowed back a sudden rise of bile in her throat. She was torn apart, half mad with fury and a blood lust for revenge while Ian sat in his chair sipping his drink, calm, teasing her, mocking her, and winning. Witnesses would have to be Africans, Europeans wouldn't know this abominable story; and the Africans would be on Ian's side. She'd never get a word out of any of them. And if he said his whore was not there in the servants' rondavels, then she wasn't. How could she track down that woman; she might be anywhere in Kenya.

'Besides,' Ian went on. 'A huge scandal wouldn't be frightfully jolly for you and Joy. Would it? Scandal has a way of sticking to everyone. People might even laugh at you, you know, people do strange things.'

Grace collapsed on the settee and covered her face. She couldn't believe what was happening. Right and justice and honour and decency were on her side, and everything Ian said was true. Ian wouldn't care about scandal, he didn't care what anyone thought of him, but Grace could imagine the Memsaabs gossiping at the Karula Sports Club, poor Grace, she's been living all those years with Ian's black tart at her back door. Her friends at the Dorset would be horrified and sympathetic but all the same embarrassed, a sex scandal with an African wasn't the sort of thing nice people got mixed up in. And if she couldn't get a divorce, she couldn't punish Ian, the only way to punish him was to drive him from Fairview.

'If you think I'm going to live here, if you think I'm going to let you do this to me,' Grace said, incoherent with despair and hatred.

'No, I wouldn't expect you to stay. I suggest a legal separation. Something quiet and discreet so you and Joy won't have any unpleasantness and then you and Joy might move to England. You won't like it here anyway when the Africans are in charge.'

'That's lovely for you, isn't it?' Grace sneered. 'Get me and Joy out of the way and bring your whore here. Fill the house with kinky-haired bastards. I daresay you'd give us a measly allowance so we could live in a cheap boarding house.'

'Why would I do that? You can have half the profits, a settlement properly drawn up. I imagine you two could live quite well on that, and I'll be doing the work that keeps the profits coming in.'

Beda entered from the kitchen with a soup tureen. Ian waved him away, saying, 'Bado, bado.'

Grace got up. 'I shall never eat with you again nor spend another night under the same roof with you. I never want to see you or hear from you. You'll get a letter from my solicitor. I mean to pack now and Joy and I will leave for Nairobi in the morning. I forbid you to see Joy. You're not fit to breathe the same air. I will take only our clothes and whatever toys Joy chooses. I don't want anything to remind me of this place and you ever. And I hope you suffer all your life as you've made me suffer.'

'Well, Grace, the main thing is that Fairview shouldn't suffer. Always remember the profits.'

Her beautiful angel was fast asleep. Grace began to pack, moving quietly. Her hands trembled so that it was difficult to fold Joy's dresses. That slow stupid man, Ian Paynter, had defeated her; she couldn't ruin him; she couldn't make him pay.

Words blazed in her mind. No wonder he wouldn't touch me, white women disgust him, the pervert, the liar, he only likes black flesh, no wonder he lived back of beyond and made no friends and kept white people away, no wonder, what did he do, go to the African lines and spend the afternoon in any hut with any fat stinking black woman he fancied, years of it, years, presents for the totos, lies, presents for his whores, married me as a smoke-screen, used me, made a fool of me, the best years, my youth, the horrible perverted sex monster, of course he let me adopt Joy, more smoke-screen while he kept his favourite bastard at hand for him, used Joy, used *Joy*, for years, all the time from the beginning, the sneaky cunning devil, no one knew, no one guessed, I'd have lived my whole life with this filth except for Joy, Joy saved me, Joy, Joy.

She had to sit down; she was exhausted by rage and bitterness. Never again sleep in that bed, I'd vomit if I thought of what had happened there, no, no, I must be calm and careful, Joy cannot know this not ever, it's my sacred duty to protect her, she must never know anything, I'll tell her we are leaving because an old friend is very ill in England, I'll think of something, she's so young, she won't question me.

Grace pulled the chair alongside Joy's bed where she could see that angelic face. Everything she loved, pure, unspoiled, and rescued thank God from this sewer of evil. Yes, rescued. Her hands had stopped trembling. She would be able to pack the last suitcases now. That was the main thing: Joy was rescued.

The ways of Providence were indeed mysterious and not painless at first sight. On second sight, the ways of Providence looked much more favourable. Joy would forget Daddy quickly; later she would tell Joy that Daddy was dead, as for any practical purpose he was. They would live in civilized England, instead of this backward country which anyway was on the verge of chaos, ruled by blacks.

Bournemouth, Cheltenham? She needn't decide in a hurry,
Joy loved living in hotels. And Joy could go to day school,
sparing her the dreaded separation of boarding school.
They would be together, she and her beloved daughter,
and comfortably off, and no depraved man and no filthy
Africans to trouble them. Grace longed for daylight, longed
to get away, knowing how thrilled Joy would be: Joy
hated Fairview, as she did. And fifty per cent was not
enough.

The house had to be disinfected before he brought Zena
to live with him. 'For the last time,' Ian said as Beda and
Mwangi unloaded Luke's old furnishings. The two farm
lorries were filled with all Grace's stuff and sent to the
Nairobi saleroom. He might have kept the red nursery for
Zena but it was Grace's doing and he wanted Grace
expunged. Ian drove to Nairobi and ambled about like a
helpless country bumpkin until he found a furniture shop.
The Asian proprietor assured him that these pale blue things
were 'a very fine suite for a young little lady'.

'I don't like the bunnies.'

The bunnies could be painted out, immediately, and
where was the Bwana buying curtains and bedspread. The
Asian's son led Ian to the Asian's cousin's shop where Ian
was astounded by the quantity and variety of repellent
material on sale and presumably bought. He was ready to
give up when he saw a bolt of cloth, more or less the same
colour as the new furniture. It was patterned with small
pink rosebuds. He showed the Asian the size of the windows as he remembered them; curtains and bedspread
would be made at once by a glum African at a pedal sewing
machine, and shipped with the very fine suite to Karula the
next day.

Ian was too preoccupied to listen. He had suddenly
thought of clothes. Since his first Nakuru effort, he had
bought no clothing for Zena. But the child wasn't naked,
how did she live? Clean little dresses, which he had taken
for granted. From where? Joy's cast-offs, it had to be. He

wanted to weep, thinking of Zena patiently accepting whatever Joy discarded all these years. He had much to learn and he must teach Zena to remind him, to ask; he couldn't bear the idea of her humility. But he also couldn't quite, as yet, bear the idea of a female clothing store. When Zena came with him, it would be different. Staring into shop windows, brooding on his carelessness, he saw a display of small shorts and striped T-shirts. Much better for the farm anyway. Zena would look enchanting, dressed like a little boy. He figured she was about the size of a seven-year-old male, and returned cheerfully to Karula with a stack of shorts and T-shirts.

He and Beda were behaving like a pair of old hens and enjoying it. Zena's room was ready, with bunches of flowers on the desk and bedside table, and the new boy's outfits in the bureau drawers. He felt a joyful elation he had markedly failed to feel long ago upon bringing Grace here. He went behind the cypress hedge, to bear the glad tidings.

'Zena, love, you're coming to live with me in the big house.'

Zena gave him a look of terror, wrenched away her hand and fled into the bush. He thrashed after her but she was well hidden. He found her sobbing in a sort of burrow behind a leleshwa bush. She must have made this hole herself and she certainly knew her way to it.

Ian carried the child in his arms to the swing under the Cape Chestnut tree and held her on his lap, soothing her while she cried as he had never seen her cry. He kept saying, 'Tell Baba, darling, tell Baba.' When she could speak, Zena said, 'No, Baba, please. The Memsaab's toto is bad to me, I don't want to live with her, please, Baba.'

So Ian learned at last the cause of Zena's unexplained sickness. If he had known, he wouldn't have let them go so easily; he would have driven them out with whips and thongs, the words springing into his mind; beaten them down the driveway, sent them bleeding and penniless from this place where the poisoned child of the poisonous woman had tormented his gentle timid little girl. How could anyone be so wicked, it was like trapping and baiting a young gazelle.

'Baba?'

'What?'

'Your face. Baba, your face is ugly.'

Hate was an ugly emotion. And now a useless one. Grace and Joy were beyond his reach, no doubt airborne. Grace had settled her business in Nairobi at speed. A letter from her solicitor demanded 60 per cent of the net profits of Fairview and he had agreed light-heartedly, with relief, by return of post. The only way he could punish Grace was by making Fairview fail. Hate was entirely useless, and a sort of victory for Grace.

He took a deep breath and let it out noisily. 'Better now? I blew the ugliness away.'

Zena nodded but she was still tense, like a little animal curled against danger

'Listen to me, Zena. They are gone. The Memsaab and her toto. They are gone forever, they will never come back. Never, you understand that, don't you? We don't have to think about them, we will forget they were ever here. There's only us, together on our farm, for the rest of our lives. Now come home with me.'

Mrs Farrell called to the barman, 'Jambo Samuel, coca cola moja, baridi sana.' She hurried across the tatty empty club room to Mrs Gordon who was reading her mail.

'Helen, have you seen Ian Paynter?'

'No, why?'

'I saw him at the post office, our throbbing social centre. He had a ravishing little brown girl with him, but ravishing. If you can imagine Nefertiti as a child, wearing khaki shorts and a red and white striped T-shirt.'

'Rose, dear, pull yourself together.'

'Why not? The Nilo-Hamitic tribes are all beautiful. How do we know that isn't what Nefertiti was? The ancient Egyptians . . .'

'I'm not up to it.'

'Neither am I, really. Anyway you sidetracked me. The point is, this beauty is obviously a half-breed. It's too extraordinary. I'm all of a twitter. Instead of staring at his feet and mumbling, Ian looked me straight in the eye, smiling all over his face, and said, "Mrs Farrell, may I present my adopted daughter, Zena." I didn't know what to do. I tried to shake hands with the child but she hid behind his legs and Ian just laughed and patted her head and said benignly, "She's a bit shy, she'll get over it." Coming from him, I ask you. And he looked radiant, I don't think I've ever seen a man look like that.'

'That's good news. Grace was not one to inspire radiance.'

'But you know, it is rather weird. Grace and her film star kiddy vanishing without a word and a few months later, Ian appearing with this new child and she's not, repeat not, full-blooded African. What can it mean?'

'Not what you think.'

'Oh, why?'

'Not Ian, anyone but Ian. I'd bet my last shilling.'

'Your opinions are universally respected, dear heart, but I'll bet my last shilling they won't be shared this time.'

'Oh really, damn it to hell, I can see it starting all over again. Poor Ian, they'll never let him alone. Why shouldn't he adopt a little girl, any colour, even green, if he wants to? You don't suppose he's had a jolly good time with Grace and Shirley Temple, do you? I've always thought he was the loneliest man I ever knew. And if he's happy now I wish to God people would just be nice for a change and let him be happy. I'm going to squash that rumour before it gets a good hold.'

'May I ask how?'

'I'll simply say I know all about the child, I've discussed it at length with Ian, and any suggestion of hanky panky is rot. If you have a spark of human decency you'll do the same. Your last good deed before you leave.'

'Okay but what do we do when they ask where Zena came from and etcetera.'

'We have the haughties, we say no one asks us about our children and it's rudimentary manners not to pry. After all, how do we know that Jenny is actually Simon's child, we take it for granted out of politeness.'

'Oh Helen!'

'Well, you get the general idea, don't you? And I'm going to have him to lunch with his new daughter as soon as Charles goes off to kill some more harmless wild animals.'

'That's a joke. He'll never come.'

'Yes, he will. He likes my garden.'

'How do you know, or has he been at your house secretly some time in the last ten years?'

'No, but he liked the garden then. And he'll need a woman friend for the girl. I'll make him come. And I long to help him with his borders, they haunt me.'

Zena had been chatting about school and gardening, for she was Helen Gordon's disciple, but grew silent as they neared Fairview. Helen Gordon could feel the child straining ahead towards home. She must have been wildly homesick this first term though Ian said her letters were cheerful. Helen Gordon felt a heavy responsibility; she had convinced Ian that Zena must go to school with other girls. She took it on herself to make the arrangements. Zena passed the scholastic tests with ease and after Independence no school could refuse a child because she had African blood. In fact, as Helen Gordon told Ian to calm him, Tanamuru Girls School accepted African students before Independence despite its reputation as the most stylish school for young ladies in East Africa.

'You don't want her to grow up knowing nobody except you and me, do you, Ian? No other children. She'll be a misfit, she won't know how to get along in the world.'

Mrs Gordon was not sure where or how the beautiful child would fit in the Republic of Kenya but then she was not sure about herself either. And it never hurt anybody to go to the right school. She had made careful inquiries and learned that the African students at Tanamuru Girls School were the daughters of Top People so she assumed the Africans were not all that different from the English in some respects.

Ian had forgotten his anxieties about Zena's solitude since they were so happy together and so sufficient to each other. Zena was blithely gay, his constant companion. The years behind the cypress hedge were unreal, part of an unreal past. He could not imagine life without her and resisted the idea of separation. But the word 'misfit' frightened him. Helen Gordon was right and he knew it though he agonized lest Zena be snubbed by white girls or mistreated; there might be other monsters like Joy. He had written to Zena every day, in every letter he told her she could come home any time she was unhappy. He didn't say that he missed her so much he felt sick, the house was a tomb, no matter how hard he worked he couldn't work off his loneliness. He pulled the pages from the calendar in his office, waiting in desolation for the Christmas holidays. Helen Gordon was to call for Zena, as she would be in Nairobi that day. She took that on herself too, guessing Ian's profound reluctance to appear at a girls' school.

Now Helen Gordon turned away and walked out of sight around the house. She couldn't watch this silent rapturous reunion; Ian and Zena clinging together as if both had just escaped drowning. Perhaps she was wrong; she'd suffered untold misery when Charles shipped the boys to England but they were boys and there was no real choice and they had never been as close as a girl would be. Perhaps she had meddled, laid another paving stone on the road to hell. Perhaps they should be left alone to live their perfectly happy absorbed lives here; but what would Zena do when Ian died? If she had never known any place other than Fairview, made no friends, grown up a recluse like Ian? Ian was forty-four, Zena was twelve; Zena had a long piece of time to live without him.

There were noises of African welcome and laughter
inside the house and then they came across the lawn, the
sweet funny pair, the small girl with her arm around the
waist of the tall man, his arm around her shoulders.

'Your roses are doing beautifully, Ian. I've never seen
a new rose garden look like this. Let me know when you
feel like coming to lunch.' She kissed them both and hurried
off. Much as they liked her, she knew they didn't want her
there a minute longer.

'Oh Baba,' Zena sighed.

'Yes.'

He understood everything Zena meant: to be together,
here where they belonged, looking at the same view.

'I'll get out of my uniform and then can we drive to
Luke's hill?'

'I thought you'd want to,' and had a picnic tea with
thermos bottle ready in the Landrover.

Zena came back in her farm uniform, khaki shorts and
shirt, saying, 'I'm only comfy like this.'

They didn't talk on the way. The afternoon was hot,
cloudless and windless. Dust hung in a curtain behind
them and dropped in the still air. Ian felt Zena's joy when
she saw a herd of grazing zebra. She was taking in the land
through her eyes, regaining her home. Ian spread a plastic
cloth on the grass at the edge of the ridge and Zena got
the tea organized; this was one of their regular treats. After
they had paid reverence to the view and their cups were
filled, Ian said, 'Tell me.'

'You know our school uniform?'

'Yes.' Lucy had worn the same in a different colour.
Apparently natural law decreed that English schoolgirls or
girls at English schools must wear that felt pot hat, blazer,
pleated skirt.

'It was called nigger brown before Independence but
now it's called dark brown.'

Ian took in his breath, all his worst fears were true; but
Zena was having a simple schoolgirl's fit of giggles.

'Who told you?'

'Betty.'

Dear God, was Zena so lonely that she still depended on an imaginary friend?

'She's an African girl,' Zena said. 'She told me because it's so funny.'

'Is she a friend of yours?'

'Oh yes, everyone's my friend.'

'That's good,' Ian said uncertainly. Zena munched cookies.

'One day,' Zena went on, 'After sports, some of the older girls were talking and they asked me to come over. One of them, she's very pretty, her name is Isabel, she asked me about my mother.'

Ian had stopped breathing; he felt tears in his eyes. She would never go back to that rotten school, better grow up a misfit than grow up tormented.

'I said I didn't know, I'd never seen her,' Zena went on, still munching cookies. 'Then she asked about my father and I said you. Another girl, I forget her name, said I must be illegitimate. I asked how to spell it, it's got two l's with e after. So I could look it up, you see. Anyway Isabel said it was very romantic, and then they all said it was romantic, and Isabel said either my father or my mother or both must be very beautiful and I said you were. I looked up illegitimate. It means a lot of things but mainly not born in lawful wedlock.'

Ian didn't know what to do; this matter-of-fact instructive conversation affected him like being kicked in the stomach.

'Weren't you in lawful wedlock with my mother?' Zena asked.

'No.' That was God's truth, but what went on in her head? Of course Zena must believe he was her real father, having known no other, and he had never said he was or wasn't. He had never explained the circumstances of her birth for the idiot reason that he didn't think it mattered.

'Oh well, that's why you adopted me,' Zena said. 'So I

could be your lawful daughter, I wasn't sure why. I wouldn't like to have a mother. I remember about the Memsaab not really but sort of.'

'Yes.' Bewildered, lost; was she telling him something he didn't hear?

'I'm the smallest girl in school. I don't mean the youngest, I mean the smallest. And I don't look like anybody else, the African girls are black and the European girls are white and then there's me. So everybody's my friend and the older girls say I'm their pet.'

'Zena, do you hate it there?'

'Oh no, Baba, I don't hate it. It's a very nice school. Lots of big trees and grass and flowers but you can't see anywhere, not like here, you can't look out and see the land and of course there aren't any wild animals. But if I can skip a form then it would only be five more years.'

Ian reached over and lifted her and sat her on his lap, enfolding her in his arms. 'You don't have to go back, you don't have to stay there five years, you can be here all the time right now.'

'Baba?' Zena said in a small voice.

'Yes, my little one?'

'Did you send me there because you were tired of me? Because you wanted to be alone on the farm?'

'Zena, how could you think that? I want you here every minute. I counted the days until the end of term. I love you better than anything in the world, the farm is terribly lonely for me without you.'

Zena snuggled closer and put her arms around his chest. 'I don't mind then.'

'Were you having sad thoughts all this time?'

'Well, I thought we lived here together and did lessons together and then all of a sudden I had to go to school, so I thought maybe.'

'No, dearest. No. Aunt Helen talked to me and said there were many things a girl needed to learn besides what she learns on a farm. I've lived here nearly twenty years now, and I don't understand much outside of Fairview. I wanted you to have more chances, but I won't keep you at that school if people hurt your feelings.'

'Nobody hurts my feelings, Baba. I told you. I was scared at first and cried in bed but so did other girls and I guessed they were scared too so I didn't feel so lonely. Then a girl called Joanna, she used to cry too, she said we'd be best friends and help each other. She lives on a farm near Thomson's Falls, they raise beef cattle, she's seen lions but she doesn't like them, she's afraid of them. Then we had parties in our dorm after lights out, you're not allowed to, eating sweets and cake and fruit and things, Aunt Helen sends me boxes so I have plenty. And they tell me funny stories and we laugh a lot. If you laugh you forget about being homesick. Anyway now I know millions of girls and they're all my friends.'

Zena unpeeled a somewhat melted bar of Cadbury's chocolate and began to lick it from the tinfoil. With chocolate on her nose, she giggled suddenly. 'I'm like Mary.'

'Mary?'

'Baba! You haven't forgotten Mary? My pet lamb?'

'Zena, love, I'm a bit confused but I think you are saying politely that Tanamuru Girls School is hell.'

'No, I'm not. Honestly. I think I'm saying that school's kind of silly, not like Fairview.' Zena licked her fingers and got up, tea and conversation finished, the sun magnificently sending afterbursts of light above the western mountains. Sounding very assured and brisk, she said, 'It's all right, Baba. Everybody has to go to school, all the girls know that. We better do what other people do. I don't suppose five years is really very long.'

They collected the remains of the picnic. Ian folded their table cloth and stowed the hamper in the Landrover.

'You write to me or send me a telegram any time and I'll come and get you. You know that, don't you?'

'Yes, Baba, I do now.'

Mwangi had prepared a feast which left them water-logged and stupefied. Zena had been reading aloud, in her dove voice, 'My Last Duchess'. They were both devoted to Browning as to Baroness d'Orczy, Conan Doyle, Robert Louis Stevenson, all the battered books in Luke's collection. Zena slept, in the curve of his arm, while Ian watched the fire burn down and tried to think of the future. After five years in that young ladies' establishment, would Zena find Fairview alien and uninteresting? A citified girl, not the responsible person Luke asked for, long ago, who'd inherit Fairview and guard it with love? Had he again got to work on building a prison for himself, a lonely old age? If so, what of it? He was trying to make sure there were no prisons for Zena. In any case, one day some sod would come along – black, white, copper-coloured – to steal Zena from him. He only hoped the sod would be a good farmer.

What's the matter with you, Ian Paynter? Use your greying head. Think of the accidents. Who could ever have foreseen, when you were Zena's age, that you'd be here, the man you are, with this particular child as the centre of your life? What about the accident that brought Zena, an infant more than half dead, to this farm? And the series of accidents that made her indeed your lawful daughter, and a bright steady little girl, able to cope with people much better than you can. Bad accidents too like going to the Karula Sports Club for the second and last time in nearly twenty years and meeting Grace. How does it cancel out? The worst, losing your family, against the best, Fairview and Zena? You won't know until you're dead, will you? And what's the point in worrying about the future? Let the future take care of itself, since you certainly can't. Be grateful now, man, be grateful.

He picked Zena up, still sleeping, and carried her to her room.

# :III: BY THE SEA

Begin at the beginning. I overheard people at the next table. Two couples, Australians or New Zealanders, I think, those accents. At breakfast in the dining room. The dining room is too big. They were talking about carmine bee-eaters. Swarms, thousands of tiny red birds, flying in to trees at the head of a creek. Making a tremendous row, thousands of them, settling for the night or squabbling over insects or whatever. Wasn't it amazing, one woman said. And the creek looks so romantic, so African. The lunch at the something Club is much better than here, a man said. Oh the whole place is much better, the woman said, I mean it looks like real Africa, that palm thatch roof and the mud-brick bungalows, I wish we'd known about it before, instead of staying here. I don't consider this place exactly hell, the man said, and they laughed. Why not hire a car again today, the other man said. One of those darling pink-and-white baby jeeps, the dark-haired woman said, probably his wife. I'll never forget those tiny red birds, the first woman said, *millions* of them.

I imagined a cloud of rosy hummingbirds moving over the sky, then breaking up, and the trees would seem to blossom with fluttering red flowers. It sounded lovely, like nothing I'd ever seen or could really imagine. They looked happy, the two couples, with their new sunburns, one of the big men had a peeling nose. They were enjoying them-selves, having fun on their holiday. Everyone here in this luxury hotel is a tourist, it's a holiday place but not all the faces look happy. Of course I haven't spoken to anyone, I wouldn't know how to start, but I watched the other guests, at the Olympic-size pool mainly. It's rather like going to the movies alone.

I was quite wrong to believe that flying off to Africa was extraordinary and a dashing thing to do. Every nationality is here, treating Africa as just another tourist resort, French people, Germans, Italians, some cruise ship Americans, all kinds of British Commonwealth, and three pairs of giggly Japanese. At the pool, the Japanese ladies wear big boudoir caps of lace and ribbons and mannish striped swim suits on their short mannish bodies.

My favourites are gone now, they only stayed five days, I'm certain they weren't tourists like the rest of us though it's odd to think of any white people living in this part of the world. Really living not here on a trip. I watched them whenever I could: a sturdy sunbaked small woman and a tall thin man, tomato-coloured with a ferocious burn which didn't seem to bother him, and two tow-headed lively boys, about eight and ten years old I'd guess, and a fearless brown baby in an infant's lifejacket. They took turns teaching the baby to swim. It was their best game, obviously they all doted on the baby. The baby was wonderful, serene and confident, not the least disturbed by being hauled and pushed by so many hands. That family looked as if they were always happy. I hoped they'd speak to me but they didn't, nor to anyone else, they were complete together.

Perhaps I was beginning to get a bit sad from watching, the single person alone here, otherwise I might not have thought about the carmine bee-eaters, charmed by the name. I realized how dull I am, I never find anything special to do. There were only a few days left and I hadn't budged from the hotel. Not that I hadn't been content with the white sand beach to walk on, and the warm sea, and the splendid pool when the tide is out, and the colours and the soft air and the sky.

After breakfast I went to the woman at the desk, the one who arranges things, car hires and visits to the game parks, and spoke of the carmine bee-eaters. She knew all about them. She suggested driving to the something Club for lunch and a swim and renting a boat to go up the creek at four in the afternoon. No, it wasn't really a Club, that just meant they could keep Africans out, no problem for Europeans. It was the season for the birds, apparently they weren't a year-long sight, only now for a month or so they came in hordes to this grove of trees. Did I have a driving licence? She could give me a nice small white Peugeot and if I started at eleven I'd be there by noon. You turn left when you leave the hotel grounds and go straight to the bridge and turn right until you see the Club sign on the right just before Kilifi creek. You can't miss it, there's only one road.

I've never driven a Peugeot but it works like any other car. Alone on an African road, I felt different. For two weeks I'd felt that I was coming alive. What do I mean? Perhaps it's very simple: physical well-being. I was at home in my body again. Glad to wake to the morning sun, golden warm but not hot because a breeze blows steadily from the sea. The breeze is called the monsoon, I learned, surprised since I thought the monsoon was some ghastly wind that happened in India. My skin felt smooth and fresh as if I was breathing all over, taking in bright air through my whole body. I slept without dreams to remember and woke to look at this beautiful world. All I could see of it from my balcony or walking on the beach. Certainly not a varied view of Africa but enough; the dazzling blue and gold and the brilliant night sky. The colours change hour by hour.

It wasn't necessary to think or feel or plan. Planning to fill time is what I always have to do. In these weeks, there wasn't any time, just the days with nothing to mark them, slow and easy and gone before I'd noticed. Time is terrible if you know there's nothing ahead but more and more time. Perhaps that's what I mean. I forgot time, I was free of it.

On the road, away from the sea, hot wind blew through the car windows. I decided it smelled of Africa, not that I know how Africa smells. This wasn't like the scented air around the hotel with its sloping gardens, the flowers, the flowering trees. Because of this new smell I felt daring, unlike myself who am not daring. All alone in darkest Africa, setting out on an adventure. There wasn't much to see at first, or nothing you could call particularly African.

The backs of hotels and a grimy grey factory with chimneys
and a few petrol stations. The sense of Africa was emptiness,
almost no cars and empty space between these uninteresting
buildings. Then there was a toll bridge over a wide river or
inlet and after that, idiotically, I began to think I was
Livingstone and Stanley, driving along a good tarmac road
at fifty miles an hour to lunch at a club for Europeans.

The trees were strange, none recognizable, surely none
planted by man. Wild trees. Despite the car noise and the
wind noise, I felt the silence. A huge silence over a huge
land. I couldn't see any distance into the huge land, only
feel it going on forever. I passed an African village by the
roadside, mud huts with pebbles stuck in the mud (why?
for ornament?) and thatched roofs. African women wearing
printed cotton cloths wrapped around them, African men
with white skull caps and gowns like nineteenth-century
nightshirts, jolly naked children. It was very picturesque
and very poor.

The idea came to me that I could make a life like this, not
all the time naturally, but as something to look forward to.
Every year, I could do this. Go away to some unknown
place and stop being me, lose my life, live by looking. It
would be a way out, or part of a way out. I must have been
mad, grabbing at hope after two weeks of feeling peaceful
and half an hour on an African road.

On both sides of the road were fields growing great
cactus plants of some kind, like giant cabbages, with spikes
that looked murderous. The ground was dry as brown
cement. The cactuses grew in long straight rows. How
could anyone get near those dangerous spikes to cultivate
them or cut them or whatever they did? Anyway there was
no sign of people. The cactus fields ended in a band of trees,
very thick, tangled, a piece of jungle which scared me into
thinking of poison snakes and spiders and malaria. The
monsoon does not reach this burned earth, the handsome
European hotels on the coast have nothing to do with what
belongs here. I hoped the something Club would show up
soon and began to have more natural emotions, natural to

me: no cars, no people, no houses, the immense silent sunstruck land, I shouldn't pretend to be adventurous and sure of myself, an experienced traveller.

It was foolish to be alarmed by the dark trees because they were a patch not a forest and the road went straight on between flat unused ground; long yellowish grass, stubby greyish bushes, unused, unlived in, much of Africa must be like this, not desert but no water, you couldn't say it's ugly but miles and miles of such emptiness would be sinister. I wasn't thinking, or telling myself hopeful stories about future journeys, I was just driving in my usual way, eyes on the road, when suddenly. From nowhere, up from the ground, suddenly, suddenly, suddenly a child leapt running. Directly in front of me, directly in front across the road, running. A second. One second. I saw his face, his profile, running . . .

A sound wrenched out of her, not from her throat, from deep inside, loud, a long rasped groan, a sound like 'NO' but not clearly a word. Mrs Jamieson did not hear it. She pressed her hands over her eyes, grinding out a picture she must not see. There were flashes of red and yellow under the pressing hands. The pain in her head that never stopped flared into defined points on the temples and at the base of her skull. She lay on the bed, rigid, watching the lights behind her eyelids, the pain numbing her mind. Then she walked to the bathroom, unsteadily, and turned on the cold shower.

She stood under the spray, holding up her long hair, gabbling to herself about the water: that's nice, nice cold water, that's nice, that's better. She dried herself, gabbling now about the thick green towels which matched the green tiles and walls of the bathroom. You'd never expect such a perfect bathroom in Africa. You'd never expect such a lovely room. Think about the room. One wall of glass, opening to the balcony. Long yellow curtains like the bedspread. White leather chairs or whatever looks like leather. Marble floor or whatever looks like marble. Big built-in cupboards, big built-in dressing table. Good lamps with plain white shades. White walls. So cool and clean and light and pretty. One painting, local work obviously, tacked on to show you where you are, an African maiden with a collar of silver rings giving her a giraffe neck, and bare breasts. All right now. Breathe quietly. Two aspirins. Ice from the thermos.

Ice cubes in a hand towel made a wet cold bag which she held against the bluish lump on her right temple, then against the unbruised left temple where the pain was worse. Raising her hair, she passed the melting ice bag across the back of her neck. The condition of her head was a fact to be ignored. The cavity inside her skull felt filled with a single hot stone, too large for the encircling bone. When the regular pain altered into pulsing jabs she sweated and was rocked by nausea so she handled this inconvenience with aspirin and ice. It did not concern her.

The mirror over the wash basin covered the wall. Another long mirror covered the bathroom door. She could not avoid seeing all of herself. She looked at her face which was unchanged except for the coloured swelling on her temple. She couldn't remember when she had stopped caring about her face. Probably when she knew she was old. Long ago. Being old did not depend on your looks or on a number of years, it was a truth you knew about yourself. Forty-three last week; she had forgotten her birthday here in those timeless days which seemed long ago too.

When she was a child her parents must have told her, or let her understand, that she was pretty so she took her face for granted but there was something wrong with it now. It was frightening. Her forehead. The dark blonde hair grew in a central point and on the sides the hair grew closely as if glued to the skin: a broad low forehead. And it was completely unlined. Nothing had happened to her forehead, nothing showed. It looked blind or worse: insane. As if it were detached from her, from life, existing alone untouched by all events, any feeling. She was wearing somebody else's forehead.

The ice had melted and there was no more in the thermos jug. She drank thirstily the last of the cold water. Food? When had she eaten? Dial 4 for room service. Ice water, iced tea, chicken sandwiches. No, the effort of speaking was too great. And she would have to find her dressing gown. Her body must be hidden from questions. Like curious sleeves, purple yellow and green bruises from shoulders to elbows; like a splotchy belt, bruises across the pelvis and back; like torn dark stockings, the discolorations on her legs. Unimportant. She put on her nightgown and went to lie on the bed.

Two days now? Three? Some day she would leave this room. It didn't matter. Time was different again. Not what she had known for so long, a ceaseless chore to attend to every day. Not like the magical drifting time of those two weeks. Time had no shape at all and she was not responsible for it. It went on, it was no business of hers.

She could tell the hours by the light flowing through the balcony window, from the silver shades of early morning to the straight white glare of noon through a slowly cooling gold to the sudden sunset. Late afternoon now, still hot on the beach. The first day here she discovered a sunset rite. A flock of green birds, miniature parrots, green with red trimmings, flew together, disorderly and playful and loud. They were evidently coming home. Home was a tree taller than the hotel, rising above her room on the top floor, to the right of her balcony. The trunk and branches were yellow, the leaves like ferns. She asked the name of the tree from the young Englishman at the front desk, an assistant manager keeping his eye on things. Fever tree, he said. She thought the name was disagreeable for the home of the sunset parrots.

Craning over the balcony she had seen the afterglow of the sun, orange and pink and streaks of pale green. Not the actual sunset, out of sight behind the hotel in a distant part of Africa far from this marvellous coast where tourists like herself were safe and snug in a tourists' Africa. By day, according to the tide, the sea looked like a map, areas of green jade and aquamarine and sapphire, a jewel map. As the sun went down, the sea darkened to purple, then to pewter while the sky briefly glowed into deep blue, glass with light behind it. You had to be quick to grasp this moment before the white line of the reef vanished and it was soft black night, but shining and crowded with stars.

These wonders continued. She had only to walk a few steps from bed to balcony to see them again but they were meaningless to her now. She must lie here and get it straight. That was all she had to do.

Begin at the beginning. It was November but already the Christmas frenzy was in the air. The year had been endless yet suddenly Christmas came round again. All my life Christmas was us together on the farm at Derry Bridge, my parents and I, then Richard after we married, and finally our son, our own private world, a special time when we had nothing to do except be happy, loving each other. The last Christmas at Derry Bridge there was only Richard and me and it doesn't count, it wasn't Christmas, bleak days while Richard talked, droned on and on, and I listened or didn't bother to listen.

He said that he had always been in third place, coming after my parents, and then definitely in fourth place since I loved Andy more than anyone in the world. I had never thought of it like this, I thought one loved different people differently, but when he said that, I agreed he must be right because I had no love left in me, not for Richard or myself or anything. He had waited through the months of my depression and hoped I'd recover and adjust – his voice droning that odious word – but he felt he was living in a cemetery, I was tending graves, and he couldn't stand it. He loved his son with his whole heart, but one had to accept what couldn't be changed, and he was not ready to die at forty-five, he meant to go on, he had to, and how was he supposed to make a life with a woman who had turned into a ghost, or a sleepwalker, who wasn't really here. I didn't care, that was all I felt. I remember his voice almost crying and almost shouting at me. Don't you think it's terrible to declare bankruptcy after eighteen years of marriage? No. The most terrible had happened, the death of an eight-year-old boy from leukaemia. What else was terrible after that?

I asked Richard to sell the farm as I would never come here again, and attend to all the other arrangements. Of course he should live, he is a successful lawyer absorbed in his work. I'll find something to do, I said, but all I want for now is to be left alone.

People say such crazy things, intended as comfort. You have the happy years to remember, they say. No one would urge a starving man to remember the fine big meals he'd had in the past. I don't understand what is expected of me. It's as if there was a fixed ration of grief and when you've used that up, you are obliged to be cheerful and act as if nothing had happened, life is back to normal again. If you grieve too much, they call in the doctors and there's the hospital, grief is a sickness, you must be cured. The funny part was all the anxious consoling words about our divorce. I was permitted an extra ration of grief when I felt nothing.

Like everyone else, Marian was distressed by the divorce. My college room-mate, always a kind bossy girl who knew exactly what to do next. She married a young English barrister about the same time I married Richard, and by now her husband is important in politics and Marian is gloriously active in London and Wiltshire being the perfect wife for a British M.P. Last spring, Marian wrote that a change would do me good. Why not move to London for a while? Why not? Anyway my departure relieved poor Richard who had a bad conscience for no reason. It's not his fault, nor even mine, if I'm queer and can't forget the face of my little boy, if I can't stop longing for my father and mother just because they're dead.

Marian took over my life, she's an organizer, a planner, she believes there's an answer to everything. She found a pleasant furnished flat and introduced me to her friends and to charity jobs, looking after lonely poor old women three afternoons a week and shoving a book trolley through hospital wards two afternoons a week. Marian thinks it noble of me to give up all my afternoons, not knowing that I'm a fraud, I have nothing to give.

Marian's answer to everything is to keep busy and no doubt she's right. If you're busy busy busy you haven't much room to think of the past and the future. My future is time, years of it, like this. I don't know any answers so I accepted Marian's: all you have to do is fill fourteen hours a day and never wonder why. When I felt sick of acting like a nice cheerful woman, I hid in my flat and doped myself on reading and the TV and nobody asked questions, I was left alone. I was getting on pretty well, I was managing, but I couldn't face Christmas.

It's just a day, it has to pass, the loudspeaker carols don't blare on forever, besides I must get used to living through Christmas. Instead I walked around London in the winter darkness thinking: there's no place to go. No one. Then I heard myself saying it out loud. A woman with an armload of parcels in Christmas wrappings stared at me. I began to run.

Soon it will be the blue hour that doesn't last an hour. Time to switch on the lamp by my bed. It would be stupid to lie in the dark trying to get it all straight. I woke last night in the dark, when the sleeping pills wore off, and was terrified, not knowing where I was or how or why. Absurd that even turning on the light, the smallest decision, requires will. Oh God why am I so thirsty? Tired. From what? Lying on a bed. I have no right to be tired.

The hotel called a doctor. I had a confused impression that my room was full of peering people, maids, waiters, the doctor, a woman who turned out to be the housekeeper. The doctor had cool hands and prodded me everywhere and took my head in his hands, twisting it. He kept asking, does this hurt? He studied my eyes with a pencil torch. He said a very serious shock, you're incredibly lucky not to, complete rest, aspirin, valium and sleeping pills. I didn't feel dazed, only exhausted. I needed to ask

him something. The people seemed to crowd and stare. I
said I wanted to see him alone. He said 'What?' and leaned
closer so I realized I was whispering. I didn't have any
voice which was peculiar and silly, why should my voice
fail? He waved the people out and I asked him what I had
to know. He frowned, looking annoyed or puzzled, and
said, 'Yes, of course.' As if it was an absurd question. After
that, the housekeeper, Miss Grant, came in several
times.

She is stocky with short stiff grey hair and tense eyes. She
must be worried, harassed, so much to remember and
supervise in this large hotel. The African waiters and maids
are young, with laughing faces. Towels and ashtrays and
wastebaskets can't be vital matters to them so Miss Grant
has to remember. She is very kind. 'Are you all right, dear?
Is there anything you want?' She ordered food that I didn't
want and cold drinks, fruit juices and iced tea and thermos
ice jugs that I did. She opened the door with her key and let
in the waiter, she told the maid to be quick and not make
any noise to disturb me.

And was sorry for me, constantly sorry for me. 'You
poor dear, so wretched for you on your holiday.' As soon
as I understood that sympathy, I couldn't stand it. Aside
from being wrong, I was afraid I might start feeling sorry
for myself and then I'd hate myself and nothing would
ever get straight in my mind. It would be wicked if I
offended Miss Grant, though I put it as unnecessary to
visit me any more since she has so much work and I am
quite all right now, I'd ring for whatever I needed, but I
really meant leave me alone, you're a danger to me. She
couldn't have guessed that. No, she seemed relieved; of
course she is overworked and I am another worrying
responsibility. She said, 'Are you sure, dear?' I am trying
to become sure, that is what I am doing.

Let's see. I can ring room service and wedge open the
door with a book and cover myself with the sheet so I
won't have to find my dressing gown or stand around
while the waiter is here. Room service? How prompt they

are. Right away Madam. The book. All ready. I'll close my
eyes and rest until the waiter arrives.

She slept instantly. All day, unaware, she slid into and out
of these lapses of consciousness. She woke to see a tall
young black waiter, tray in hand, by her bedside.
    'You better, Memsaab?' A wide smile, uneasy.
    'Yes thank you.'
    But he couldn't figure out what to do with the tray. She
couldn't figure out what to do with the tray. He stood there,
holding it with one hand, looking at her flat on the bed
while she looked at him. She thought: I don't know what
to do. I'm going to cry because I don't know what to do.
I can't tell him, I can't think. I'm going to cry over a tray,
not knowing where to put it. I'm going to cry over a tray
and I can't stop. He must go. Tell him to go. Tell him to
stop standing there. Don't look at me. He must go. I can't
help it, I can't stop, I can't.
    The waiter turned and laid the tray on the long empty
dressing table. He brought the square stool, padded in
imitation white leather, to the bed. He deposited the tray
on the stool and straightened up, beaming. A triumph of
intelligence and competence. She was breathing with
difficulty through a tight throat, against pressure in her
chest.
    'I come later, Memsaab?'
    'No thank you. Tomorrow.'
    Her voice was a whisper again. Draught from the open
balcony slammed the door hard behind the waiter. She lay,
unmoving, and got her breath back, refusing to think of
that insane panic over a tray. Iced tea filled a parched
hollow, even inside her head felt cooler. She munched small
chicken sandwiches, determined to eat them all.

I was hungry. I have hardly eaten these days. I must eat
regularly and tomorrow I'll get up and go on the beach.
Lying here and not eating is ridiculous. My head is simply
bruised and bruises take time to heal or evaporate or

whatever bruises do. In a few days I'll be quite all right and then I'll leave. The fever tree assistant manager will fix everything. This is ridiculous, lying in bed, weak from hunger.

That's what I needed, just a little food. I'm much better, I'll finish now, I'll get it all clear. But what baffles me is the advertisements on the back page of *The Times*. Holiday in the Sunny Caribbean. A Villa on Glamorous Corfu. Ski in Andorra. Cruise to the Canary Islands. Cheap Flights to Johannesburg, Singapore, Hongkong. That page fascinated me from my very first day in London. Births and deaths on the left, then all the personal ads, people wanting to sell pianos or sending mysterious messages to each other, and even announcements about how much money the lately deceased had left behind and would their nearest kin apply to the Treasury. The right-hand columns are travel bargains.

I read that page every morning, it was like a very odd fascinating gossip column, reading about unknown people being born and dying, and places I'd never been nor wanted to be. So why, one morning, did I get the idea of going on a trip alone, and staying in a hotel alone which I've never done, and on a continent I've never dreamed of seeing? What drove me to this lunatic scheme? I told myself that I was yearning for hot sun, I needed a change from the dismal wet grey London winter.

Agnes Markham asked me for Christmas dinner. The Denbeighs invited me to stay in Dorset. New friends, inherited from Marian. And of course Marian, looking worried, begged me to come down to Wiltshire. I am lucky to have kind friends. I know that, I'm always grateful, I don't earn the kindness by being clever or amusing or interesting. I'm an extra woman. At Christmas, family people are specially sorry for extra people. They think they can take you into their home and make you feel you belong in their family. They don't understand this is the most dreadful of all. They don't understand that you cannot bear it. I have learned how to be an extra woman if no one fusses, if I am left alone to manage the way I have learned. Perhaps other extra people are happy to be asked to join in someone else's Christmas.

And I am afraid of being a burden, of people saying to each other, 'Poor Diana, she's alone, we must do something about Diana.' On the worst days, I imagine voices talking about me with pity, and also boredom. A duty, a burden. I fear that. But even more I fear I will not always be able to behave properly. Cheerfully. It is essential to behave cheerfully.

I lied to everyone, saying more or less the same thing. 'How lovely, thank you so much, what fun it would be, but I'm meeting American chums in Switzerland, ski-ing for a few weeks.' Nobody could check on this harmless lie and nobody would. The English don't pry, that's one of their best points. Marian was delighted, I could see she felt I'd cheered up wonderfully if I was planning to go off on a ski party. I didn't want to speak of Africa, explanations, comments, excitement. Switzerland is usual but it would sound very eccentric to say I'd read an advertisement on the back page of *The Times* and was launching myself alone into the blue. I meant to sneak off quietly and come back quietly. No one knows where I am. I am lying on a bed in a luxury hotel by the Indian Ocean and I don't understand why.

But I do understand. Sun was an excuse. I was swamped in loneliness, drowning, it gets worse all the time, not better the way people tell you. I ran away as far as I could, running from everyone and everything that reminds me of Christmas when I had a child and a family. I knew it would be easier alone in a place so strange that I'd be a stranger to myself. Why do I have to go on acting like a normal woman? 'Adjusted' is the word. Why do I have to get up and wash and work at my time-filling jobs and shop for food and telephone about repairing the fridge or the TV and buy clothes and pay bills and chat with friends and smile and pretend to care when I don't care about anything on earth? Why can't I scream and scream and scream I hate it all, I don't want to be here, I want to die, *leave me alone*.

No. NO. Peering people. Doctors. The hospital. Be quiet. Be orderly. Calm. Now I have to start again, I've made it harder for myself. Marian will be astonished when I tell her how I planned my trip and kept it as a surprise for when I got back. The night flight was appalling, wedged between two men, cramped, I was so worn out that Nairobi was just blinding sun and the smell of the warm wind and a blank wait in the airport. Another plane, yellow empty land, blue grey hills, too tired to look, and the airport here, jungle trees, terribly hot, the hotel car, the hotel room and sleep.

Then it worked better than I'd dared imagine. I didn't mind being a lone woman, the hotel didn't make me nervous, I was invisible anyway. I'm the invisible age, too old for flirtations around the pool, too young to be motherly, a nice old lady that people talk to. It was fine, wasn't it, and so clever to have thought of this, and so energetic to pull it off.

One morning I decided to make a short trip to see some birds I'd heard about and lunch at another smaller hotel. I felt the car plunging into the ditch, a split second, not enough time to think, and I was knocked unconscious. When I came to I was in the passenger seat covered with dust and dry grass. Facing back the way I'd come which was impossible but it seems the car turned over on its top and then rolled back on its wheels. Someone told the police and they told me. The windscreen didn't shatter. A freak accident. There are millions of road accidents every year all over the world. I never had an accident before but millions of people have an accident the first time. It was just another road accident. That's all it was. That's absolutely all it was and now I've got it straight and tomorrow I'll talk to the assistant manager about a plane to London.

The two African policemen wore grey uniform shirts and shorts and long black knee socks and black boots and they were very kind, driving me back in their Landrover, and they saw my filthy dress, my hair half down, my general condition I suppose, and said very kindly, don't worry, everything's all right, you just relax. Everything's all right. I started to laugh, my face cracked across the middle, and they said now now there's nothing to cry about and I thought how weird that laughing looks like crying in Africa.

Stop, please stop, please, stop, *stop!* What? Am I talking out loud again? That sound, I can't bear it, that sound like a sick kitten mewing. No, no, it's not here, it's all right, there's only the sea. I fell asleep. I had a dream, very bad, but I don't remember it. I heard the sound in my sleep. So hot, stifling, what's the matter with the wind? My pillow's soaking and my nightgown. Fell asleep, forgot to turn on the light, stupid. Turn on the light; what time is it? Now my watch isn't working. Maybe it's midnight, that would be a piece of luck, the night half gone. If I'm always going to hear that sound in my sleep, I'll go mad. Be quiet. Listen to the sea.

Slap, thud, pause, slap, thud, pause. Small waves, the ocean held back by the reef. The long shallow beach, white sand churned into the small waves, but the water is transparent. You can see the bottom as you wade in, and warm as a bath until you swim far out and then it's cool and silky. I never saw or felt such water; bliss. There's no wind at all and the insects are quiet. Do they go to sleep at night? Is that possible? They're always here, unseen, never still; I imagine hundreds of millions of them, making a high crackling buzzing whine all over Africa.

I could go out on the balcony, it would be cooler there. But the truth is the night sky frightens me, it's too big with more stars than anywhere else, enormous and far away and silent. I don't think people were meant to live on this huge empty land under this huge sky. I feel I'm lost, nowhere, nothing to hold to, the truth is it's terrifying to be alone beneath that enormous beautiful black sky.

What am I going to do, lie here bathed in sweat, and

wait for morning? And count over the different pains in my body and have a nice slobbering cry because I hurt so much? I wish I were like Marian. She'd make a plan. She'd know what to do next.

'May I come in, Mrs Jamieson?'

This is the limit. Why can anyone get a key to open my door?

'Who is it?'

'Dr Burke. May I come in?'

The young doctor, with red hair and a dark beard, the one the hotel sent for. He ought to shave that beard; perhaps he wears it to look older.

'What time is it, Dr Burke?'

'Nearly seven. I thought I'd pop in on my way home to see how you're getting on. Miss Grant reported at noon that you were resting nicely. That's the best treatment. You had a mammoth shake-up yesterday.'

'*Yesterday?* How long have I been here?'

'In Kenya?'

'No, no, here, now, in bed.'

'Why, since yesterday afternoon.'

'I thought I'd been here for days, two or three days.'

'There's nothing like a big bang on the head to muddle one. How does your head feel?'

I'll tell you how it feels. Right now it feels as if steel clamps were fastened on my head above my ears, and a loop of steel joined them across the back of my skull, low down, and the clamps and the loop are being tightened and tightened until they'll squeeze my head so the top bursts open. This is brand new, I didn't know there was such a style of headache.

'Not too bad.'

'And the bruises?'

Any movement hurts. However I lie hurts. I feel as if I'd been beaten all over with a bicycle chain. That's how the bruises are. 'A bit stiff. What's happened to the wind?'

'It always drops at sunset and sunrise. Hadn't you noticed? This is the hottest time of year, the monsoon's changing. Shall I close the balcony door and turn on the air-conditioner?'

'Please, no.' I want to hear the sea, it keeps out that other sound. Now thermometer and pulse and the doctor look on his face, studying, puzzling, calculating. There's something I have to ask him, and I dread the words. He's got his pencil torch, to peer at my eyes.

'Dr Burke.' My voice has failed again, it comes out as a whisper. I seem to have no control over my voice. 'Can an unconscious body make a sound?'

'Yes, of course, Mrs Jamieson. You asked that yesterday.'

So it wasn't pain. Thank God it wasn't pain.

'I heard a sound after the accident. Like . . . like a whimper.'

He's watching, he knows that's a lie, but I can't say how it really was, I can't speak.

'Yes, I guessed something of the sort. Not a whimper. What you heard was the last automatic exhalation of air from the lungs.'

My eyes feel they're being burned. I try not to understand what he's said. Because then it's true, what I didn't know or didn't dare to know. Afterwards, sitting in the car in the ditch with the sun beating down, the road was empty. The little body on the road, nearer to the right than the middle, and the sun and that sound in the silence. I could not move and there was dust over my eyes, or in the air, I saw through a haze. Africans came from nowhere, from the empty land, and lined the road close to the child's body, but none stepped out on to the road. Women wailed, a wild up and down wailing that didn't break the silence. No one came near me. I was miles away, not there or anywhere. Nothing happened; nothing changed. I thought I would stay there always, alone with the little curled-up body.

The police spoke to me but I couldn't answer. I didn't watch what they were doing, I closed my eyes and saw the same thing: the empty road and the child and me, alone. The police helped me into their Landrover; in back were children, I didn't see them but I knew there were children

and on the floor something, a bundle. I didn't look or hear.
Everything was very slow, under the sun, the light and
heat of the sun were part of it and it would never end. I was
a an office on a chair by a desk and a young black policeman was talking but I don't know what he said. He took
my bag which he must have found in the car and copied
things from my passport and driver's licence.

I was trying to explain to myself what happened but I
couldn't because what happened was not believable. I don't
know if I was talking to myself or out loud. The same
words went on, over and over, in my mind. I was driving
on the left the way you do in this country and a child ran
out from the left from nowhere and I swerved as hard as I
could to the right to get away from him and I heard a soft
plop, like a cloth flapping against the car behind me, and
I saw the ditch and then I saw nothing until.

The policeman took my arm to move me from the chair
and led me to the Landrover and helped me in and it was
all very slow, with the sun beating down, but I didn't feel
pain in my head or body and I didn't see anything except
the empty road and the child and I didn't hear anything
except that sound. But I must have known he was dead only
I didn't ask and no one told me. Now I know he is dead,
a beautiful little brown boy, not black, dark brown, six
years old I think, naked to the waist, running like a deer,
running faster than I could get away from him.

'But I didn't run over him. I know that. I swear I didn't
run over him. How can he be dead?'

'Apparently he slammed head-on against the rear fender
of your car. Broke his neck instantly. He can't have seen
anything or known anything, otherwise he'd have stopped.
You mustn't think of it, Mrs Jamieson. It wasn't in any way
your fault.'

'If I'd pulled the wheel one second faster.'

'From what the police say, impossible in that distance.
Mrs Jamieson, listen to me. You did all anyone could do
and more than most would. It's a miracle your neck wasn't
broken too.'

'I'm alive. And he's dead. A child.'

'You don't know this country, Mrs Jamieson, and I do. I was born here. Believe me, if the Africans out there thought it was your fault they'd have torn you apart before the police got to you, and disappeared back into the bush. And I might add the police wouldn't have been all that amiable.'

'He's dead.'

'And so are any number of children every day of the week on the roads here, and even in the towns. They rush out without looking and get killed. It's the parents' fault. They don't teach their children, they don't train them, they don't keep track of them. They're ignorant and irresponsible. They're entirely to blame for this sort of needless accident.'

'The mother? Blame the mother?'

'Yes indeed. No one else. It's her duty to explain to her children about traffic. Yours wasn't the first car ever to pass on that road. They've had years to learn and they don't bother. Children have no business playing alongside a highway. The mother is at fault. It happens all the time and still they don't look after their children properly.'

He's insane. I don't want him near me. *Blame the mother?* A woman from a poor mud village. What does he know about the mother? I know. I know she's looking at her child and saying *why*, screaming *why*, until there's nothing else in the world but that, why, *why* is my child dead. She'll hold his body in her arms and try to make it come back to life and then she'll start to die too, and she'll go on dying and she'll never remember when he was beautiful and ran like a deer, she'll only remember him as he looked dead. She'll remember that always, she'll have lost all the happiness of him because she can't forget the last, the worst.

'Mrs Jamieson, please stop crying. You must, really. You're tormenting yourself and making yourself ill. It isn't doing your head any good. You want to get well and go home, don't you? I'm giving you a stronger sedative for tonight and I want you to swallow these pills now. I'll be back in the morning.'

Leave me alone. Go away. Don't talk to me. How can you blame the mother, you're insane, you're inhuman, you don't understand anything. All right, I'll swallow the pills, I don't care what I do, only go away.

'Goodnight, Mrs Jamieson. Take these capsules later. You must get a good night's rest. You'll feel better in the morning. You're still badly shocked but I can assure you there's nothing wrong, no damage that won't heal naturally.'

No damage. Bruises and a headache. And knowing that if I'd been one second faster, the one second when I saw the child directly in front of me, the stunned one second when I shouted NO, the paralysed one second of horror. Why couldn't I have died? Always someone else, but not me. Maybe wherever I go someone will die. Maybe I bring death.

'You've had a nice nap, dear?'

Everyone has a key. Anyone can come into my room. As long as I lie here I can't stop them. It's Miss Grant, I thought she understood I wanted to be left alone.

'Dr Burke told me you were hot and uncomfortable. Shall we freshen up a bit? Could you take a shower while I change your bed? Here, let me give you a hand.'

I feel dull and heavy. It's too much trouble to argue. She's treating me the way they do in hospital, as if you're frail and half-witted. Ah yes, the shower is nice, I'd like to stand here under the cool water until morning.

'I found a clean nightdress. Is that all right, dear? We'll have this one laundered and ready tomorrow. Now your bed's all fixed. There you are. Dr Burke says you don't like air-conditioning. Neither do I. The wind's coming up again, it'll soon be nice and cool.'

She is kind and it's much better like this, in dry smooth sheets. If I could read, time would pass quicker. This day has lasted several days already.

'May I sit down a minute, dear?'

'Yes of course, Miss Grant. Thank you for making my bed.'

She seems nervous, or is that the way she always is, the strain of her job.

'Mrs Jamieson, Dr Burke thinks it would be better if you went to Nairobi as soon as you feel able to move.'

'Nairobi? What for? I'll fly back to London.'

'Well, there may be a delay. And Dr Burke thinks Nairobi would be better, where your Embassy is, so they can look after you.'

'The Embassy? Why should the Embassy be expected to?'

'Oh they will. We've spoken to the Duty Officer. He's very nice. He suggested it might be a good thing if some relative came out to keep you company. We could send a cable or telephone for you.'

What is she talking about? She doesn't make sense.

'Miss Grant, I'm filled with some dope Dr Burke gave me so my brain isn't working. I don't follow you. I'm a grown woman, I'll simply get on a plane and fly back to London. All this about Embassies and relatives is ridiculous.'

'You see the point is, dear, you can't right away. The police have your passport. Don't worry, no one's going to charge you with anything. But there are formalities, paperwork, and I'm afraid Africans are frightfully slow.'

The police?

'Really don't worry, Mrs Jamieson. The police spoke to Mr Hammond yesterday. He's our assistant manager. The manager, Mr Burckhardt from Switzerland, is in Nairobi for a meeting. The police explained to Mr Hammond what happened and they were very sympathetic about you. But Africans love paperwork and they're not much good at it. It's such an awful stupid story.'

'What is?'

'According to the police, the boy's sisters were in the ditch on the other side of the road.'

'There wasn't anyone anywhere. And I didn't see any ditches.'

'No, you wouldn't, they're so overgrown. Old drainage ditches. It looks as if the bush grows right up to the tarmac. But they're quite deep, well, you know that, you poor dear. Naturally you wouldn't see children down below the road level, hidden in that long grass. Anyway the two girls called to their brother to run across quick before the car came.'

'There weren't any other cars, ahead of me or behind.'

'I know, that's what makes it so stupid. The boy only had to wait a second and you'd have passed and the road was clear. But evidently he heard his sisters and just jumped up and ran without looking.'

I cannot endure it. I cannot. It's as if there was some crazy cruel plan, tied to one second in time, for no reason, for nothing. It could just as easily not have happened. But it did, that will never change. It did.

'Are you all right, Mrs Jamieson?'

'The sisters, where are they?'

'At home, I suppose. The police said they deserved a good beating. They were older, they didn't have to be so stupid.'

I hope they're not old enough to understand. I hope they can forget. Because if they were somewhere in the ditch, they'd have seen what I didn't, the instant when the boy and the car, and they'd have heard that sound. I don't know how long I was unconscious so I don't know how long that sound went on. I heard it twice. Or three times? I'll never be able to forget it. But no one was there, no one on the road. Then they were hiding. Afraid. Afraid of death that came when they were only playing.

'Mrs Jamieson, here, have a drink of water, please. I shouldn't have told you all this. You look terribly pale. My dear, it's been a dreadful shock for you but it's different for these people. They have so many children, one a year, they die as easily as they're born and the women just go on making more. They don't feel about life the way we do.'

They're trying to tell me a black woman doesn't love her children. A woman loves her child, I know, I'm the one who knows. Nobody understands anything except that black woman, that mother, and me. We're the only ones who know.

'If the police want to arrest me, I'll stay here.'

'Mrs Jamieson! Don't say such a thing! There's no question of arrest, merely delay. And you'd be much happier with someone to keep you company. Your husband perhaps?'

'I haven't got a husband.' She looks scandalized, poor plain Miss Grant, I want to laugh. I shouldn't laugh, there's nothing to laugh about but I can't help it. Now she looks frightened. Why? Does she think Richard's dead too and I'm laughing? Oh God what a mess, I'll have to explain, more talk, I'm too tired to talk.

'It's all right, Miss Grant, really, he's not dead. He's fine, really. He's married again to a much younger woman and she's pregnant so he'll have another son. People thought I was upset about the divorce but I wasn't. Honestly. There wasn't anything left to be married for.'

Why on earth is she patting my hand and saying, 'There, there.' I've got hiccups from laughing. Her face was so funny at first but it isn't now. I don't want to be a nuisance, she's an overworked middle-aged woman and it's night and she ought to be in her own room with her shoes off.

'Miss Grant, you've been working all day. You needn't stay here. You must be tired.'

'No dear, I'd rather stay with you a while. Could you eat something?'

'No thank you.'

'How about ice cream? And a pitcher of fruit juice? They make a very nice mixture of fresh pineapple and lime and a little mango.'

'That sounds lovely. And then you can go, I'll be all right.'

Dial 4 for room service. Miss Grant speaks Swahili and her voice is brisk and stern, talking to Africans.

'Now then, Mrs Jamieson, let's see who could come out and be with you. Perhaps your mother?'

'My mother is dead. Is your mother alive?'

'No.'

She doesn't know about being a mother, but she knows about being without a mother. It's natural, it's inevitable, parents die before their children, it happens to everyone. If something happens to everyone it's not special and you mustn't show what you feel because you embarrass others, you're a grown woman, not a defenceless child. Long ago, people wore mourning for a year. They were allowed a year at least. But we go faster, we have no time to mourn, mourning is shameful.

All your life there is someone to talk to and be heard. One person is never indifferent; one person is always there and looks at you as no one else ever can; you are not alone. Richard said we were unusually close, my mother and I, but Diana you knew it had to happen one day. Oh yes I knew, it was the only thing I feared, I feared it from childhood. Knowing something will happen does not prepare you for how it is when it actually happens.

I understood I should not speak of this and besides the one person I could tell was her, and she was dead. The roof and the walls and the warmth inside are gone. It's up to you, there's no one between you and all the space, all the space of the world. A husband is a man of your own age, he has his own fears and needs and loneliness, and he can't hear everything, even when you don't speak. Richard disliked his mother and his father died when he was a boy. Richard tried not to be impatient with me but he wanted me to hurry and get used to the fact that I would never see her again. Not even in dreams. My dreams are filled with strangers.

But Andy was there, my son Andrew, six years old and discovering each day as if it were a new country. I knew that though I had lost my safety I must provide the same safety for him. That's the order of life, obviously. You don't tell a child that you are homesick and heartsick and weak, you tell a child comforting lies for both of you, and you try to become yourself the necessary roof and walls. I am glad my mother did not see Andy die.

'Did you love your mother, Miss Grant?'

'Yes.'

For a moment, we look at each other, not like a responsible housekeeper and a problem tourist, but like two extra women. Someone banged on the door.

Miss Grant says crossly, 'That idiot, Juma.' The moment is over. I want Miss Grant to go, I can't talk any longer. The same young waiter comes in but his face is different, not lit up by the wide grin that I remember, and he seems even more awkward with the tray. Miss Grant snaps at him in Swahili and he shuffles to the dressing table stool and brings it, with the tray, to my bed. Miss Grant must have put the used tray outside. More Swahili and he is gone, letting the door slam. Miss Grant makes a little annoyed click and shakes her head.

'Juma? Is that his name? He was here before. He seems very friendly and obliging.'

'He's not bright but he's a nice enough boy, though he was better when he began here, last year. Now he keeps bad company, one of the handymen, a coast Arab, a real trouble-maker, but the union loves trouble-makers so we daren't sack him. Oh well, anyway I'm pleased that Juma's been giving you decent service. They've sent three kinds of ice cream. I recommend the coffee, if you like that flavour.'

I mean to eat so she will be reassured and leave me. I pull myself up to a sitting position and let out a snivelly moan before I can stop it. Moving my head suddenly tightened that clamp arrangement.

Miss Grant cries, 'You're in pain. It's too miserable for you.'

And I say angrily, 'I am not. Nothing has happened to me. Can't you see? No bones broken, no vital organs crushed, nothing, nothing, nothing.'

In silence, but hurt, Miss Grant hands me a glass bowl of coffee ice cream. She only intends to be kind and has again thought of the helpful gesture. The ice cream is cold in my mouth, cold going down my throat, the coldness soothes my damned head. I am ashamed to feel pain, I have no right. I eat ice cream and try to think of a way to apologize to Miss Grant but I can't concentrate and find the words.

'All I ever wanted was what the African women have, a baby every year. That's all I ever really wanted.' I don't know whether I was thinking that or saying it out loud. Either Dr Burke's pills or the bang on my head are making me worse, more confused. I must have been thinking it because Miss Grant says nothing, though she observes me warily, but perhaps that is due to my rudeness. Rudeness is a great offence to the English, another point in their favour.

'This is delicious, Miss Grant. I'll finish it slowly and drink the fruit juice but please don't wait. You've done everything for me. I'm very grateful and you must go now, you need your rest too.'

'Are you sure, dear?'

'Quite sure.' Poor creature, what a burden I've been. Why did she come in the first place when I told her I was all right yesterday, no, today, but hours and hours and hours ago. She has left a glass filled with fruit juice and ice cubes so I won't have to lift the pitcher. Considerate Miss Grant. The stuff is too sweet, I'll suck the ice cubes and plod on with the ice cream and then I'll go to the bathroom and brush my teeth and swallow these new red and green capsules and get rid of this horrible day.

It's true about only always wanting what African women have, a baby each year. Through my whole childhood, I told myself a long continuous story about Diana and her six babies. I invented those six when I was practically a baby myself. An only child is supposed to crave brothers and sisters, but not me, I was perfectly happy having my parents to myself and my own six babies, three boys and three girls, roly-poly butter balls all the same age, dressed alike in bright coloured caps and mittens and zip-up woolly suits. I played with them, gave them baths, fed them and instructed them in good behaviour. Since I didn't know how babies were made, there was no provision for a Daddy. Besides I had the best Daddy in the world already, he served for my babies too.

When I got the hang of things, my six babies changed into the most ordinary female dream. I would grow up and marry a gentle good man and have four children, one each year, and live happily ever after. My friends at school weren't interested in babies and in college everyone was thinking of some sort of career, thinking and worrying. I had no worries, I knew exactly what I wanted and never doubted I would get it; I never really abandoned my childhood fantasy.

In due course, as expected, with no effort on my part, the gentle good man appeared and we fell in love and married. All I had to do was wait for the tumbling laughing babies. Instead of them, I had miscarriages. Three. They would have broken my heart except for my mother. I couldn't have survived without her. The great hope and then the failure and hope lost in a hospital bed, sick in my body and my mind, and all the doctors I consulted and the waiting to try again and fail again. She knew I had to have a child, she gave me courage, telling me it had been just as difficult for her, she promised I would succeed with patience. How I needed her and how I leaned on her. And on the loving steadiness of my father. He understood too. Poor Richard. But Richard had his work, he had a meaning for his life and for me there was only one.

With patience for seven years, and seven months in bed and a Caesarian, I got Andy. My first born and my last, the doctors said, and I didn't mind at all. Thirty-two isn't exactly a young mother but I felt something I'd never known in my life before. I think it was joy, I didn't know anyone could feel such rejoicing. From the moment I saw my son. He was beautiful and perfect, he was everything I wanted. I couldn't have loved another child as much, it was right to have only Andy. And I thought now it's come true at last and we'll live happily ever after.

Why not? Why shouldn't we? What did I know of unhappiness except for three miscarriages? I didn't spend all the time between those failures in abject gloom. In between times, Richard and I enjoyed ourselves like any lucky young married couple. Christmas and summer at Derry Bridge with my father and mother were always heaven. Why not expect to live happily ever after if you've been as happy as a cabbage all your life aside from three temporary setbacks. And I was happy when I had my son in a way I can no longer believe or remember. I've often wondered if I am being punished because I had too much, when life is so terrible for millions upon millions of people. But punished by whom? And is happiness a sin?

October is a beautiful month, the red and yellow leaves and the special clean blue of the sky, but it's sad too, the beautiful ending of the year. I've always wanted to hold the days back in October, make them stretch, before November and winter set in. November is an ugly month. Ugly, ugly, hated. On weekends that October, Andy and I used to play explorers in the woods at Derry Bridge, or on our bikes on the dirt back roads, meeting imaginary animals, climbing trees to spy out unknown territory, but Andy tired quickly which he'd never done. I worried and he loathed being worried over and anyway I had trained myself since his infancy not to be a smothering Mum. He'd become a great reader and I thought perhaps he was in one of the many mysterious phases of growing, and books seemed more manly than make-believe games with Mummy.

Then one morning in New York my little boy crept into my bed and said he felt sick, he had a sore throat, it hurt to swallow. I took his temperature, 103, and called the doctor in panic. The doctor came within an hour and didn't do much that I could see. He checked Andy's temperature, gently poked places below his waist, studied his skin and inside his mouth, and telephoned for an ambulance. They knew right away, though they made all the tests before they told me. My brain froze. I heard but could not believe or accept the words. Acute leukaemia on a fulminating course. Those words. From nowhere, from nothing, for no reason.

I had a bed in Andy's hospital room, I never left him, I sat beside him and watched while he shook with chills and poured sweat as the fever rose and dropped and always rose again. I could never take him in my arms, that was my torment, I felt him so alone, I wanted desperately to hold him so he would know I was close, but the pain in his bones had started and the slightest pressure on his chest and ribs caused him anguish. I could only hold his hand, kiss his hands, kiss his forehead lightly lightly, I felt everything in him was breaking. Needles in his arms, transfusions, antibiotics; he cried from all the different pains, he vomited and cried. He cried weakly, hopelessly. He couldn't understand what had happened to him of course. He must have thought no one heard his weeping because no one came to save him.

Was consciousness worse than delirium? How can I know? Burning with fever, my little boy raved in fear about animals which he'd always loved. He had a mission in life already; when he grew up he planned to take the animals in Central Park Zoo back to their homes where they belonged so they could be free and happy among their relatives. Delirious from fever, he saw his friends, the animals, as monsters threatening him. It was too cruel that he should lose his friends.

When his temperature dropped and his mind cleared, he would beg me to make this agony stop. His voice always fainter, Mummy make it stop. And then he gave up, I had failed him. His eyes were dark and despairing; I had failed him. I wanted him to die, to escape the murderous fever and pain in his child's bones, I sat by him day and night, helpless, watching him die, in nineteen days, in November. His face wasn't his face, wasted, old and lonely. Because I couldn't make it stop, I couldn't take the pain for myself, he suffered alone. There was nothing left of Andy that was like him except his shaggy yellow hair. I held his little wrecked body in my arms and died too. I went away into the darkness where Andy had gone.

Why did they give me shock treatment and force me to come back when there was nothing to come back to except the memory of his face, his eyes, begging me. It is useless to weep though it goes on all the time, like internal bleeding; she'll learn that too, that other woman, that African mother. She'll hate me as I hate the disease that took Andy from me and she'll never know how gladly I'd have died instead.

The land was grey and flat and wide, nothing grew on the hard ash-coloured ground. The road was a lighter grey, narrow, cutting straight through the vast distance of the land to the horizon. The sky was grey too, paler than the road. There was no movement anywhere, the air silent. Far away at first, then nearer, she saw grey figures on the road. She did not move, nor did they, yet they grew in size so that she recognized them. Her throat ached with the need to cry out, she felt the tears on her cheeks, but she could not speak or move.

Her mother was bending over a little curled-up body on the grey road. The body looked shapeless, a small bundle of grey rags. Her mother's face was gaunt, shrunken, not her face in life, her face in death. Her eyes, which had been a shining cornflower blue, were black and dull. She did not touch the child's body. She was dressed in rags with her arms showing stick-thin through the dirty grey cloth. She was on her knees, staring dry-eyed at the bundle on the road.

The child's face was hidden, the only colour in the greyness of the world was his shaggy yellow hair. Softly, from somewhere inside the little hump of rags, a sound came out, a single mewing sound like a sick kitten, a hurt kitten. It came again louder. Her mother did not touch the child, or hear, her mother's face was unchanged, fixed in exhaustion and defeat. The sound came again and now louder and louder, a cry of fatal pain, an agonized cry for help.

She struggled to move, she had to run to them, she wrenched and tore against some unseen force that held her, she tried to scream to stop the sound, to scream for them to wait, stop, wait, *Mother help him*, I am coming, I am coming to you, only wait! Shouting, sobbing, but could not move . . .

'Wake, Memsaab! You wake! No sleep!' A hot damp hand pushed her shoulder. She looked up, through half closed eyes, stunned by the dream and barbiturates, dazzled by the lamplight, to see the face of the young waiter close to her. She smelled him, a foul heavy odour of sweat. She saw the road and her mother and the child, helpless, and understood the waiter was holding her so she could not run to them. She shrank away from him, from his red-veined eyes, and his black sweating face, she had to get away from him and run.

Ali thought of this. Ali was born in Mombasa, a sharp city boy, not an ignorant bush fellow. Ali made him say it four times so he would remember. Get the key from the night houseboy on the floor below. Tell him you have to pick up a tray. Not *her* tray, *a* tray. Tell the woman you are the cousin of the boy's father. She killed the boy. She must give you one thousand shillings for the father. She is rich. But Ali did not say the woman would be twisting like a snake on her bed and crying strange words and that her eyes would look as if she was crazy from bhang.

'I am cousin of father of that boy. You kill that boy. You give one thousand shillings for father.' He was whispering but the whisper shocked him, it was as loud as the steam whistle at the cement factory. He stank of fear, he couldn't remember whether Ali said one thousand or ten thousand. It was not easy, as Ali said. It was bad. She would call him a liar and Memsaab Grant would come and know he was lying. The police. He wanted to run from this room but was too full of fear. And the woman watched him with those crazy eyes, she wouldn't let him go, she was watching him.

'You give me money. Ten thousand shillings. You kill that boy.'

'No!' She slipped her shoulder free of his hand and rolled off the bed, crouching on the other side by the open balcony door.

He could not remember how to say the words Ali told him, father, cousin, shillings, only 'You kill that boy.'

She was crying the strange words of her sleep. 'No, I didn't! Mother knows, she knows, *don't run wait Andy!* I didn't, I didn't!'

They would hear her, they would all come, and the police would beat him until he was covered with blood. He had to stop her, sweat poured from his face, from his armpits, his clothes were wet and cold, he was wild with fear. He had forgotten all the other words, he moved around the bed, to reach her, to stop her making that bad bad noise, whispering insanely, 'You kill that boy, you kill that boy.'

The woman screamed 'NO!', and ran so fast he barely saw her in the dim light, ran out to the balcony, ran. Far below, in that same instant he heard something, nothing, not as much as the sound of the waves. He stood, shaking, his hands over his mouth to shut in the terror. Shaking, he backed slowly to the door. The door, the door. With one hand still holding the terror inside, he opened the door and began to run. He threw the key away on the stairs and ran down five flights to the big empty dark dining room.

Less than an hour after sunrise, Miss Grant and Dr Burke stood on the path along the north side of the hotel. The air was sweet with the scent of frangipani and jasmine and mimosa, birds sang, the morning breeze ruffled the leaves of the fever tree. Dr Burke had signed the form; while the balance of her mind was disturbed. The police had come and gone. Nothing marked the place except a mashed oleander bush and some stains on the coral rock bordering the path. Miss Grant looked as old as she was, without make-up in an orange kimono. Dr Burke had grabbed the nearest clothing, bathing trunks, beach sandals, a T-shirt. He felt hollow, sick from discouragement. He tilted his head to study the balconies above him. All the wide glass panels were closed, the curtains drawn.

'Lucky they like air-conditioning,' he said.

'Most of them would have been on the terrace on the other side. There was a dance last night.'

'Lucky none of them are early risers.'

Miss Grant could not take her eyes from the oleander bush and the coral rocks.

'Bad for tourism,' Dr Burke said bitterly. 'Mustn't upset the tourists. Our great national industry.'

'To think I was the last person to see her,' Miss Grant said. 'I could so easily have stayed. I'll never forgive myself.'

'You? I could just as easily have sent a night nurse and a day nurse or put her in the hospital whether she liked it or not. I knew she was over-emotional about that damned stupid accident but she wasn't concussed, she wasn't off her head. In God's name, how could anyone guess? Oh Mary, it's so *useless*. Why can't these bloody morons keep their kids off the roads!'

'I'd better get dressed before they start coming down for breakfast.' She couldn't afford to let go, the working day began at seven thirty when the dining room opened. Not now, later. And how would she handle the memory of the path and the broken body? Miss Grant took Dr Burke's arm for company, for comfort; she was shivering.

'Poor woman,' Miss Grant said. 'Poor woman. She should never have come to Africa.'

## THEOPHILUS NORTH
**Thornton Wilder**                    53108   $3.95
Thornton Wilder, America's most honored writer, explores through young Theophilus North the lives of the saints and sinners, the rich and the servants, the gigolos and the fortune hunters in Newport, Rhode Island in the 1920's.

## A CHARMED LIFE, Mary McCarthy   53884   $2.95
Mary McCarthy's celebrated novel of 20th Century love and decadence is set against the backdrop of a New England artists' colony. "A glittering tragedy."
*The New York Times*

## AMERICAN BAROQUE
**Lamar Herrin**                       77362   $3.50
An unforgettable story of the 1960's, and of the imperfect ideals and inescapable truths which sparked the imaginations and sensibilities of American youth. "Herrins's writing has vitality, humor, intelligence and vividness."                *The Washington Post*

## THE WELL OF LONELINESS
**Radclyffe Hall**                     54247   $3.95
This is the controversial and eloquent classic that movingly portrays a woman's love. It paved the way for the popularity of Virginia Woolf and of works such as Vita Sackville-West's THE DARK ISLAND, and Rita Mae Brown's THE RUBYFRUIT JUNGLE.

## MASS APPEAL, Bill C. Davis         77396   $2.50
The stormy but underlying tender conflict between a middle-aged priest and a rebellious, idealistic young seminarian is explored in this "wise, moving and very funny comedy."        *The New York Times*

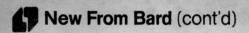 **New From Bard** (cont'd)

**DESERT NOTES:**
**Reflections In The Eye Of A Raven**
**Barry Holstun Lopez**          53819   $2.25
In this collection of narrative contemplation, natu-
ralist Lopez invites the reader to discover the beauty
of the desert. "A magic evocation, Castenada purged
of chemistry and trappings."          *Publishers Weekly*

**PRINCIPLES OF AMERICAN NUCLEAR**
**CHEMISTRY: A NOVEL**
**Thomas McMahon**          54122   $2.95
Set in Los Alamos, New Mexico in 1943, this is the
story of the intellectual, emotional and sexual fer-
ment that grips a group of American scientists at
work on the atomic bomb. "A brilliant and important
novel." Kurt Vonnegut, Jr.

**A SHORT WALK, Alice Childress**          54239   $3.50
From the rustic life of the rural South to the chaos
of a Harlem riot to the revelry of a Depression
Christmas, this is the moving story of one woman's
passionate life, and a striking portrayal of 50 years
of the black experience in America.

**THE GROVES OF ACADEME**
**Mary McCarthy**          52522   $2.95
In this wicked and witty bestseller Mary McCarthy
deftly satirizes American intellectual life. "Brilliant
...funny...bitterly tongue-in-cheek."          *New Yorker*

Available wherever paperbacks are sold, or directly from
the publisher. Include 50¢ per copy for postage and
handling: allow 6–8 weeks for delivery. Avon Books,
Mail Order Dept., 224 West 57th St., N.Y., N.Y. 10019.

**AVON Paperback**